SP♦TLIGHT
A SAINT SQUAD NOVEL

OTHER BOOKS AND AUDIO BOOKS BY TRACI HUNTER ABRAMSON

UNDERCURRENTS SERIES

Undercurrents

Ripple Effect

The Deep End

SAINT SQUAD SERIES

Freefall

Lockdown

Crossfire

Backlash

Smoke Screen

CodeWord

Lock and Key

Drop Zone

ROYAL SERIES

Royal Target

Royal Secrets

Obsession

Deep Cover

Failsafe

Chances Are

Twisted Fate

SPOTLIGHT

A SAINT SQUAD NOVEL

TRACI HUNTER ABRAMSON

Covenant Communications, Inc.

Published by Covenant Communications, Inc.
American Fork, Utah

Printed in the United States of America
First Printing: October 2015

21 20 19 18   10 9 8 7 6 5 4 3

ISBN 978-1-68047-618-7

For Gabriel

You are stronger than you know and loved more than you
ever dreamed possible.

ACKNOWLEDGMENTS

THIS BOOK WAS WRITTEN AMIDST many trials, and I can't possibly name everyone who has helped me carve out time to escape into my fictional world, even when it was for only a few minutes at a time. My sincere thanks to you all. A special thanks to Jen Leigh for all of the quiet acts of service over the past few months. I don't know how I would have survived without you.

Thanks to Kanani Cox for helping me prepare this novel for submission and to Paige Edwards, Kathryn Brown, Jen Leigh, and Mandy Abramson for your invaluable insights. Thank you to Stephanie Read, Darlene Sullivan, and Jenn Wolfe for your help and support in all that I do. Also, thank you to Tiffany Hunter for your insights into the movie industry and for sharing that knowledge with me.

I also want to thank Samantha Millburn and the many people with the Covenant family who have been so supportive of my writing. Thank you for your patience and for making this career such a joy.

Finally, thank you to the many readers who have written to me over the years and asked that the Saint Squad stories continue. I admit that I have enjoyed sharing the journey with you, even if it has resulted in far too many sleepless nights. May we share many more sleepless nights in the years to come.

1

CRAIG SIMMONS CROUCHED BEHIND THE shrubbery on the side of the modest house and watched four men emerge from the vehicle parked by the curb. His objective was simple: assess and identify any threats, specifically men who were armed.

"Here they come," Damian Schmitt said through the communications headset.

From their hiding places on opposite sides of the yard, they watched the men continue up the front walk. Craig's thoughts went to the past six months, during which he had undergone the grueling training of BUD/S, the Navy SEAL training program. He had learned so much: how to scuba dive, jump out of helicopters, disarm explosives. His flight skills and defensive driving abilities had improved, and he'd mastered his weapon skills and evasion techniques.

What he hadn't expected during those months was to spend his first week with his new squad doing nothing but surveillance. Yet here he was freezing on a cold February day while he sat around and watched the people who walked by.

The enormous black man looked dangerous even without his weapon. With a muscular build and broad shoulders, he stood over six and a half feet tall, but the slight bulge of a shoulder holster revealed he didn't have to rely on brute strength today. The lankier man on his left was nearly equal in height and appeared to be unarmed. The same wasn't true for the man on his right—six feet tall, with dark hair—who was also carrying.

Craig analyzed the fourth member of the group: a tall, sandy-haired man who strolled casually past his position. No weapons visible on him either. Craig spoke into the microphone on his headset. "I've got one with a gun in the back of his waistband and a shoulder holster on another. That's all I'm seeing. How about you?"

Damian's response was instant. "Looks like there's also one wearing an ankle holster."

Craig was so focused on the men in front of him he almost missed the movement off to his left. "I've got something at the back of the house."

"Drop back and intercept," Damian instructed him. "I'll keep an eye on the others."

Craig drew his weapon and silently slipped out of his hiding place. His heartbeat picked up speed, and his palms would have gone damp had his gloves not absorbed the increased moisture. He was trained for this, he reminded himself.

Keeping the barrel of the gun aimed down, he crept along the side of the house, then stopped at the corner to peek around the edge before committing himself forward. For all he knew, it was some neighbor's kid taking a shortcut through the yard.

He ducked the moment he spotted the figure on the back patio, a weapon in his hand. Craig took a split second to identify the threat. The moment he saw the intruder begin to turn, weapon first, Craig fired. A sense of satisfaction pulsed through him when he heard the high-pitched beeping from his new commanding officer's sensor vest.

Craig lowered his modified weapon equipped with a laser rather than bullets as Brent Miller disengaged the sensors.

"Not bad," Brent said. "I wasn't sure if you would see me."

"I thought this exercise was to identify weapons."

"No. This exercise was to make sure that while you're trying to spot concealed weapons, you're also alert and aware of your surroundings," Brent told him. "You passed."

"Isn't it about time you tell us about the mission we're prepping for?"

"Tomorrow," Brent said. "I'll explain everything tomorrow."

* * *

Sienna walked along the beach, the hood of her sweatshirt covering her dark hair. Her sunglasses cut the glare off the water and hid her blue eyes.

She loved a winter beach. The crash of the waves, the scent of the sea, and the lack of people. Especially the lack of people.

She knew she could go home anytime to enjoy the private beach near her parents' home in Malibu, but inevitably the paparazzi would figure out some way to snap photos while she was there. Just another constant challenge that came from being the daughter of one of the most famous men in the world.

She supposed she and her sister were gluttons for punishment. Both of them, despite their desire for privacy and normalcy, had chosen careers that put them in the public eye too. Kendra had decided to carve out a spot for herself as a successful singer and songwriter. At twenty-six years old, she already had three Grammys. Sienna had taken the more expected route by following their father into acting.

The year Sienna spent at UCLA had been a great experience, but when her dad handed her a script at the end of her freshman year she had altered her course, launching her acting career earlier than planned by winning a supporting role in one of her father's movies.

She had tried to ignore the claims that her last name had landed her the role and looked on the bright side. The attention, though negative, had brought her into the public eye as an actress. She knew there was an element of truth to the statement, but she also knew she had earned every role since. Her recent Oscar nomination for supporting actress served as proof that she belonged in this crazy world called Hollywood.

The college courses she took online were as much to prove she could complete her education as they were to help her learn to take control of her career. If she had her way, she would graduate with her degree in business in three years. At twenty-two years old, she knew many of her old friends would finish college in a few months, but she would never trade the experiences she'd had because of her choice to pursue a career earlier than expected.

A seagull cried out in the distance, and Sienna let herself enjoy the moment. She knew this was one of the last times she would have the opportunity to be alone for the foreseeable future.

Her sister's wedding would take place in less than a week, and immediately following the wedding, Sienna would begin filming her next movie.

She had to admit she was nervous about this one. Every role she'd had so far had been similar to the one before. Romantic comedy had been a natural fit, with an occasional drama thrown in. After nearly four years, that was what her fans expected. So playing a starring role in a military thriller had been completely unexpected. She had auditioned for the movie on a whim. She might have turned down the role if it hadn't been for one thing: the filming would take place primarily in the Virginia Beach and Norfolk area, providing her with a public reason to be in Virginia. Eventually people would learn she was also here for her sister's wedding, but she loved knowing her presence wouldn't be reason for the press to become suspicious of her true motives.

Besides, this would also give her the opportunity to act opposite Adam Pratt, one of the top leading men in the industry. Undoubtedly, Adam's presence would bring the paparazzi out in droves, especially after his recent breakup with his actress girlfriend of two years.

Sienna could understand her sister's desire to keep her wedding out of the public eye. Though she and Kendra had grown up in the spotlight, their parents had gone to great lengths to keep them safe. Often the security their father forced upon them made them feel isolated, but the summers they spent with their grandparents gave them a taste of middle-class America. Both sisters found they liked their grandparents' lifestyle. They loved the sense of accomplishment they found in doing things for themselves as well as the presence of the gospel in their lives.

Their father had been raised a member of The Church of Jesus Christ of Latter-day Saints, but he had stopped practicing shortly after beginning his acting career. Thankfully, he continued to embrace the strong family values of his youth and had not objected to his daughters joining the Church, provided they always took their bodyguards with them. The one thing he cared about more than his public image was keeping his little girls safe. Sienna doubted he would ever truly consider them able to take care of themselves.

Sienna hoped her father would continue to be supportive of their church activity when he discovered Kendra was getting married in the temple in a ceremony he wouldn't be able to attend.

Kendra's engagement was already well-known, but so far no one had been able to come up with the details of when the vows would be exchanged. That wasn't surprising considering how tightly Kendra was controlling that information. Even their own parents didn't know the date. Their father never had been able to keep a secret, and though their mother was slightly better, she couldn't hide anything from their father, so Kendra and her fiancé, Charlie, had kept both of them in the dark.

The scheme seemed so elaborate, inviting their parents to Virginia to meet the future in-laws. Luckily, Kendra's future father-in-law was a U.S. senator, a high enough social ranking to entice Kendra's father to make the effort. In addition, Charlie and his siblings had been planning a big anniversary party for their parents for over a year. No one would know the family was coming to a combined anniversary party and wedding reception until they actually arrived.

Sienna thought for a moment about what she would want to do for her own wedding, if that day ever came. Her last boyfriend, Joseph, had been too self-absorbed to ever be capable of being in a serious relationship. He had been convenient, especially when she'd been shooting her last movie in London. As soon as she had returned to the United States, their relationship had fizzled, and their breakup occurred only weeks later. In reality, the emotional ties had been severed much earlier.

She smiled slightly when she thought of her grandfather's reaction when she'd told him about the breakup. William Blake didn't have many demands of his grandchildren, but striving for a temple marriage was high on his list. Since Joseph wasn't a Latter-day Saint, nor was he inclined to explore any religion, he had never met with her grandfather's approval.

* * *

Craig sat on the beach, a sketchpad in his hand. He penciled in two seagulls on the horizon and shaded the crest of an incoming wave. The woman heading toward him caught his attention. Petite in stature, confident in stride, she looked content in her solitude. A hooded sweatshirt covered her head, and her hands were tucked into the front pocket.

Her face was tilted away from him, a pair of sunglasses hiding her eyes as she gazed out toward the horizon. A strand of dark hair danced in the wind, and she reached a hand up to brush it out of the way. Fascinated, he sketched the outline of her profile, waiting until she drew closer to fill in her features.

In his peripheral vision, he caught a glimpse of a dark-haired man wearing a Dodgers cap a short distance away, following behind her. Craig didn't pay much attention to him until the woman stopped to pick up a shell from the sand and the man stopped as well, not resuming his forward progress until the woman began walking once more.

Craig supposed it could have been a coincidence that the only other two people on the beach had stopped at almost the exact same time, but now his curiosity was piqued. He watched the woman stop once more, this time to simply look out at the horizon. Again, the man mirrored her movement.

Craig's attention no longer on his artwork, he studied the man lurking behind his current subject of interest. The man appeared to be around forty, but he had the look of someone who made exercise a regular part of his routine. Without realizing he was doing it, Craig did a quick threat assessment of the man and noticed the telltale sign of a holster in the waistband of his jeans.

Another man of about thirty appeared from the opposite direction and jogged toward the woman. Immediately, the man in the ball cap hastened his steps. Concerned by the suspicious behavior, Craig tucked his sketchpad into his backpack and pushed to a stand.

The jogger passed them without incident, but Craig didn't trust the woman would be able to depart as easily. He left his backpack where it lay and strolled casually toward the woman with the intent of putting himself between her and the potential stalker. His concern heightened when the man behind her again quickened his pace.

Craig was ten feet from the woman when he saw the man reach for what was surely a weapon.

"Gun! Get down!" Craig shouted, racing toward the suspect. Craig didn't give the man the chance to fully draw the weapon before he launched himself at him and tackled him to the ground. The man managed to get the gun in his hand, but Craig wrenched it away from him rather than drawing his own weapon.

Using the skills he had learned during his Navy SEAL training, he quickly rolled the man onto his stomach, pressed one knee into the center of his back as he secured his arms, and pinned him to the ground. Then he looked up at the woman, who was now staring at him, stunned. "Are you okay, miss?"

He saw her dark eyebrows lift above the sunglasses. "I'm fine, but I don't think George appreciates being tackled," she said, and Craig thought he sensed amusement.

"You know him?"

"Yeah. He's my bodyguard."

"Bodyguard?" Craig repeated, an unspeakable embarrassment washing over him.

She pulled her sunglasses free and pushed her sweatshirt hood down to reveal shoulder-length dark hair. It took him a second to recognize her, seeing her completely out of context. After all, this wasn't a woman he expected to see walking around town. He expected her to be on movie screens and red carpets. Yet there was no doubt about it. The woman he had been sketching as she walked along the beach was none other than actress Sienna Blake.

"I am so sorry," Craig said uneasily, releasing the bodyguard and standing up beside her. "I saw him reach for his gun. I thought you were his intended target." Craig shifted his attention to the man who was still sprawled on the ground. He reached his hand out and offered to help him up. "I really am sorry."

George didn't say anything but continued to glower at Craig. He ignored the offered hand and pushed himself to a stand, brushing the sand off his jeans and retrieving the ball cap Craig had knocked to the ground. Craig decided he would hold on to the gun for a moment longer until he was sure George didn't intend to use it on him as retribution for the embarrassment he had caused.

"How did you even know I had a gun?" George asked, obviously annoyed.

"I guess you could say I've been trained to spot them."

"Let me guess. You're navy," George said dryly.

"Yeah." Craig glanced down at his clothes, assuring himself that his jeans and sweatshirt didn't have any identifying marks on them. He guessed the bodyguard identified him from his actions as well as the military haircut he had just started to grow out so he could blend in. So much for blending in today. "How did you know I was navy?"

"Because we're next to a couple naval bases."

Satisfied with George's explanation, Craig continued. "I really am sorry." The repeated apology eased some of Craig's embarrassment and seemed to help George as well. The man's posture relaxed, and Craig handed the gun back to its rightful owner. "This isn't somewhere I expected to see a bodyguard."

"What's your name?" Sienna asked.

"Craig Simmons."

"Sienna Blake." She extended her hand to him, and he grasped it in his own, noticing the smoothness of her skin. "I appreciate you trying to come to the rescue like that, even though I didn't need rescuing."

He caught a whiff of coconut and had the sudden image of summer despite the cold breeze coming off the water. He forced himself to let go of her hand and took a second to realign his thoughts with what she had just said. "Glad to know you didn't need rescuing. I hope you never do."

"That's his job. To make sure I don't." Sienna jerked a thumb at George. "Right, George?"

"Let's hope I do a better job the next time someone chases after you."

"I wasn't chasing her. I was just going to make sure she knew there was someone behind her with a gun."

"Same difference."

"I'll let you get back to your walk." Craig took a step back, and he thought he saw surprise register on her face.

"Thank you," Sienna said. "It was nice meeting you, Craig."

"You too." Craig took another step back. "See you around."

He headed back to where he'd left his backpack, thinking how ridiculous his last comment had been. *See you around?* Like he would ever run into Sienna Blake again. The fact that he'd just been talking to her still hadn't quite sunk in.

A part of him wished he'd thought to ask for a photo of them together, but that would have made him feel like even more of an idiot. Plopping back down on the beach, he retrieved his sketchpad once more and decided he would have to go for the next best thing.

Turning a new page over, he retrieved his pencil and started to sketch. Only this time, Sienna Blake's eyes weren't hidden behind sunglasses.

2

SIENNA STUDIED THE WOMAN ON the other side of the threshold. She wasn't much older than she was, maybe twenty-five, and hardly looked old enough to own a design business. Of course, for years, Sienna's entire family had favored the same designer, a man in his fifties. Had it not been for Kendra's insistence on keeping her wedding a secret, she would likely have used him for her wedding dress instead of gambling on a brand-new talent.

After a brief study, Sienna said, "You must be Carina."

"Yes, it's so nice to finally meet you." Carina offered a hand before escorting Sienna through the living room of the modest-sized house and down a hall. "Kendra got here a few minutes ago. She's trying on her dress now."

They reached the back of the house, and Carina showed her into the home studio. Kendra stood in the middle of the room, her blue eyes alight with anticipation and her blonde hair pulled back in a ponytail. The hairstyle definitely didn't go with what she was wearing.

Kendra's princess-style wedding dress flowed to the floor in an elegant sheet of satin. The gown could have come straight out of a fairy tale, with its billowing skirt and sweetheart neckline, but a few unique touches made it unlike anything Sienna had ever seen before.

"What do you think?" Kendra asked, turning to give her a glimpse of the pearl buttons up the back and the flattering line of the dress that accentuated her waist.

"It's stunning," Sienna said with complete sincerity. "Absolutely perfect."

Carina Wellman's face flushed with pleasure at the compliment. Sienna had questioned her sister's judgment with this designer, but now she understood what a hidden talent Carina was, especially considering her age.

"Would you like to see yours?" Carina asked.

Sienna had fully expected to be disappointed in their dresses. She had come prepared to be excited no matter what, even if she had to dig deep into her well of acting abilities to hide her disappointment. Instead she hummed with anticipation, her skepticism erased. "I'd love to see it."

Carina crossed to a closet on the far side of her studio and retrieved a gown covered in white plastic. She hung the dress on a rack and slowly peeled away the protective covering to reveal a gown the color of daffodils. The design was similar to Kendra's dress, except the skirt was straight and draped elegantly to the floor.

"Oh, wow." Sienna reached out a hand, pulling the skirt out to further examine the line of the dress. Her delight came naturally, no acting talent needed.

"Do you like it?"

Sienna smiled. This wasn't a hardened Hollywood designer with ego oozing from every pore. This woman had no idea how truly talented she was, and Sienna's desire mirrored her sister's to see Carina rise in the ranks of the fashion world.

"I love it, Carina. You truly have a gift." Sienna looked up from the dress, and a smile broke out on her face. "I honestly didn't expect to like it this much . . . or for it to be something I would want to wear a second time."

"See, Carina," Kendra said. "I told you."

"What?" Sienna asked.

"You thought I was going to pick something you'd hate."

"Okay, so you got me," Sienna admitted. "After Bridget's wedding, I was starting to think no one knew how to design a bridesmaid's dress that had any style."

Sienna moved closer, studying her dress. She looked over at Carina. "So how long does it take for you to create a new design?"

Carina motioned to the drawing table in the corner of the room. "I actually have quite a few designs already completed. To make something from those or an easy adaptation of one of them would take me a few days to a week. Did you have something particular in mind?"

"Actually, I'm not really thrilled with the dress I was going to wear to the Oscars in three weeks." Sienna ran a finger along the dress. "Something similar to this in a different color would be perfect."

"*The Oscars?*" Carina choked on the words. "You want me to design a dress for you to wear to the Oscars?"

"If you think you can fit me into your schedule." Sienna nodded firmly. "The director of this new film is giving us a few days off from filming since both Adam Pratt and I are up for awards. I'd need the dress a couple days before."

"I'd love to try," Carina said. "Now that all of the dresses are done for the wedding, I don't have anything else pending."

"You have to look at her design book," Kendra told Sienna. She grinned before adding, "I have a feeling Carina may be putting a serious dent in a few designers' businesses."

Sienna chuckled. "After you leak the wedding photos, Carina is going to be swamped with new orders."

"That's what I keep telling her," Kendra said.

"Can I look at your sketches today?" Sienna asked. "I think I'd better get a few orders in now before I have to stand in line."

Her face glowing with pleasure, Carina crossed to her design table and lifted a thick folder. "I'd love to get started on some orders for you, but I can guarantee that no matter what, the Blake sisters will always be my favorite clients."

"Excellent." Sienna took the folder, flipped it open, and immediately approved of the design on top. "Oh yeah, you are going to be very busy."

* * *

Craig looked at his cell phone to see his mother calling. Thursday at nineteen hundred hours. His mother was certainly predictable. Of course, she probably had an alarm set that reminded her to make this weekly call. "Hi, Mom."

"Hi, sweetie. How are you doing?"

Craig cringed at the nickname, one she refused to let die no matter how old he got. "I'm fine. Just got back from the beach."

"I thought you navy types didn't have time for such things."

Craig wasn't going to tell her the things he normally did within sight of a beach: disarm underwater explosives, perform boat maneuvers, take ridiculously long runs, swim with a hundred pounds of gear on his back. "We had an early morning, so I had time today. I decided I'd take advantage of the time off to get better acquainted with the town."

"Undoubtedly with a sketchpad in your hand."

He thought about whom he had been drawing today and decided he probably shouldn't answer the way he usually did. As much as he loved his mother, she had a tendency to key in on certain things of interest, especially tidbits of gossip she could share with her friends.

The last thing he needed was his personal life splashed on his mom's social media pages. Even worse was the idea of Sienna Blake's name being associated with his just because of their random meeting.

"You know me. I like to be ready in case anything catches my eye." He changed the subject smoothly. "Tell me what's going on at home. How's the farm? How's everyone in town?"

"I ran into Teresa yesterday, and she asked about you. She's still single, you know."

Craig rolled his eyes. "Mom, Teresa and I broke up over a year ago. I think it's time you move on. Just because we're both single doesn't mean we should be together. Enough about Teresa. How is everyone else doing?"

"Your brother is getting ready to start planting in another week, and Mr. Standen's mare foaled last night. You remember that pretty quarter horse you had your eye on in high school?"

Craig let himself fall into the familiar routine of country gossip as his mother gave him the latest on his family and the neighboring farms outside Indianola. When Damian knocked on his door, Craig used his teammate's arrival as an excuse to end the call.

As soon as he hung up, Damian said, "I didn't mean to interrupt."

"You didn't. My mom had already told me everything that's happened in Warren County over the past week. If you hadn't gotten here when you did, she would have moved on to the surrounding counties." Craig gave a mock shudder.

"In that case, I'm happy I could help." Damian motioned down the hall. "Paige and I are going to check out that new seafood place down the street. Did you want to join us?"

Craig considered the offer. He genuinely liked Damian's fiancé, but sometimes it was awkward being the third wheel. Glancing at his backpack, he shook his head. "I have a couple things I want to take care of tonight. Thanks for the offer though."

"No problem. We aren't leaving for another hour, so let me know if you change your mind."

"I will."

Damian left, and Craig pulled out his sketch pad and looked down at the rough drawings. The memories of the afternoon still fresh in his mind, he settled down at his desk and retrieved a pencil. Within minutes, he was lost in the images he was determined to create.

* * *

From the back of the restaurant, Bruce watched the same exchange occur over and over. Big-name celebrity enters. Maître d' smoothly shows him or her to a prime table. The waiters arrive only moments later, discreetly taking orders and standing by to fulfill any need.

He hadn't received that kind of treatment when he'd arrived. Even though he'd called in a reservation, he had waited nearly fifteen minutes to be seated. Though he would have typically been annoyed at such a slight, the possibility of this dinner meeting turning into a job opportunity helped him downplay the negative emotions.

Once he'd been seated at his table, service had been adequate at best. Now he waited with his drink in hand and watched the door. Apparently his dining companion, a former A-list actor, anticipated such an event and had decided to be fashionably late.

As minutes ticked by, worry crept in that perhaps this opportunity was going to slip away from him before the interview even began. He checked his cell phone, verifying that he was indeed in the right place at the right time. When he looked up, the man he had been waiting for walked inside.

Though he had starred in countless movies in his youth, his entrance was treated with indifference. He had been out of the limelight for the past few years, but he clearly still spent a good deal of time in the gym, and his sandy-colored hair was perfectly styled. Bruce suspected the actor anticipated another big break any minute. He knew the feeling.

The maître d' appeared to recover quickly when the man gave his name, then, after a brief conversation, showed him to his table.

Bruce stood to shake his hand. "Good to see you again."

"You too."

Both men took their seats, and Bruce bit back his impatience as the man across from him decided to read the entire menu before making a selection. When their orders were finally placed,

Bruce said, "You mentioned on the phone that you had a job opportunity I might be a good fit for."

He took his time answering. "I understand you worked for the Blake family for some time."

"That's right."

"Tell me about your duties there."

Bruce studied the man across from him, taking his own time before formulating a response. Then he answered the man's question, hoping he could tell him what he wanted to hear and that this would be his last night of unemployment.

* * *

Craig was still thinking about his run-in with Sienna Blake when he walked into the conference room the next morning. Part of him wanted to share the experience with his teammates, but he suspected no one would believe him. He also figured everyone would give him a hard time for not asking for her phone number. As if someone like her would give her number to a complete stranger.

Brent and Seth were already inside when he arrived. He looked up at the two men, and the thought crossed his mind that he wasn't used to looking up to people. At six two he was normally at least at eye level or looking down a bit at others, but on this squad, he was on the shorter side. Only Quinn and Damian were shorter than he was. Even Amy, their intelligence officer, was six feet tall.

"How's it going, Craig?" Seth asked. He had a Southern accent and an easy demeanor that contrasted his obvious size and strength.

"Good, thanks. So when do we find out what's going on?"

"Everyone should be here in a minute."

The minute dragged into five as several of his teammates took their time getting there. Even Quinn, who always seemed to hum with energy, was among the last ones to arrive. He sauntered in without any sense of urgency, confirming Craig's suspicions that everyone else already knew what was going on.

They all took their seats, and Tristan offered their morning prayer. Not for the first time, Craig thought how odd it was that he ended up on a squad that was almost entirely made up of Latter-day Saints. He hadn't expected to find any other Mormons in the teams, much less a whole squad of them. Only Damian didn't share his religion.

Brent had explained that when the original squad was formed, they had started this unique ritual to ask for the Lord's guidance as they went through their day. With the squad's continued success, no one was about to change that now.

After the amens, Brent got right to the point. "This morning we're taking our turn on the shooting range at oh eight hundred. Following that, we have PT." He continued to outline their schedule for the day. "Tomorrow we leave on assignment at oh nine hundred."

"Where are we going?" Damian asked.

"Northern Virginia. We'll be based out of a bed-and-breakfast near Great Falls."

"A bed and breakfast?" Craig looked skeptical. "What will we be doing there?"

"You and Damian will be working security detail for a formal event on Friday night."

"What about the rest of you?"

"We'll be attending that event."

"Excuse me?" Craig wondered if he had heard Brent correctly. "This doesn't sound like a job for a Navy SEAL. Is this normal?"

"Not normal, but this particular event has the potential of garnering a lot of attention. There will be quite a few high-level government officials in attendance as well as some Hollywood types," Brent told them.

"Secret service will run the main detail, but their priority will be government officials," Seth put in. "We've been asked to help augment security on the interior for the other guests."

Craig didn't try to hide his confusion. "The interior? I'd think with how we've been trained, we would be outside."

"No. Secret service will work with a private security firm to cover the perimeter."

"Wow. That's a lot of manpower." Craig leaned forward slightly. "What are we expected to do?"

"Basically you'll be blending into the crowd while you watch for anyone who might make it inside armed." Brent waved a hand to encompass the original members of the squad. "Even though the rest of us will be guests, we'll all be watching out for anything suspicious. You'll get further details when we go through our briefings tomorrow. Former FBI agent William Blake has outlined a detailed security plan. In the meantime, you all need to get fitted for your tuxes."

"Any reason why you didn't tell us what we were prepping for yesterday?"

"Yes," Brent said without expounding further. He handed everyone a business card. "Here's the address where you'll get your tuxes, along with the purchase order number."

Craig took the business card and looked down at it to see the shop was located a short distance from base.

"Did you want to ride over with me?" Damian asked as the rest of their squad filtered out of the room.

"Yeah, sure." Now alone in the room with Damian, Craig asked, "Is this normal? The commander springing things on us last minute with no apparent reason?"

Damian shrugged his shoulders. "Don't look at me. I've only been here a few weeks longer than you. Lots of secrets in this squad."

"You're telling me."

3

SIENNA JOGGED ALONG THE BEACH, her thigh and calf muscles burning. Though she much preferred how she looked and felt when she could fit a run into her daily routine, her schedule during her last movie had rarely given her the opportunity. As a result, her muscles were protesting at the increasing demand.

With filming beginning next week, she wanted to make sure she was ready for the physical requirements of her new role.

She glanced out at the water and noticed a pontoon boat in the distance, a half dozen men aboard in addition to the driver. Two at a time, the men dropped into the water, all of them laden with some sort of backpack.

She was astonished to see the boat continue on, leaving the men behind to swim ashore. They were angling away from her, apparently to a stretch of beach out of her view.

She glanced around, a little surprised at herself when she realized she was looking for Craig, the guy who had attacked George the other day. Even more surprising was her disappointment that he wasn't anywhere in sight. She wondered why his name stuck with her after only one brief encounter.

She was just lonely, she thought. There wasn't any particular reason to look for Craig except that he was the only person she knew in town besides Carina. The idea of her sister getting married must be affecting her more than she wanted to admit. She was happy for Kendra, but she also knew things were about to change. Charlie was Kendra's first priority now, not her.

Sienna chastised herself for that thought. She was being selfish. For the past few years, her social life had revolved around work, and this was one of the rare occasions when she hadn't brought her personal assistant with her on location. She couldn't remember the last time she had gone somewhere new without the crutch of either a boyfriend or an assistant to help occupy her time. She supposed it was time to expand her network of friends.

Again she thought of Craig. He intrigued her in more ways than one. She suspected she would have noticed him yesterday even if he hadn't tackled George. He was attractive in his own rough-and-tumble way. The dark shadow of the beard on his face contrasted with the military-short haircut. She didn't know if he was starting to grow a beard or if he didn't want to bother with a close shave. Regardless, the look suited him well.

Beyond his looks, though, he'd caught her attention because of how he had acted so blessedly normal when they'd met. He hadn't pretended not to know her, but he also hadn't exhibited the typical fan behavior. Rarely did she meet someone who didn't at least ask for a photo or an autograph. He hadn't even tried to get her phone number, a ploy many men had attempted over the years.

She also appreciated knowing he would jump to a stranger's rescue. If she trusted his actions, he had already proven himself to be a good, truly selfless guy.

She finished her run and turned to walk back the way she had come. In the distance, she saw a familiar dark-haired figure strolling down the boardwalk, a backpack over his shoulder. She could almost see his deep green eyes from here.

Her face lit with pleasure when he drew closer and confirmed her suspicion. She changed direction and headed toward the man she hoped would become her first real friend in Virginia.

* * *

Craig knew he should be back at the barracks packing, but he needed a few minutes to clear his head. As soon as Brent had released them from their last training exercise of the day, Craig had showered and promptly headed out to his car. He could have jogged to the beach near base, but instead he drove to the one in town, where he had run into Sienna Blake.

He knew he couldn't expect to run into her again just because she happened to be here yesterday, but that didn't stop him from thinking about her. Perhaps it was his inability to talk to anyone about meeting her yesterday that kept her so firmly on his mind.

He strolled down the boardwalk toward the nearest entrance to the beach. His eyes were drawn to the water, and he squinted when he saw Sienna a short distance away. His heartbeat instantly quickened.

Was she waving at him? He looked behind him to see if the greeting was intended for someone else. A sense of wonder and amazement lifted his spirits. Sienna Blake was here, and she remembered him.

Hoping he appeared more calm than he felt, Craig continued forward and headed toward her.

"I was wondering if I would see you again today," she said.

Craig considered playing it cool but didn't manage it. "Really? I was just thinking the same thing about you."

Her blue eyes warmed, and her lips curved. "Do you come here every day?"

"No. I just finished some appointments and have an hour before I have to head back over to base, so I decided to go for a walk to clear my head," Craig told her. "What about you? You don't live around here, do you?"

"No. I start filming a movie next week."

Craig looked over at George, who was standing several yards away. He lowered his voice. "He's not still mad about what happened yesterday, is he?"

She leaned closer and whispered, "I think he's over it."

"I hope so."

She smiled. "You definitely made an impression though."

"I'm not sure if that's a good thing or a bad thing."

Glancing over at George, she said, "I think it was a little of both but mostly good."

Craig let his gaze sweep over the beach. "Did I interrupt your run?"

"I was just finishing up." Sienna motioned to the water. "Do you want to walk with me for a bit, or do you have plans?"

Like he would turn down the chance to get to know her better. "A walk sounds good."

They started across the sand, taking a path near the water without getting close enough to get wet. George dropped back behind them, strolling along as though he just happened to be heading in the same direction.

"I hadn't heard there was a movie shooting around here," Craig said conversationally.

"Yeah. It's one of those military action films."

"Not your usual role."

"I know. I'm actually a little worried about how this is going to work out," Sienna confessed. "I don't normally have to deal with stunt doubles and action scenes."

"I'm sure you'll be fine."

She shrugged. "Yeah. I guess."

Craig looked over at her, still not quite able to believe this was real. A beautiful, interesting woman had waved him down, and now she was giving him glimpses into what was behind her famous persona. "You sound worried."

She took a deep breath, her shoulders rising and falling on a sigh. "My character is supposed to be a highly trained CIA agent who knows how to take care of herself. It's been a while since I took a self-defense class."

"I have to tell you, this is feeling a little surreal to me," Craig said. He saw her answering smile and pressed on. "But I do know a bit about that kind of stuff. Let me know if you need any help."

She looked over at him, clearly considering. "Does that mean you're offering me your phone number?"

"Do you want it?"

She looked over at him, the epitome of a woman who was completely in control of her destiny. Yet he could have sworn he saw a flash of vulnerability in her eyes. "I think I do. You know, in case I really do need some help."

She retrieved her phone from where it was strapped to her upper arm. Craig expected her to hand it to him so he could put in his information and save her from the embarrassment of asking for his name again. Instead, she opened up the contacts herself. "Craig, what's your last name again?"

"Simmons." As soon as she typed it in, he rattled off his number.

"Great. Thanks."

"Fair warning. I'm happy to help when I'm here, but tomorrow I'm going out of town for work."

"What are you doing tonight?"

"I need to pack, but that's about it."

"Any chance you could spare a couple hours?"

Craig nodded at George. "I'm surprised you don't have him help you."

"He's funny about that kind of stuff. He's afraid that if he tries to work with me, he'll lose his focus and let someone get too close to me."

"I can see his point."

"I need to go get cleaned up." Sienna looked at her watch. "Maybe we could meet at my hotel in a couple hours? We can look at the script over dinner."

"Sounds great."

She held up her phone and took a step back. "I guess I'll call you later, then."

"Talk to you soon." Craig watched her head back the way she had come. For the second time in two days, he wondered if he was living in some kind of dream world.

4

Sienna held her phone in her hand, her heart racing with a combination of nerves and anticipation. Stalling, she checked her e-mail and read through a couple of old text messages.

"Are you going to call him?" George asked.

"Call who?"

"The guy from the beach. I know you want to call him."

She let out a sigh. "It feels weird. I hardly know him."

"But you like him, or you wouldn't have spent the last fifteen minutes staring at your phone. Besides, you know he's fine, and it's not like you're going to be by yourself with him."

"Why do you think I know he's fine?"

George gave her a deliberate stare. "Any guy who runs to the rescue of someone he doesn't know can't be all bad."

Sienna caught a glint of something in his eyes. "You ran his background check, didn't you?"

"Well, yeah. That's my job."

Sienna didn't dispute his words, nor did she put her phone down. "You know, you really could help me get ready for this role."

"You don't want me to help you, and we both know it. You want to call that boy."

"He's hardly a boy."

"He's more than ten years younger than me. That means he's still a kid."

Sienna chuckled, some of her nerves easing. "You're acting like forty is old."

"Yesterday on the beach, it felt like it."

"Are you still mad about that?" Sienna asked.

"Just a bruised ego. I'll get over it." He pointed to her phone and spoke in his I-know-best tone. "Go ahead and call him. I'll talk to hotel management about setting up a place for the two of you to meet."

"I can have him come up here."

George looked around the hotel suite. "You may have plenty of space up here, but I'm not ready to have some random guy in your hotel room, even if I am sitting right next to you."

"I thought you said he was okay."

"Saying he's okay is one thing. Having him in your room is another. Let's not forget that your father still pays my salary."

Her eyebrows lifted. "Don't tell me you're afraid of my father."

"I'm more afraid of getting caught between you two. Neither one of us needs the fallout that would come from you ending up in the press right now. Having some guy seen coming or going from your hotel room would not be a good thing."

"True."

"Go ahead and make your phone call. I'll be back in a minute." He crossed the room. "Don't leave your room, and don't unlock the door for anyone."

"I know the drill." Sienna followed George to the door. As soon as he closed it behind him, she flipped the lock. With another glance at her cell phone, she mustered her courage. "I guess it's now or never," she muttered to herself.

She scrolled through her contacts and found Craig's number. Still, she hesitated. She knew few people would believe she was shy at heart. Once she got to know people, she was fine, but those initial contacts made her stomach curl with dread and anxiety.

She'd been forced to learn to push through it, especially growing up under the microscope of the paparazzi.

She was a little surprised that so far the press was leaving her alone. She wasn't sure if she had been successful in avoiding them when she traveled to Virginia or if they hadn't discovered where she was staying yet, but as far as she knew, no one had splashed her photo on the Internet or in print since her arrival.

Crossing to the glass door leading to the balcony, she stared out at the ocean. Even through the glass, she could hear the roar of the waves and the squawk of seagulls flying overhead. She looked down at the few people jogging along the beach and let herself remember her earlier meeting with Craig.

George was right. She did want to call him. She felt the promise of a friendship, one that might give her some semblance of normalcy, something she had often searched for but had never seemed to find.

Her palms dampened, not unlike they did every time she stepped in front of the camera. With her heart racing, she forced herself to push the talk button.

* * *

"All of this practice has been for Amy's parents' anniversary party?" Craig asked skeptically. Surely he had heard Brent wrong. "I assume there's more to it than that. Are you aware of some threat we should know about?"

"Nothing specific, but Amy's family has some unique quirks."

"Such as?"

Brent looked over at Amy. She picked up the unspoken signal and answered the question for him. "My father is a U.S. senator, my oldest brother is the starting first baseman for the Marlins, and my sister-in-law used to be in the Witness Protection Program after she helped break up a smuggling ring."

"Wow. You guys know how to make things interesting," Damian said.

Craig looked from Amy to Brent. "So we're going to be there to help your family?"

"Not just my family. Our squad has made some enemies over the years, and unfortunately, a few of our targets know who we are. We don't want to take any chances that our professional lives will spill over and make this night anything less than perfect," Brent said. "Besides, it will be great training for both of you. I prefer not to take any rookies into the field without a dry run."

"I can vouch for that," Damian said.

Craig lifted his eyebrows in question.

"We don't need to go into details," Brent said, clearly referring to a specific incident rather than his general policies.

"Whatever you say, Brent," Damian agreed obediently.

"Is everyone all set for departure tomorrow morning?" Brent asked. When they all nodded in the affirmative, he continued. "After we settle in tomorrow afternoon, we'll have a briefing at the site of the anniversary party, followed by an outing I think you'll enjoy."

"What kind of outing?"

"You'll find out soon enough. Just consider it a bonus for being willing to help us out this weekend."

"You do realize you haven't exactly given us a choice, right?" Damian asked.

"I promise it will be a weekend worth remembering." Brent stood up. "I think that's everything for now."

"If everyone is already packed . . ." Seth began.

Craig's phone rang, and Seth turned to look at him inquisitively. Embarrassed that he'd forgotten to silence his phone, he quickly retrieved it from his pocket. "Sorry," he mumbled.

"Do you need to get that?" Brent asked.

He started to say no, but when he saw the California prefix, he looked at Brent apologetically. "Actually, if you don't mind, I think I should take this."

"Go ahead. We're finished here anyway," Brent said.

Craig stepped out of the room, answering the phone as soon as he entered the hall. "Hello?"

"Hi, Craig. It's Sienna."

"Hey, I was wondering if you were going to call." He cringed inwardly as once again he realized how lame his response must sound to her, as though he was sitting around waiting by the phone, hoping to hear from her. Why was it that every time he spoke to her, the first thing that entered his mind popped out of his mouth?

"Are you still free tonight?"

Craig could have sworn he heard a hint of insecurity in her voice again, but he brushed it off. Surely he was mistaken. "Yeah. Did you still want some help?"

"That would be great, if you don't mind."

"I just finished my last meeting of the day. Let me know when and where you want to meet, and I'll be there."

"How about if we meet at my hotel? How soon can you come over?"

"I can come right now if you want. Where are you staying?"

"I'll text you the address."

"Okay. I'll see you in a little while."

"I look forward to it."

He was halfway to his car when he heard his name being called. "Craig. *Esperate*!"

Craig turned to see Damian jogging across the parking lot toward him. He wondered briefly if Damian realized he was telling him to wait in Spanish rather than English.

Even though Damian had the look of his German ancestors, he had grown up in Venezuela until his teenage years. Craig had quickly discovered that this particular teammate didn't always remember which language he was speaking.

"What's up?" Craig asked him in English.

"A bunch of the guys are getting together to watch the Capitals game on TV at Seth's house tonight. Do you want to drive over with me?"

"No, thanks. I have plans tonight."

"Plans?" Damian looked at him suspiciously. "What plans?"

"Just plans." Craig slid the key into the lock and unlocked his vehicle the old-fashioned way. He had bought the used truck when he was sixteen, and it didn't have such amenities as keyless entry or even working air conditioning. Living in Virginia, he might have to rethink his decision to forgo repairing the A/C.

Damian continued to stare at Craig as he pulled the door open. "Do you have a date?"

Since he wasn't exactly sure how to classify his meeting with Sienna, he decided avoidance would be the best course of action. He climbed into the driver's seat and called out, "See you later."

Before Damian could respond, Craig slammed his door shut, started the truck, and pulled out of the lot, leaving his teammate to stare after him.

5

CRAIG READ THROUGH THE TEXT message from Sienna one more time. He approached the front desk at the hotel, not sure why in the world Sienna would tell him to ask for Elizabeth Hancock instead of her. Maybe Elizabeth was her personal assistant or something.

The sharply dressed woman behind the counter smiled in greeting. "May I help you?"

Half expecting to be told he was in the wrong place, he said, "Yes. I'm supposed to meet Elizabeth Hancock here."

"Your name?"

"Craig Simmons."

"I'll let Miss Hancock know you're here. She'll meet you in the Oak Room." She pointed to her left. "Follow that hallway past the elevators, and it will be the second door on the right."

"Thank you." Craig made his way to the room she indicated. When he arrived, he was surprised to find a large room with only one round table set up. Atop the white linen tablecloth, there was a single red rose in a vase, along with two place settings.

He took a few steps into the room, still not sure he was in the right place. Sienna had mentioned going through her script over dinner, but he expected they would meet in the hotel restaurant or perhaps in a hotel suite with George watching over them. He glanced down at his BDUs, the battle dress uniform he had worn to work, and instantly felt underdressed.

When he had talked to Sienna, he had gotten the impression that their dinner would be casual. Now he wondered if he should have dug out his Sunday suit. He was still second-guessing himself when he heard movement behind him. He turned to see Sienna walk in wearing jeans and a button-up shirt.

Relieved to see her casual attire, he motioned to the table. "Is this for us?"

"Yeah. I figured it would be easier to go over the script if we had some privacy, and George is funny about me having men in my hotel room."

He gave a half smile. "I can understand that. I have a feeling he's still a little leery of me."

"You've got that right." George's voice sounded from the hall.

"Hi, George," Craig called out. He motioned to the table. "There are only two place settings. Isn't George joining us?"

"No, he'll eat later, after he's sure I'm safely tucked away somewhere." Sienna lifted the script in her hand. "Dinner should be here in about fifteen minutes. Do you mind if we start looking through this?"

"Not at all." Craig crossed to the table and pulled out a chair for Sienna. After she sat down, he took the seat beside her. He noticed several bright-orange tabs protruding from the script.

She flipped to the first one. "Here. Look at this." Sienna set the open script on the table between them and shifted closer. "This is one that has me worried. It's probably the first scene we'll shoot."

Craig read through the scene she had highlighted. The stage direction called for Sienna's character to defend herself from an attacker who would approach from behind. "Oh, this won't be hard."

Sienna's eyebrows lifted. "Easy for you to say. The guy I'm supposed to be defending myself against is as tall as you are."

"Like I said, this won't be hard."

"Care to demonstrate?"

"No problem." Craig stood up and motioned for her to join him in the open part of the room. "First of all, if this were a real situation and not just a movie, you would want to go for the pressure point." Craig demonstrated on his own arm, placing his thumb on the underside of his bicep. "If you dig your thumb in right there, I don't care how big your attacker is, he'll stop and pay attention."

"Really?" Sienna asked.

Craig nodded. "It might leave some bruising, but you can bet his hold will loosen." He instructed her on some basic defensive measures, such as tucking her chin to keep her attacker from getting her in a choke hold and the movements she would likely want to use to break free of his grasp.

"Since this is for Hollywood, let me show you what your director is probably looking for," Craig said. He took position behind her and put one arm loosely around her neck. Her hair brushed against his cheek, and the smell of her shampoo tickled his senses. His stomach jumped when she leaned back against him, and he tried to convince himself he wasn't affected by being so close to her.

He rolled his eyes to the ceiling. Who was he kidding? He had his arm around one of the most beautiful women he'd ever seen, and his entire nervous system was going haywire.

"Now what?" Sienna asked, her own voice low.

"Assuming you're trying to break free, like the script says, here's what you want to do." He tried to pretend he was helping one of his teammates but failed completely. He took a steadying breath and guided her hands to where they would be most effective.

"Like this?" she asked.

"Exactly. Now you're going to pull both hands down and throw your hips back."

"That seems easy enough."

He kept his grip loose so she would be able to break free with ease. She did so successfully, but when she turned to face him, her expression was wary. "You're taking it too easy on me. I don't think my costar will be so kind. He'll want to flex his muscles."

The surge of jealousy was instant, as was Craig's surprise. "Your costar is supposed to attack you? I thought it would be one of the bad guys."

"Not in this particular scene. This one is a case of mistaken identity." Her eyebrows lifted, and her eyes sparked. "Kind of like when my bodyguard was recently tackled on the beach."

"I heard that," George called out.

"Just making sure you were paying attention," Sienna said.

Craig felt himself relax. "I gather he's been with you for a while."

"Yeah. Since I was a teenager."

George poked his head in. "Dinner's here."

A waiter walked in a moment later, pushing a cart with several covered dishes on top of it. While the waiter busied himself with setting their meal on the table, Craig once again pulled out Sienna's chair for her.

"Your mother sure raised you right," she said with a smile.

Craig waited for her to sit and helped her shift her chair forward before taking the seat beside her. He watched the waiter serve them their meal, which consisted of fresh bread, a green salad, steak, roasted baby potatoes, and steamed vegetables.

Sienna motioned to the food. "I hope this is okay. You looked like a meat-and-potatoes kind of guy, but if you don't like it, we can have the kitchen send something else."

"This looks great," Craig assured her, the smell of freshly baked bread complementing the scent of grilled meat. "Although I have to admit, I'm not used to a woman treating me to dinner."

"I figured it's the least I can do since you're going to the trouble of helping me out."

"Trust me. It's no trouble. It's actually nice to get off base for a while."

Sienna lowered her head as though offering a silent prayer as he and his teammates often did when they were eating in the mess hall. Craig sent up a prayer of his own, not sure what to think of the woman across from him. When he looked up, Sienna started the conversation again without missing a beat.

She speared a piece of lettuce with her fork. "How long have you been stationed here?"

"Only a couple weeks." Craig broke open a roll, steam escaping from it.

"Where did you grow up?" Sienna asked before taking a bite of her salad.

"Iowa."

"Iowa?" she repeated. "So you're a farm boy?"

"You know, there are some people who live in Iowa who aren't farmers."

Sienna's eyebrows lifted. "I guess that is a bit of a stereotype. Kind of like everyone from Hollywood must work in the movies." She shrugged good-naturedly. "If you weren't a farmer, what did you do in Iowa?"

"Actually, I was a farm boy," Craig said and was rewarded with her laughter. He loved the way her face lit up with humor, and he tried not to think about how different his hometown was from the world Sienna had grown up in. "I'm from a little tiny town in the middle of nowhere."

"I always wondered what it would be like to live in the middle of nowhere."

"You do a lot of driving."

Sienna chuckled. "I guess that would be true if you don't live near the store."

Craig nodded. "The closest one was forty-five minutes away."

"Do your parents still live there?"

"My mom does. My dad passed away when I was in college."

Sienna set her fork down, her focus now entirely on Craig. "I'm sorry. What happened?"

"Cancer."

"That must have been rough."

"It was. Especially on my mom and younger sister. They were the ones who took care of him at the end."

"Does your sister still live at home?" She picked her fork back up and took a bite of her vegetables.

"No. After my dad passed away, my sister went to college. She works as a nurse in Des Moines now."

"That must have been tough for your mom, trying to put two kids through college at the same time after your dad died."

"I didn't finish school." Craig fought back the frustration that always surfaced when he thought of the one thing he had started and failed to finish. "When Dad got sick, I dropped out to help my brother run the farm."

"You never went back?"

"No. It wasn't meant to be." Craig's shoulders lifted. "The main reason I went to college was to get out of town. My sister had a purpose, so it made sense to help her through instead. I met with a recruiter a couple months after my dad died and decided the navy was a better fit for me."

"How did your mom feel about that?"

"I think she understood I needed to get out of town. I know how to farm, but I was never a farmer."

"Have you ever thought about going back to school?" she asked.

"Not really. I go through so much training with work that I don't think I'd have time even if I wanted to," Craig said. "What about you? Did you ever go to college?"

"I did a year at UCLA."

"I gather college wasn't for you either?"

"Actually, I loved it, but the opportunity to start my career came sooner than I expected."

"Have you ever thought about going back?" Craig asked.

She hesitated as though trying to decide how much to share. "I never really left. I've been taking classes, mostly online, so I can finish my degree. It's taking forever, but I'm hoping to finish in a few more years."

"That's great."

They fell into easy conversation as they ate their dinner. When they finished, Sienna asked, "Do you know yet where you're going for work tomorrow?"

"Not yet. I guess I'll find out when I get there." Craig shrugged. "Of course, I probably couldn't tell you even if I did know."

"Oh, so you're one of *those* kind of military guys, the kind who has to go on highly classified missions?" She phrased it as a question, but her tone was light.

Craig didn't answer.

Her expression grew more serious. "Are you one of those guys who goes on highly classified missions?"

Craig's response this time was to change the subject. "How do you like Virginia so far?"

Sienna stared for a moment, clearly aware that he was deliberately avoiding her question. "I like it. I especially like the solitude of the beach. It will probably get crazy, though, once the rest of the cast arrives."

"When does that happen?"

"Next week sometime. Some of the crew is already here. They've been working on the house they rented that we'll use for our main set."

Craig motioned to the script. "Do you want to look at some more of the action scenes?"

"Might as well." They read through several, and Craig gave her more pointers on how real-life scenarios would typically play out. They had to skip some of the moves since they would have needed mats to make sure no one got hurt.

As soon as they finished, Sienna asked, "Do you have to get back to base, or do you have time to go out for some dessert?"

"I have time."

Sienna walked to the door and spoke to George. "What do you think, George? Do you want to grab some dinner at that restaurant down the street while Craig and I get dessert?"

"I think I could be persuaded." He eyed Craig. "Are you carrying?"

Recognizing that he was asking him if he was armed, Craig nodded. "Yeah. It's standard procedure for my squad."

"Good. That way I can relax a bit over dinner and let you play bodyguard for a while." George motioned down the hall. "We'll meet you in the lobby in a few minutes after I take Sienna up to get her coat."

"See you then."

6

Sienna couldn't believe how easy everything was with Craig. She walked beside him like they'd known each other for years. He didn't seem to care that George tagged along behind them, nor did he act like some starstruck groupie who was only interested in her because of her fame.

She had worried things would be awkward when he was helping her with the action scenes, but he had helped her feel at ease, all except for the rush of attraction that had flowed through her when he had held her against him. For a moment, she had forgotten he was supposed to be her attacker, instead letting her mind get carried away by the warmth of his body against her back and the sudden leap in her stomach.

Craig had seemed unaffected by their close proximity, and for the first time in years, she found herself unsure of where she stood with someone. Yet she couldn't deny she felt more herself with Craig than she did with most people.

When they reached the restaurant, Craig pulled the door open for her, and the thought struck her that her grandfather would approve of her current companion. If Craig was LDS, her grandfather would probably start planning a wedding, right after conducting an old-fashioned interrogation while cleaning his shotgun.

The fact that she desired her grandparents' approval more than her parents' only served as a reminder of how different their values were. Her father would be just as happy to see her with some A-list actor who would keep her name in the social pages as he would to know she was with someone who offered her true friendship. She knew publicity was part of her job, but that didn't mean she always had to be in the news.

She didn't doubt that her father wanted her to be happy, but he often got so caught up with keeping Kendra and her safe that he didn't take the time to understand what she needed for true happiness. She wanted what her sister was about to have: a temple marriage to someone who loved her, a companion who cared about her more than anything else. Not that she expected to find that anytime soon, but she liked to think she could find the dream someday.

They stepped inside, George following right behind them. Immediately, Sienna reveled in the scent of freshly baked pastries and homestyle cooking. "I ordered dinner from here yesterday. The apple pie is amazing."

"I'm surprised you indulge in dessert. I thought people in your profession lived off salads and celery sticks."

"I've heard that." Sienna looked at him thoughtfully. "I tried it once, but I didn't like it, so I decided not to do it again." Craig chuckled, and Sienna felt a sense of satisfaction that he appreciated her humor.

"I'm glad to hear that. I've never really understood people who live off of vegetables."

"What about fruit? Apple pie counts as a fruit, doesn't it?" Sienna asked.

"I guess you could say that."

When they approached the hostess, Sienna saw the light of recognition in the woman's eyes.

Craig stepped up before the hostess could say anything. "Would it be possible for us to get a quiet booth in the back? We just wanted to get some dessert."

The woman took a second to respond, as though she had to gain her composure before speaking. "Of course, sir." She fumbled with the menus before leading the way to their booth. "Is this okay?"

"This is great. Thanks," Craig said, waiting for Sienna to sit before sliding in across from her.

"Your waitress will be right with you." The hostess handed them each a menu and disappeared back the way she had come.

"Did you want apple pie again, or do you want to try something new?" Craig asked.

"I know it may sound boring, but I just want apple pie." Sienna noticed the hostess talking to a waitress, the two women turning to look in their direction. Sienna offered a little wave.

"You realize you just made their night."

"I doubt that."

The waitress approached with a hesitant smile and took their order. Out of the corner of her eye, Sienna saw the hostess show George to a table across the room. The simple fact that George wasn't in hearing distance afforded her a sense of privacy she wasn't accustomed to enjoying.

The waitress served their pie in record time. Sienna scooped up a bite, savoring the warm apple contrasted with the cold ice cream. Glancing across the table, she couldn't help comparing Craig to her last boyfriend. She wouldn't have been able to order dessert in front of Joseph. He would have criticized her for taking in so many calories, always quick to remind her the camera added pounds.

She swallowed and lifted her fork for another bite. "Do you have any idea how long you're going to be out of town?"

"I'm not sure. From what I've heard, I should be back early next week."

"That's good. I'm actually heading out of town for a few days myself."

Craig's eyes sharpened with interest, but it wasn't the greedy self-serving look she often saw from the reporters who too frequently followed her around. Instead, Craig's expression revealed simple curiosity. "Where are you going?"

"My sister has a concert tomorrow night in DC. We're going to meet up so we can hang out for a few days together."

"That'll be fun."

She saw the way his curiosity melted into acceptance, and he seemed to pick up on her excitement about the upcoming weekend. "It will be. We don't get a lot of time together, especially since she got engaged."

"I heard about that. She's marrying a cop, right?"

"An FBI agent, actually."

"I remember seeing it in the news when she had that stalker go after her." His eyes met Sienna's and held a quiet understanding. "That must have been terrifying for your family."

Sienna's fingers tightened on her fork. "Definitely. I actually didn't know much about it until afterward because I was in Europe at the time."

"Still, just knowing what your sister was going through must have been really stressful."

Not wanting to dwell on such a negative topic, she asked, "Will you be able to call or text me while you're traveling?"

"It's possible, but I won't be sure until I get there." Craig's eyes met hers. A touch of uncertainty flashed in his expression, but when he spoke, his tone was flirtatious. "Do you want to talk to me while I'm on assignment?"

She felt color rising in her cheeks and hoped he wouldn't notice. "It would be nice to hear from you."

"I didn't think you'd want any interruptions while you're with your sister."

"Her fiancé will be with us too, so it's not like I'm going to have her undivided attention."

"You can always text me if you get bored," Craig suggested.

"Would you get in trouble if I texted you while you're working?"

"If I'm in a situation where I can't take calls, my phone will be off."

She took another bite of pie and then gestured with her fork. "So you're telling me not to get annoyed if you don't respond right away."

"Exactly."

* * *

He stared at the computer screen, the vibrant images of last year's Oscars filling all twenty-seven inches of space. There had been a time when he would have been in the middle of the action, rubbing elbows with all of the biggest names in Hollywood and in the music industry. He had been somebody once. Now he was somebody no one wanted.

A sleek black limousine had pulled to the curb, and he saw the photographers jostling for position. He remembered that particular moment like it was yesterday. The driver had circled to open the door, and a moment later, Sterling Blake had exited the vehicle, dressed in his latest Armani suit. He'd smiled and waved at the crowd before turning to offer a hand to his wife, the lovely brunette wearing a column of white silk. The daughters came next, Kendra and Sienna.

The entire family had come together for a group photograph, indulging the press and creating an image that would be one of the highlights of the evening. They had become the poster children of the night, and he had walked by unnoticed. How had everything changed so quickly? How had he faded so completely into the background among the people he had once considered his peers and the people who had made a living photographing them?

He wasn't blind to the way the entire Blake family exuded elegance and class. After all, he knew firsthand how closely their public image mirrored their private lives. Sure, the daughters liked their privacy. That was undoubtedly one of the reasons Kendra Blake had graced the red carpet without her FBI boyfriend at her side. Still, they were good people. If only they hadn't ruined his life.

He clicked off the image and fought against the memories. The newspaper articles on the corner of his desk described his fall from grace in agonizing detail. That was the past, he reminded himself. Now was the time to create his future.

Beside the articles lay one possible key to his return to his former life. Four letters, each one constructed from words cut out of magazines, outlined the threats toward the Blake family and one member in particular. The plastic bags that encased them would ensure they remained free of any unwanted fingerprints.

He'd hoped it wouldn't come to this, but he was running out of options. He opened a new search on the Internet. Typing each of the Blake family names into the search bar, he began compiling their upcoming schedules. He couldn't go on living like this much longer. He had to make a change, or he would disappear into oblivion. He wasn't about to let that happen.

Jotting down all the family had planned, he lifted his eyebrows when he saw the moment everyone's paths would cross. Interesting. He looked at the calendar, considering. Was it coincidence or design that the entire Blake family would be on the East Coast at the same time? Speculating to himself, he opened another tab and typed in his preferred travel site. Time to make some airline reservations.

* * *

"I know you want to keep your plans secret, but I still can't believe you're having a concert only days before your wedding." Sienna dropped into a chair in her sister's current bedroom. She had settled into her own room when they'd first arrived at the elegant estate where Kendra's wedding reception would take place. Now she watched as Kendra sorted through her extensive wardrobe in preparation for the night's concert.

"Can you think of a better excuse to be here in Virginia than this? It's perfect."

"Yeah, but I would think that the Whitmores' anniversary party would be reason enough."

"It might be, but I didn't want to take a chance of people figuring out what's really going on," Kendra said. "Besides, you, Grandma, and Grandpa aren't named on the guest list. You know the paparazzi would notice if you were in DC without a reason."

"True. Not to mention Dad still thinks he's coming out here to meet the Whitmores and get a tour of the White House."

Kendra sniggered. "Dad is so gullible sometimes."

"I can't believe you managed to clear his schedule long enough for him to be here."

"That wasn't easy."

A knock sounded at the door.

"Come in," Kendra called out.

The door opened, and both girls heard the familiar deep voice before they saw their grandfather. "There are my girls," William Blake said as he walked inside.

"Grandpa!" Sienna leaped up and threw her arms around him. "I didn't know you were already here."

"I figured I'd better show up early to make sure everything is all squared away for the events of the next couple days." He released Sienna and hugged Kendra in turn. "Are you all ready for your concert tonight?"

"I think so."

"That man of yours is skulking outside. I think he's getting impatient waiting for you to decide what to wear."

"Charlie doesn't skulk. He's protective." Kendra shot him a knowing look. "Kind of like someone else I know."

"Being protective is a good trait for an FBI agent," William said without missing a beat. "Didn't I pick you out a nice future husband?"

"Yes, Grandpa. You did a great job," Kendra said with a grin. "Thank you for that."

"You're welcome. It was the least I could do for my favorite granddaughter."

"Hey! What about me?"

"You're my favorite too." William cocked his head to one side. "Of course, you'll be more my favorite when you dump all of those Hollywood boyfriends of yours and find a nice Mormon boy to date."

"I'll get right on that," Sienna said sarcastically. "Because, of course, there are so many Mormons in Hollywood."

"You always have had a sharp tongue on you," he said with affection. "Don't worry. I'm keeping an eye out for you. We'll find you a nice boy."

Kendra nudged her. "Watch out for him. He's sneaky."

"I know."

William's eyebrows furrowed. "You do know I'm standing right here."

"Yeah. We noticed that," Kendra said.

William shook his head and reached for the doorknob. "Kendra, good luck tonight, or break a leg, or whatever it is I'm supposed to say before a concert."

"Thanks, Grandpa. I'm sure we'll see you before we leave."

"You can count on it."

7

CRAIG LOOKED THROUGH THE WINDSHIELD at the enormous white house in front of him. The structure sprawled across the bluff that overlooked the large property. A thin layer of snow covered the wide slope of lawn, but the long driveway was clear.

"We're staying here?" Damian asked from the seat beside him.

"This is the right address." Craig pulled up the drive and into a small parking area off to the left of the main entrance. He climbed out of the car, stepping out of the way so Seth and Jay could park beside them.

"This is where we're doing security?" Jay asked as soon as Seth managed to extract himself from the car.

"For now."

"I thought we were going to be at a bed and breakfast. This looks more like a private resort."

"Call it what you want. This is our home for the next few days." Seth popped the trunk, and he and Jay collected their duffels and their tuxedo garment bags. "Grab your gear, and I'll show you where you'll be staying."

Craig and Damian did as they were told and followed Seth and Jay inside. Black and white marble covered the floor of the main entrance, and two sweeping staircases flowed opposite one another to the second level.

Seth headed for the stairwell to the right. "This way."

The others followed him up the stairs and into a long, wide hallway.

Seth opened the first door on the right. "Damian and Craig, you'll be in here. Jay and I are in the identical room in the other wing."

Seth stepped aside to let Damian and Craig enter first. Both men walked in and stared. The living room was a pleasant combination of elegance and comfort. The rolltop desk in the corner appeared to be antique, while the two chairs facing the fireplace on the far wall were oversized as though begging the occupants to settle in and enjoy the warmth of the fire.

Two bedrooms opened off the living room. Craig peeked into the closest one, noting the plush pillows artistically arranged on the bed and the jack-and-jill bathroom joining the bedrooms.

"This place is incredible!" Craig set down his bag, the tan canvas contrasting against the pristine surroundings. "Who's paying for all this?"

"Don't worry about that. You two had better get settled while you can. It's going to be a crazy couple of days." Seth motioned toward the stairs. "We have a briefing downstairs in the main entrance in twenty minutes."

Seth and Jay left, and Craig looked over at Damian. "I don't know about you, but I sure never expected an assignment like this when I was going through hell week."

"We'd better enjoy it while we can. For all we know, we could be freezing our butts off in Afghanistan this time next week."

"Let's hope not." Craig hoisted his bag onto his shoulder and headed for the closest bedroom. "I think I could get used to this."

* * *

Marble floors, sweeping staircases, miniature palm trees in ceramic urns. An excellent watercolor hung on the wall to his left. William Blake looked past all that, instead focusing on the men gathered in the foyer. From what he'd been told, this entire squad was made up of Mormons. He hoped some of them were single. After all, it was time Sienna started socializing with men like these: men who knew how to handle themselves, who also had a testimony of the gospel.

He knew his granddaughter would be appalled if she knew he was thinking of meddling in her social life, but someone had to, or she might keep drifting for the next ten years. Besides, it was time she left those Hollywood boyfriends behind and started remembering what was important in life. And how was she ever going to find a good man if she never met any?

William approached the group, recognizing the woman standing with them as Amy Miller, Kendra's future sister-in-law. Amy's husband, Brent, stepped forward and shook his hand before he addressed the rest of the group.

"Everyone, this is William Blake. He's in charge of security for this weekend."

"So these are the Mormon boys I've heard so much about," William said, shaking hands with Seth and Tristan as they introduced themselves to him. He was disappointed when he noticed the wedding bands they both wore. The next man in line, Craig, was the first one with any promise, his left hand bare.

"Where do you come from, Craig?"

"Iowa."

"Really? Have you been with the squad long?"

"No, sir. This is my second week."

"I see. Did you serve a mission for the Church?"

"Yes, sir. I served in Geneva, Switzerland."

"It's very nice to meet you." William continued down the line and replayed the same conversation. When he asked Damian if he too had served a mission, Damian shook his head.

"No, sir. I'm not Mormon."

"Really? How did you end up in the Saint Squad?"

Damian cast an amused sidelong glance at his team. "Just lucky, I guess."

"So it appears. I've heard great things about this squad."

"Shall we go over your plan?" Brent interrupted, cutting William off before he could continue his inquisition.

"Here's what we've got." William passed a folder to each of them. "There's a complete guest list included here. I would like each of you to familiarize yourself with it."

Craig opened his folder and tapped a finger on the photos that accompanied each name. "This is great."

William was all business now. "We aren't taking any chances."

* * *

Craig listened to William and Brent discuss the various security plans for the upcoming events, though it was clear that William was most definitely the man in charge.

"Everyone will have to show ID to come in, but the private security firm will take care of that, as well as the metal detectors at the entrances," William said.

"How many guests are on this list?" Seth asked.

"Two hundred and fifty-seven," William said. "We're lucky this event is on the small side."

Craig wondered what William would consider a large party.

William motioned them toward a set of double doors a short distance away. "The main event will take place in here."

Everyone walked into the large banquet hall. A bank of windows stretched along the far wall, and a portable stage had been set up on one end of the room in front of a single door. On the opposite end, another set of double doors appeared to lead to the kitchen.

"That entrance will also be equipped with a metal detector, and a guard from the security detail will be stationed there." William motioned to a third set of doors on the same wall as the entrance they had emerged through. "The security company will also ID all of the service personnel."

"What about access to the grounds beyond those windows?" Seth asked.

"I have men assigned to cover the outside perimeter," William said.

"So the only way to get a weapon inside would be to plant it before security is in place," Brent added.

"Correct," William said. "The facility will be completely evacuated when we do a thorough sweep tomorrow morning."

Brent nodded his approval. "Sounds like you have all the bases covered."

"That's my job."

Seth looked at William inquisitively. "I thought you were retired."

"You'll find out eventually that you never truly retire."

Brent motioned to Damian and Craig. "The areas next to the entrances are the most vulnerable. We'll have you start out in the hall as people come through. If anyone's planning to try anything, you should be able to spot them as soon as they see the metal detectors."

"Actually, I'd like to have one of these men stand in as my granddaughter's date. She's one of the people I'm most concerned about," William said.

Craig felt a surge of apprehension. It wasn't like he was dating Sienna, but he certainly didn't want to be someone's date for hire while she was so firmly on his mind.

"Since Damian is recently engaged, I think Craig is the logical choice," Brent said.

"Perfect." William nodded in agreement.

"Is there anything else we need to know?"

"That should cover it," William said. "This is the main event, but we'll also have security details at a couple of smaller events off site. I'll give you more details on those when I have them finalized."

Once again, Craig wondered if the constant secrecy was common when planning missions. "Is there anyone in particular we are supposed to be protecting? I know secret service is usually assigned individuals to protect, and you mentioned your granddaughter."

William stepped forward. "Craig and Damian, I want you two to primarily focus on my family members. We've had a few issues in the past, which is why I would like to have your squad accompany my granddaughters tonight."

"We can certainly accommodate that," Brent said. "I've already outlined a watch schedule for tonight for the four team members who will be staying here."

The door across the room opened, and Craig looked on in wonder when they saw the beautiful Kendra Blake enter. Walking beside her was the man who was well known to be her fiancé.

"Here they come now." William waved for the newcomers to join them.

Before he could make introductions, the man beside Kendra rushed forward and scooped Amy into a hug. "Hey, sis."

"Charlie! I've missed you."

"I've missed you too." Charlie turned to shake hands with Brent as Craig stared, perplexed. Kendra's fiancé was Amy's brother?

"Thanks so much for being willing to help out with this," Charlie said to Brent.

"It's our pleasure."

Charlie proceeded to greet the rest of the squad by name, except for the two new members.

"Charlie, these are the new guys I was telling you about, Damian Schmitt and Craig Simmons. This is Charlie Whitmore, my brother-in-law, and that's his fiancé, Kendra Blake."

"Nice to meet you," Charlie said, extending his hand.

"You too," Craig said, nodding a greeting to Kendra. His mind spun, putting facts together as Damian fumbled through his greeting. Kendra Blake. The daughter of renowned actor Sterling Blake. The older sister of Sienna Blake.

He thought of his encounter with Sienna and George, finding it odd that Kendra didn't have a bodyguard trailing behind her.

Perhaps she didn't feel one was necessary when she was with her FBI agent fiancé.

The door opened once more, and Craig saw the familiar hulking figure fill the doorway. George stepped aside, and Sienna walked in behind him.

"Sienna, come meet the guys," William called out.

She took several steps before her eyes landed on Craig, surprise reflecting in them. His own surprise increased when instead of waiting to be introduced, Sienna shifted and walked directly to him.

"It's you," Craig said before he thought to play it cool in front of his squad. Sure enough, he could hear the snickers behind him.

"It is me," Sienna said. "It's good to see you again, Craig."

The snickers stopped, immediately replaced by stunned silence.

"I didn't know you were going to be here," Sienna continued.

"I didn't know I was going to be here either."

Sienna waved in Amy's direction. "Hi, Amy."

Amy nodded a greeting, apparently as stunned as everyone else in the room.

Hoping to fill the awkward silence, Craig motioned to the men beside him. "Have you already met the rest of my squad?"

"No, I haven't."

Craig went down the line, starting with Damian and ending with Brent.

Brent shook her hand. "It's nice to finally meet you."

"You too." Sienna looked over at William. "Am I interrupting, Grandpa?"

"Always, darling, but we'll forgive you."

Sienna flashed a smile. "You always do."

"Any sign of your parents yet?"

"No. You would have heard by now if they'd arrived."

"True. Very true," William agreed.

"We're heading upstairs to our suite. The manicurist just arrived. Can you let Mom know when she gets here?"

"No problem," William said. "You girls enjoy getting pampered."

"We'll do our best." Sienna kissed him on the cheek. "Come on, Kendra."

"See you all later." Kendra gave Charlie a quick kiss on his cheek before falling in step with her sister.

"Bye," Sienna said to everyone, but her eyes landed on Craig.

Craig watched her go and wondered how long it would take before the interrogation started.

8

"Okay, spill." Quinn was the first to make the demand, following Craig and Damian into their room, Tristan right behind them.

Enjoying himself, Craig looked at him innocently. "Spill what?"

"You know perfectly well what I'm talking about." Quinn closed the door to ensure some privacy. "How long have you known Sienna Blake?"

"I met her a few days ago." Craig pasted his best I-don't-know-what-the-big-deal-is look on his face.

"And you didn't tell us?" Damian rolled his eyes in disbelief.

Craig's left eyebrow lifted. "Would you have believed me?"

"Probably not," Quinn admitted. "But we would have had a great time razzing you."

Craig fought the grin trying to form. "Which is exactly why I didn't say anything."

"So what happened?" Tristan asked.

"Do you want me to tell you the truth, or should I make something up so you can razz me some more?"

Quinn seemed to consider his options, and Craig wisely didn't give him time to formulate an answer. "Quinn, I think I'm going to let you use your imagination."

"Now that's living dangerously," Tristan said.

Craig took his room key out of his pocket and dropped it on the dresser. "We need to get ready to go."

"I can't believe we got added to the security detail for the concert tonight," Damian responded, clearly thrilled with the development.

"I can't believe Craig is going to be Sienna Blake's date on Saturday," Quinn countered. Mischief lit his eyes. "The real question is if this is his first date with her."

Craig ignored him, stripping off his shirt and retrieving a clean one from the closet. He debated between jeans and tan slacks, grateful that he'd been told to dress casually for the concert tonight.

"Go with the jeans," Tristan said, apparently keying in on Craig's thoughts.

"Well?" Quinn asked impatiently.

"Well what?"

"You are no fun."

Tristan motioned to Quinn. "Come on. I guess we should get ready too."

Quinn hesitated briefly before taking a step toward the door, then he turned to Tristan. "You know, you really need to work on your interrogation techniques. You didn't help at all with him."

Tristan glanced back at Craig. "Yeah, I don't think he's cracking."

Now Quinn looked at Craig too. "We could use force."

"He's on our side, remember?"

"Oh yeah. I keep forgetting that."

"Maybe you should plan your tactics when I'm not standing in the same room," Craig suggested.

"He may have a point," Tristan said lightheartedly. Then he turned businesslike. "See you in twenty minutes out front. Don't be late."

* * *

Sienna walked toward the limousine that would take her to her sister's concert. She still couldn't believe Craig was here. What she didn't understand was why.

Craig had said he was with the navy, but guys in the military didn't typically hang out with celebrities. When they were talking in Virginia Beach, she had gotten the impression that he was with some kind of special forces unit. Had he exaggerated what he did for a living to impress her? It had happened before, too many times, but she hadn't gotten that sense with him. In fact, he'd seemed hesitant to tell her anything about his work.

She caught a glimpse of him standing with a couple of his friends. They were an interesting-looking bunch. Though they all exuded an air of confidence, she wouldn't have necessarily pegged them for military types. They all had short hair, but except for Craig, none of them had the traditional military-style crew cut. Even Craig's hair was a little longer than she suspected would normally be acceptable in the more rigid military units.

Craig looked toward her and offered a wave. She waved back, noticing the way one of his teammates elbowed him in the ribs good-naturedly. She suspected she had already become the topic of conversation between them. That was normal, she reminded herself, even as her heart sank a little.

When, she wondered, would she get the chance to know someone who liked her for herself instead of for the image her publicists had created? She'd thought Craig was different, but with the way his teammates were clearly joking around with him, now she wondered if he was like all the other men who had paraded through her life.

"Let's go," William said, motioning her into the car.

Turning her attention back to her family, she slid into the limousine and tried to look forward to the concert.

* * *

Throngs of people jostled in the long lines, an air of excitement humming when the doors opened and the first few disappeared inside. The wind picked up just then, causing many to catch their breath and huddle against the frigid air. The fact that so many had been standing in line for hours to ensure a good seat for Kendra Blake's concert only reinforced the truth that she continued to be one of the top stars in the industry.

He watched from a distance, standing in the sheltered doorway of a nearby building. He didn't stand in lines. He never had, and he wasn't about to start now. His hand gripped a single concert ticket, annoyed at the reminder of how much his life had changed over the past year. Always, in the past, he had sported a backstage pass, and tickets had been unnecessary.

The crowd continued to move forward with anticipation, taking a frustratingly long time to finally filter inside. When the line was nothing more than a handful of stragglers, he moved forward and relinquished his ticket to gain admittance to the warmth inside. Blending in with the crowd, he walked into the Patriot Center and took a critical look around.

He had been here before and was pleased to see that nothing appeared to have changed in how the facility operated their security. His stern face relaxed slightly, his confidence rising with each passing moment. He was going to make it backstage today. He was sure of it. And when he did, the Blake family was finally going to understand what they had done to him. Tonight was the night his life was finally going to change.

* * *

Craig felt like he was on another training exercise, only this time, instead of checking a handful of people for weapons, he was searching a crowd of ten thousand. He'd spent his first two hours at the Patriot Center at George Mason University watching the mass of people making their way inside, all the while searching for any sign of a problem and trying not to think about the biting February wind.

The concert was already underway when he received his current assignment: watching the back door. His teammates were scattered throughout the facility, rotating through the various sections in the crowd and the area by the main entrance.

"Any chance I get to come inside sometime soon?" Craig asked, using his headset to communicate with his squad. "It's freezing out here."

"Is there any activity in your area?" Brent asked. With his voice came the background noise of the concert in progress.

"Nothing," Craig responded. "I haven't seen anyone for ten minutes."

"We'll let the local security take care of everything outside. Go to the backstage area. I've got the area to stage left. You take stage right."

"Will do." Craig rubbed his hands together, despite the gloves he wore, in an effort to get the blood flowing again. He approached the door he had been guarding, knocked, and showed his backstage pass to the security officer inside.

"Finally coming in from the cold, huh?" the large Polynesian man asked. The little gold name tag on his uniform identified him as Kalani, and Craig's quick analysis of him indicated Kalani used his size rather than a weapon to protect the back entrance.

"Yeah." Craig pulled the door closed behind him. He tugged off his gloves and rubbed his hands together again. "The temperature is dropping fast out there."

"That's not a problem in here."

Craig unzipped his jacket, welcoming the warmth radiating from the heating system as well as the crowd. A roar of applause sounded.

"The opening act is finishing up," Kalani said. "It'll take the crew a few minutes to change the set before Kendra Blake's performance begins."

"I'm going to take a look around. I assume you haven't had any problems back here."

"So far, so good."

"Hopefully it will stay that way." Craig started down a wide corridor leading toward the stage. Stagehands scurried back and forth, mostly carrying pieces of equipment. Instinctively Craig scanned the area for anyone who wasn't actively engaged in the concert set change.

He saw Charlie from a distance, standing down the hall outside what appeared to be a dressing room. The door behind him opened, and Kendra emerged, followed by Sienna.

Craig let his gaze linger long enough to see Kendra give Sienna a hug. Kendra then reached up to give Charlie a kiss a moment before Craig caught movement on the edge of his peripheral vision. He sized up the man walking toward Kendra, Charlie, and Sienna. He appeared to be in his fifties, and the way he carried himself made Craig think he was part of the Blake family's private security staff. Only he hadn't been in the briefing before the concert.

A lanyard hung around his neck, but what appeared to be a backstage pass was flipped around so the front wasn't visible. He didn't appear to be carrying a weapon, which sent a sense of unease through Craig. The family's security staff was armed, which made it unlikely that this man was a bodyguard. He also didn't appear to be part of the backstage crew.

"Charlie, do you know the guy heading toward you?" Craig asked. "He's at your three o'clock. I haven't seen him before."

"Yeah, I know him." Charlie stiffened. "I need some backup here."

"Craig, go," Brent ordered. "You're the closest."

Brent needn't have said a word. Charlie's defensive posture was enough to quicken Craig's steps. He was already within earshot when the man approached only to find himself facing Charlie's gun.

Craig drew his own weapon, not sure why Charlie considered this man a threat. Adrenaline rushed through him, and Craig scanned the backstage area, realizing this man might not be alone.

The presence of drawn weapons was enough to send most of the backstage crew scampering for cover behind the heavy curtains separating the main stage from the backstage area.

"What are you doing here, Bruce?" Charlie asked, his voice surprisingly calm considering he was pointing a gun at the man. "And how did you get back here?"

"I'm not armed." Bruce held his hands out in a gesture of submission. "I only wanted to talk to Kendra."

Charlie lowered his weapon slightly. "I thought her father made it clear when he let you go that he didn't want you anywhere near the Blake family."

"I wanted to apologize." Bruce shifted his gaze to Kendra. "I had no idea what my son was doing. You have to know I would have done anything to protect you and your family."

"Bruce, I appreciate the sentiment, but that doesn't answer Charlie's question," Kendra said. "Why are you here now? You already sent me a letter telling me all this."

Bruce's skin flushed slightly. "I've had some difficulty securing employment this past year. I hoped you might be willing to talk to your dad, maybe see if he would give me another chance."

"You've got to be kidding me," Charlie said before Kendra could respond. "Your own son tried to kill her. How can the Blakes ever trust you again?"

"I didn't know," Bruce insisted. "I swear I didn't."

"It was your job to know," Charlie countered.

Bruce stood a little taller. "I kept the Blake family safe for over a decade. Shouldn't that count for something?" He drew a breath and seemed to muster his courage before adding, "My son was sick, and he hid the symptoms well. I wasn't the only one who missed the signs."

Kendra put her hand on Charlie's arm before speaking. "Bruce, I will tell my father we spoke, but I doubt anything I say will change his mind. Like you said, you worked for my family for more than ten years. You of all people know how protective he is."

"I see." Bruce took a step back. "I'm sorry I bothered you."

Charlie motioned in Craig's direction. "Craig, would you please escort Bruce out?"

"Yeah, sure." Craig did another quick analysis of the situation before he holstered his weapon and reached out to take the older man's arm. "This way."

Bruce didn't offer any resistance as Craig led him to the door he had entered a few minutes earlier.

"Where did he come from?" Kalani asked.

"I'm not sure, but he's leaving."

Kalani gave a curt nod and pulled open the door.

Bruce turned to face Craig. "Whether they know it or not, the Blakes need me."

Craig's blood ran cold with Bruce's certainty. "What do you mean?"

"They'll figure it out eventually," Bruce said as though Craig hadn't spoken. "I just hope it's not too late when they do."

Craig's grip on Bruce's arm tightened. "Is that a threat?"

"It's a fact." Bruce shook his arm loose and walked outside. "Enjoy the concert."

* * *

Sienna had felt invisible as she'd watched the exchange between Bruce and Charlie. The attempt on her sister's life last year still seemed like a bad dream she had heard about only in bits and pieces. Kendra had gone into hiding last winter, unsure at the time who had planted a bomb at her concert, but Sienna had been on the other side of the world, filming a movie in London.

Seeing her father's longtime head of security for the first time in over a year had been both unexpected and unnerving. Bruce Parsons had always been a quiet presence in their home, and a frustrating one at times. He had often been behind restricting her movements, keeping her from going to various parties and events, even when she and Kendra wanted nothing more than to attend a Church activity on a weeknight.

So much had changed since that attempt had been made on Kendra's life, an attempt that had resulted in Bruce's son becoming paralyzed and ultimately being committed to a mental institution. Though Sienna couldn't say she had ever been terribly fond of Bruce, she felt bad for him because of the situation he was in now. What must it be like, she wondered, for him to suddenly find himself without a job? And to be blacklisted on top of it.

Her father hadn't specifically done anything to prevent Bruce from working elsewhere, but he hadn't helped him find other employment either.

Visibly shaken by the unexpected visitor, Kendra took a few minutes to settle herself emotionally before taking the stage. Sienna stayed with Charlie and watched the performance from the wings, but she knew where Charlie's attention was focused. Her few attempts at conversation went unanswered as Charlie kept one eye on the backstage area and one on his bride-to-be.

Sienna found her own eyes wandering as one song led to another. It didn't take long for her to realize she was looking for Craig. He hadn't reappeared after escorting Bruce to the door.

The concert was nearly over when Sienna caught sight of Craig talking to Brent. The two men spoke briefly, and then Craig looked around, his eyes landing on her. He lifted his chin in a brief acknowledgment and then headed toward the exit, disappearing once more.

Kendra started her final number, and several members of the crew gathered for the inevitable encores that would follow. Sienna looked around the crowded backstage area, realizing she was surrounded by people but felt completely alone.

9

CRAIG SAW HER IN THE moonlight, recognizing Sienna by her
stride rather than by her features. He had barely seen her at the
concert, and he had been disappointed that their paths hadn't
crossed except for the brief moment when Bruce Parsons had
shown up. After escorting the man out, Craig had learned from
William that the intruder had been fired as Sterling Blake's head
of security after an attempt had been made on Kendra's life.

The buzz of conversation after Bruce's departure had filled
in a lot more details, including the information that Bruce's
son had also worked for the Blake family until they'd learned
the man was a serial killer who had fixated on Kendra. The
details of the attempt on Kendra's life were sketchy, but one of
the family's bodyguards had mentioned that Charlie had been
one of the agents responsible for taking the man into custody
before the killer had the chance to hurt Kendra.

The idea that such danger could exist for Sienna's sister left a
sick feeling in Craig's stomach and made him uneasy about the
fact that someone might try to hurt either of the Blake sisters for
any reason. Throughout the concert, Craig's protective instincts
had remained heightened. He'd quietly worked with his team in
the background, staying in the shadows and seeing everything.

Positions shifted throughout the night, and Craig had wished he could personally keep an eye on Sienna. At least she had been standing beside Charlie when he had traded places with Quinn in the audience.

The rest of the evening had gone by without incident, except for a couple of minor scuffles in the parking lot and a trio of teenagers who had tried to sneak backstage. Tristan had put an end to that.

Shortly before the Blakes left the concert, they sent Craig and Seth back to the estate where the family was staying to secure the premises and make sure security was in place before their arrival. Checking out the house itself didn't take long, but the grounds were more challenging.

They made their rounds through the surrounding woods and searched the house a second time. A few minutes after they finished, Brent and Damian arrived with William. When Craig was assigned the first watch shift, he resigned himself to the reality that he and Sienna might be in the same place, but he was here to work and wasn't likely to see her as much as he would like.

He reminded himself of that fact as he watched her heading slowly down one of the sidewalks encircling the resort. Not wanting to intrude on her private thoughts, he stayed in the shadows as she approached the fountain in the center of the courtyard. She was wearing a sweatshirt again, her hood up, her hands tucked in the pocket. He wondered if she ever considered wearing a coat to ward off the winter chill. Even as he had that thought, he saw a shiver run through her.

Craig shrugged out of his overcoat and stepped forward. "Here. I think you need this more than I do."

She whirled around to face him, her hand lifting to her heart.

"Sorry. Didn't mean to startle you, but you look like you're cold." He draped the coat around her shoulders.

"Thanks."

"What are you doing out here?" Craig glanced around the area again. "And where is George?"

"I didn't want to wake him. He needs his rest for tomorrow."

"Even if George was sleeping, I know your grandfather assigned one of your parents' bodyguards to watch the upstairs hallway. Didn't he question you before you came downstairs?"

"He never saw me." At Craig's confused look, she added, "Let's just say I'm well practiced in slipping past security when I need some time alone."

"You realize the bodyguards are there for your protection, right?" When Sienna simply shrugged, he asked, "Exactly how did you get past your bodyguard tonight?"

"It wasn't complicated. I gave Bernie a big cup of his favorite hot chocolate. Ten minutes later, when he went to the bathroom, I came down here."

"That's sneaky."

"When you live your whole life with security, you learn the tricks. Sometimes desperate times call for desperate measures."

Craig took a half step back and studied her. "You don't look desperate to me."

Her eyes lifted to meet his. "I'll take that as a compliment."

"As it was intended."

"What are you doing down here?" Sienna asked.

"I'm here for when you and your sister sneak past your usual security." Realizing he had let his focus center on Sienna, he glanced around the courtyard to make sure they were still alone.

"Seriously?"

"Seriously." Craig winked at her. "I guess your grandfather is on to you."

"My grandfather?"

"Yeah. He's the one who set us up here."

"I see." Sienna folded her arms across her chest. "And exactly what do you do? Don't tell me you're a bodyguard. I thought you were in the navy."

"I am in the navy."

"Why would my grandfather enlist the navy's help in keeping the Blake family in line?"

"Excellent question. It's not one I'm really sure I can answer though."

"Why not?" She lowered her voice. "Is it classified?"

"No. I just don't know the answer."

Sienna chuckled. "Then why are you doing it?"

"Following orders." His gaze swept the area before he turned his attention back to her. "I have to think it has something to do with my commanding officer being your sister's future brother-in-law."

Her face lit with understanding. "Ahh. So you think Brent called in a favor."

"Something like that. Plus, we're always doing training exercises, so he probably sold the higher-ups on the need for Damian and me to get some hands-on experience."

"You and Damian? What about the others?"

"We're the new guys."

"Oh, really?"

"Yeah. Our squad just expanded from five to seven members. The other guys have been together for a long time, so we're still the stepchildren."

"What kind of squad do you belong to? I assume you have some kind of specialty."

"The Saint Squad is trained in a lot of different areas." He debated whether he should keep his career path from her, then decided it wouldn't hurt to be honest with her. "We're Navy SEALs."

"SEALs? Wow, Brent really pulled in some favors." She tilted her head as though his declaration might have changed him somehow. "Why are you called the Saint Squad?"

"Apparently when the squad was formed, most of them were the same religion. The nickname comes from Latter-day Saint."

Her eyebrows lifted. "Are you all Mormon?"

"All of us except Damian."

"That was unexpected. I'm a member too."

"You're kidding. I had no idea."

"I'm surprised you missed that little tidbit." She fell silent for a moment. "How much do you know about what's going on this weekend?"

"All I know is that we're supposed to be on protection detail for the next forty-eight to seventy-two hours."

"Really?"

Craig sensed her surprise, which only reinforced his suspicion that the rest of his squad was keeping some pertinent facts from him.

"When is your shift up?"

He glanced at his watch to see it was nearly 3:00 a.m. "Seth should be here to relieve me in a few minutes."

"Do you think we could go for a walk?"

"A walk where? It's the middle of the night."

"You do realize that most people would jump at the prospect of going for a walk with a famous movie star."

Craig considered that. "I guess you're right."

"You guess?" She was being playful, but a touch of insecurity illuminated her face. "Are you saying you don't want to go for a walk with me?"

"I'm telling you that my concern right now is to make sure you stay safe. That is my job at the moment."

She straightened slightly. "I see. So you really are acting like a bodyguard."

"For the next forty-eight to seventy-two hours, I am." Something changed around him. He turned, putting his body between Sienna and the space where he felt someone's presence.

Seth emerged from the sidewalk behind him.

"I gather you're here to relieve me."

"That's right." Seth motioned to Sienna. "How did you get out here?"

"She wanted to go for a walk," Craig answered for her.

"And her bodyguard was okay with that?"

"Kind of."

Seth shook his head. "I don't feel comfortable with you out walking by yourself."

72 — Traci Hunter Abramson

"What if Craig is with me?" Sienna asked.

Seth reached out and tugged on the hood of her sweatshirt. "Keep the hood up, keep Craig with you, and stay on the grounds."

"Really?" Sienna said, delighted.

"I'm not a prison warden. I just look like one," Seth said, his lips twitching into a brief smile. "Craig, keep your comm gear with you in case you run into any trouble."

"Will do." Craig watched Seth cross the courtyard to check the perimeter of the resort grounds. He turned to Sienna. "Where to?"

"I don't know. I didn't think anyone would say yes." Sienna looked up at him. "Do you mind going for a walk with me?"

"It depends. Am I going on a walk with Sienna Blake or a famous movie star?"

"Is there a difference?"

"I would think so."

Genuine surprise reflected on her face. "I knew I liked you."

"I hope so." Craig shifted beside her and put a hand on her back to guide her down a path. The naturalness of the gesture surprised him, and a glimmer of hope for something beyond friendship took hold. He smiled slightly. "After all, I am your date for Saturday night."

* * *

Sienna took a moment to process Craig's words. At first she thought he was asking to be her date for Saturday. Disappointment and irritation surfaced when she realized he had been assigned to play the part.

Silence fell between them, and Craig must have sensed her mood change. He reached out, touched her arm, and slowed his pace. She could imagine acting out such a scene for the cameras, but the tingling sensation shooting through her at Craig's touch wasn't something she could summon at will. Every time he touched her, she experienced a similar response, yet now she wondered if the growing attraction was real on his part or only hers.

"You didn't know?" he asked.

Sienna shook her head. "This is the first I've heard of it."

"I'm sorry. I assumed your grandfather had already talked to you about having someone stand in as your date."

"Knowing Grandpa, he was planning to wait until we were on our way to the reception to mention it."

They reached the edge of the woods, the moonlight casting shadows on the path. Craig stopped and turned to face her. "If you would rather I not be your date, I can talk to your grandfather."

"If he has it in his mind that I need a personal bodyguard, nothing is going to change it," Sienna said, not bothering to disguise her frustration. She couldn't be sure if her grandfather was being overprotective or if he was trying to play matchmaker like he had for her sister.

Embarrassment bubbled to the surface, and she could feel her public persona settling over her, that thick shield she often used to protect her real feelings from being seen. "How did you end up being the lucky one? Did you draw straws? Pick numbers? What?" Sienna watched Craig's expression, searching for any clues that he might be holding something back. She might not be an FBI agent like her grandfather, but over the years, she had learned how to read people.

"Hardly. I was the logical choice," Craig said. "After I survived your grandfather's interrogation, he realized I was the only single member of the squad. That's how you got stuck with me."

"It sounds like you're the one who got stuck with me." Sienna questioned Craig's motivation. It seemed everyone always wanted something from her. Why should he be any different? "You realize this could make you famous," she continued. "One kiss on the cheek, a few too many dances, or even holding hands could put you on the front page of all the gossip websites."

"Thanks for the warning."

"What? You don't want to be famous?" She cringed inwardly at the way she sounded like the epitome of a Hollywood diva.

"Not particularly," Craig answered as though he truly didn't care about her fame. "My line of work and fame aren't terribly compatible."

The realization that his words were uncomfortably true overshadowed her annoyance, and she felt her defenses ease. "Now you sound like Charlie."

"FBI agents can work successfully without going undercover. SEALs don't typically announce where they work. If we get noticed by the wrong people in another country, it could turn deadly."

"Then why are you doing this?"

"Because I was asked to." Craig stopped walking and took her hand. He held it until she turned to face him. "I hope you know I would have volunteered, given the opportunity."

His sincerity sent a flutter through her. "In my world, most people plan everything they do with the press in mind. I'm not used to being around someone who isn't trying to get their name in print one way or another."

"I promise you'll never have to worry about that with me. In fact, I would appreciate it if you wouldn't tell anyone I'm in the military."

"What am I supposed to say when people ask me what you do?" Sienna asked. "That question is bound to come up."

"We could always say I work on my family's farm. Technically I still own an interest in my mom's place," Craig told her. "Of course, if I'm standing next to you, I doubt I'll be the focus of the conversation. We both know you'll be the center of attention."

"Not this time. Saturday belongs to Kendra and Charlie."

"What do you mean?"

Sienna debated briefly whether she could confide in Craig. She wanted desperately to be able to talk to someone about her roller coaster of emotions surrounding her sister's upcoming wedding. Though she didn't know Craig well, he was clearly being invited into her inner circle. After all, he was being trusted with her safety by one of the people who loved her most. Still, knowing her own parents weren't aware that Kendra and Charlie were getting married this weekend held her back. "You'll see soon enough."

"See what?" Craig's eyes narrowed. "I'm so tired of not knowing what's really going on."

"How good are you at keeping a secret?"

"I'm a Navy SEAL. That's part of the job."

"You have to understand, not even my parents know what's really happening," Sienna began.

"What *is* really happening?"

She looked around to make sure they were alone. "The Whitmores' anniversary party is an excuse for us to all be here." She shifted closer to Craig. "We're really here for Kendra's wedding."

Though she caught a glimpse of Craig's surprise, she saw him quickly mask it with understanding. "Now everything is starting to make sense."

"You can't tell anyone I told you."

"Don't worry. Your secrets are safe with me."

Sienna stared up at him, finding a sense of calm she hadn't felt since arriving in Virginia. Suddenly the idea of going to Kendra's wedding with Craig at her side didn't feel like an imposition. Instead, she looked forward to the prospect.

"Come on." Craig motioned back toward the resort. "We should both get some sleep while we can. It sounds like the next couple days are going to be even crazier than I thought."

When he took her hand and a bevy of butterflies erupted in her stomach, Sienna found new meaning in his words. "*That* you can count on."

10

"You want me to do what?" Craig was certain he hadn't heard Brent right.

"We have to secure Sterling's cell phone," Brent repeated. He had used those exact same words a moment ago when Craig had arrived in his room to find Brent waiting for him with William and Sienna.

"You mean steal," Craig corrected. "You want me to steal Sterling's cell phone."

"If my son has his cell phone when he finds out Kendra is getting married this weekend, word will get out. We have to make sure he and Monica don't have any way to communicate with the outside world until after the reception is over."

"How are we getting Mrs. Blake's phone?" Craig asked.

"Kendra and Charlie already took care of that. Kendra borrowed Monica's phone this morning when they were at breakfast and gave it to me instead of giving it back to her mom," William said. "I'll give it back after the wedding."

"Won't she notice it's missing?"

William shook his head. "She loses her phone all the time, so she probably won't realize it's missing until we get ready to leave."

"What about your son? He'll notice his phone is gone."

"He's so used to his assistant taking care of his phone, there's a good chance he won't notice. Besides, I plan to keep him distracted tonight at the White House. Hopefully, by the time he does notice, it will be too late for him to do anything about it.

"Now, this is how it's going to work," William continued. "Sienna will introduce you to her dad and let him know that you'll be her date for tomorrow."

"*This* should be interesting," Sienna mumbled under her breath.

Craig read her expression. "I gather he's the protective type."

"Maybe a bit," William answered for her before continuing. "I'll call Sterling to tell him I'm coming to see him. That way we'll know where his phone is. One of you will text me that information, and when I get to his room, I'll give him a hug and pickpocket his phone."

"Grandpa, you're making this way too complicated," Sienna said. "What happens if Dad keeps his phone in his hand after you call him? You can't lift it off him if he's holding it."

"Do you have a better idea?"

Sienna gave them all a winning smile. "Watch and learn."

Twenty minutes later, Craig stood outside Sterling's hotel suite with Sienna by his side. "I can't believe we're doing this."

"Just follow my lead." She slipped one hand into his and lifted the other to knock.

"As long as it doesn't get me killed." He hoped the flutter of nerves rushing through him was a result of holding Sienna's hand rather than preparing to meet her father.

She grinned at him and sent his stomach somersaulting. "Don't worry. My dad doesn't carry a gun."

Sterling's door swung open, and in a flash, his expression went from welcoming to glowering. Craig had seen both expressions in various movies over the years. He found this man even more intimidating in person than he was when facing down terrorists on the big screen. Apparently Sienna wasn't joking when she said her dad was overprotective.

"Hi, Dad." Sienna released Craig's hand long enough to give her dad a hug. "This is my boyfriend, Craig."

"Boyfriend? When did this happen?" Sterling demanded. "I was just getting used to you going out with Joseph Hurst."

"Let's go inside, and I'll tell you all about it." Expertly, Sienna nudged her father aside, took Craig's hand, and led both men into Sterling's sitting room.

After Sterling closed the door, Craig once again found himself facing the man who seemed larger than life, even in the informal setting of a hotel suite. Mustering his courage and trying not to think about the fact that this was one of the most famous men in the world, Craig continued to grip Sienna's hand and extended his right hand to Sterling. "It's an honor to meet you, sir."

"Craig Simmons, this is my father, Sterling Blake," Sienna said to ease the introduction.

Sterling waited two heartbeats before shaking hands.

"Why don't we sit?" Sienna suggested.

Sterling conceded by lowering himself onto the love seat, strategically ensuring that Craig and Sienna couldn't sit together. Sienna sat beside her father, and Craig took one of the two chairs facing them.

"Where did the two of you meet? And how long have you been dating?"

"I guess you could say George introduced us," Sienna answered without missing a beat. "Craig has been helping me get ready for my next movie."

"How so?"

"He's been teaching me some of the moves I'll need for my character."

Sterling relaxed marginally. "And how is that going?"

"Very well," Craig answered. "Your daughter is a natural."

Sterling's phone rang, and he answered it. As expected, it was William. They already knew the gist of the conversation: William was making plans with Sterling for their trip to the White House that evening.

As soon as their plans were set, Sterling handed his phone to Sienna. "Your grandpa wants to talk to you."

Sienna took the phone and stood. "Hi, Grandpa."

She listened for a moment before saying, "Just a minute." She then turned her attention back to her father. "I'm going to take this in the other room so you two can talk."

Craig watched her disappear into the bedroom. When he turned his attention back to Sterling, the man was sizing him up once more.

"My daughter said you're helping her prepare for her movie role. Have you been working in the industry long?"

"Actually, no. This is my first time."

"Then how did you come to George's attention?"

"I guess you could say he didn't have a choice but to notice me." Not wanting to elaborate on his first encounter with Sienna and her bodyguard, Craig changed the subject. "I understand you're going to tour the White House today."

"Yes. We'll have a tour and an informal dinner with the president and his family."

"I hadn't heard that. I wasn't aware you knew the president."

"I met him once when he was campaigning in California. Senator Whitmore actually arranged for our visit when he found out we were coming into town."

"I'm sure it will be an experience to remember."

Not easily distracted, Sterling steered the conversation back to Craig. "If this is your first time working in the film business, what do you normally do for a living?"

"I'm a farmer."

The man across from him didn't utilize his acting talents to hide his surprise. "A farmer?"

"Yes, sir."

"I see. And exactly how does a farmer gain the expertise needed to train an actress for an action movie?"

"Ten years of martial-arts training didn't hurt," Craig said.

"I wouldn't think farmers would have easy access to that kind of thing."

"I started learning from my dad. He was in the navy for a few years when he was younger. When I got into high school, I started driving to Des Moines to train."

Sterling shifted forward in his seat and pinned Craig with a hard stare. "What exactly are your intentions toward my daughter?"

Craig didn't have to pretend to be nervous. He clasped his hands together tightly in his lap, remembering that he was only playing a part . . . Never mind that he was making his first acting debut in front of a man who had ruled Hollywood for decades.

"Actually, I hope to marry her."

"*What?*"

"Sienna and I are here to ask for your blessing." Craig forced the words through his mouth. He wondered if they would have been any easier to say if William and Sienna hadn't fed them to him. He seriously doubted it.

Sterling's jaw hung open, and it took him a moment to recover. When he did, he opened and closed his mouth twice before any words came out. "You expect me to give you my blessing when I had never even heard of you before today?" He pushed to a stand and paced across the room, circling the limited space until he once again stood in front of Craig.

"I know it may seem sudden," Craig said, judging that Sterling had worked off the worst of his shock. "We've actually known each other for some time. We just wanted to keep our relationship private until we had a chance to talk to you."

"Exactly how long has that been?"

"Fourteen months," Craig recited his next line. "I hope you can support us in this," he continued. "I love your daughter very much."

"Do you love my daughter or her bank account?"

Craig bristled now, no longer acting. He stood in an effort to put himself back on equal ground with the man across from him. "I can't say that I've ever met Sienna's bank account, nor do I see any reason why I would need to."

"You can't seriously expect me to believe you plan to support her on a farmer's income."

"I have a few other plans for my future that go beyond farming." Craig shoved his hands in his pockets, fisting them there. He heard the bedroom door open and saw Sienna enter once more.

As Sienna had predicted he would, Sterling rounded on her. "You can't honestly expect me to believe you want to marry this guy."

"Of course I can." Rather than move to the couch, she crossed to Craig, linked her arm through his, and adopted a wounded look. "I thought you wanted me to be happy."

"Of course I want you to be happy, but I don't know anything about this guy."

"Grandpa knows him."

On cue, a knock sounded at the door. Sterling stomped to the door and threw it open to reveal William standing in the hall.

William evaluated the situation in about three seconds. "I gather Craig has already talked to you."

"What is it with you?" Sterling demanded. "This is twice you've known my girls were dating seriously without telling me."

"Sorry, son, but you tend to meddle in your daughters' lives."

As Sterling blustered, William stepped inside and tapped at his watch. "I think we may need to table your discussion with these two until later. We don't want to keep the president waiting."

"Did you know they're planning to get married?" Sterling demanded.

"I had a feeling." William put his hand on his son's arm. "Come on. We can talk on the way."

Sienna gave her grandfather a kiss on the cheek and repeated the gesture with her dad. "I'll go make sure Kendra and Charlie are ready to go."

"It was good to meet you, sir," Craig said. He thought about offering to shake hands again but decided against it. Somehow he didn't think Sterling was feeling particularly friendly toward him at the moment. He followed Sienna to the door. "I hope you all enjoy your evening."

"Aren't you coming with us?" Sterling asked, stunning everyone in the room.

"I don't think I was included on the invitation."

William stepped in before Sterling could respond. "Secret Service is very strict on having advance notice of everyone visiting the White House. I'm afraid we didn't know Craig was going to be able to join us this weekend until a few days ago."

"Come on, Craig." Sienna tugged on his arm. "You can keep Charlie company while Kendra and I finish getting ready."

Craig followed her into the hall, not saying a word until they were well away from her father's suite. He looked over his shoulder. "I think I deserve hazard pay for that."

"But it worked." Sienna grinned and held up her father's cell phone. "My dad was so distracted he totally forgot I had it."

"That's fine for you. I'm the one who had to face an irate father who isn't ready to give up his little girl."

"Just think of it as practice for when you do decide to get married."

"That's not funny."

Sienna stopped and looked up at him, a smile still on her face. "Yeah, it was."

"It would have been funny . . . had it been someone else going through it."

"That's the price you pay for being the only single guy on your squad." Sienna reached up on her toes to kiss his cheek. "I'll see you later."

The gesture was so natural Craig almost forgot he and Sienna had been playing out a scene. She was halfway down the hall by the time he recovered, and he wondered again if there was a chance something could develop between them beyond friendship.

11

SIENNA THOUGHT OF THE NIGHT before at the White House, of the history of the building and the novelty of dining with the president. Her father had clearly been as impressed with the intimate dinner party as she had been. Otherwise, there was no way he would have made it through the evening without noticing his cell phone was missing.

She considered it a good sign that he hadn't mentioned anything about his phone when they had left the resort that morning. Logically he should have realized he didn't have it when he went to bed last night since that's when he normally took the time to charge it. She could only imagine that the excitement of touring the White House had thrown his routine off enough that he had been too tired to worry about such things.

She supposed the news of what their real plans were for this morning distracted him further. Now she sat with her parents inside a rented limousine, the glory of the Washington D.C. Temple rising into the blue sky behind them. Any moment, Kendra and Charlie would emerge for the first time as husband and wife.

The privacy window between them and their driver was raised, even though their driver was Damian, a member of the Saint Squad.

In keeping with the engagement story Sienna had invented, Craig sat beside her, both of her parents across from them.

"I still can't believe no one told us," Monica Blake said.

"Mom, I'm sorry, but it was really important to Kendra and Charlie that their wedding day not turn into a media circus."

"How would telling us have made a difference? We wouldn't have told anyone," Monica insisted.

Sienna let that comment linger in the air.

"And I want to know who is handling security. We should bring in extra personnel to make sure everyone is safe." Sterling reached into his pant pocket and then the other one, a wrinkle of confusion appearing on his face when he didn't find what he was looking for.

"First of all, Grandpa took care of security. Second of all, your incessant need for more bodyguards is why you only found out about the wedding an hour ago."

"What does that have to do with anything? What's wrong with having extra security?" He patted his shirt pocket. "And where is my blasted phone?"

Sienna ignored his last question and zeroed in on his previous ones. "If you knew about the wedding, you would have told your head of security why we needed extra bodyguards. Undoubtedly, someone would have leaked it to the press."

"You don't know that," Sterling insisted. "My people can be trusted."

"You can trust them all you want, but today is about Kendra and Charlie," Sienna countered. "Please help them enjoy it. They went to a lot of effort to make sure you would be here."

"I need to at least call my publicist to make sure he knows I'll have a press release to send out tomorrow," Sterling said. He patted his wife's knee. "Monica, let me borrow your phone."

She picked up her purse and started rummaging through it.

Craig reached over and took Sienna's hand, giving it a squeeze in silent communication. Sienna looked up at him, seeing the same question reflected on his face as the one running through her mind. When would her parents realize they had taken their phones?

She gave a little shrug and decided it was time for some distraction. "Mom, you are going to love the dress Kendra had made for you for the reception tonight. This new designer Kendra discovered is amazing."

Monica gave up on her search. "I hope it fits. You know how hard it is for me to get things to fit me right in the waist."

"Don't worry. The designer is going to meet us back at the resort in case anyone needs any alterations made."

Sterling redirected his wife's attention. "Your phone?"

"Sorry, honey. I don't see it in there. I must have left it in our room."

"Sienna, let me borrow yours." Her father held out his hand.

"I don't have mine either."

"What about you, Craig? Are you going to tell me you aren't carrying your cell phone either?"

"No, sir." Craig pulled his phone free of his pocket, unlocked the screen and, to Sienna's surprise, handed it over.

"Finally." Sterling took the phone, prepared to dial, and hesitated. He turned to his wife. "What's Nate's phone number?"

"I don't know. I have it in my phone."

"Great," Sterling muttered and handed Craig his phone back. "I guess I can call later."

Craig pocketed the phone once more.

"Kendra and Charlie should be coming out soon. Should we go wait by the door?" Sienna asked.

"Good idea," her mother agreed.

Craig exited first. Sienna took the hand Craig offered her and let him help her from the car. They walked toward the temple, taking up a position where they could see through the glass doors into the lobby. They were there only a few minutes before she caught her first glimpse of Kendra.

"Look, here they come." She shifted closer to Craig as her sister emerged in a vision of white, hand in hand with her husband.

Something tugged inside her, an unusual combination of joy, wonder, and longing. When Craig rubbed his thumb over the back of her hand, the wonder dominated. The magic of the moment, seeing such happiness on Kendra's face, gave her hope that someday she too could find someone she would want to spend eternity with.

Within moments, they were all exchanging hugs while the photographer Charlie had hired captured their emotions on film.

* * *

"Smile."

Craig forced himself to comply with the photographer's direction, not terribly happy with the prospect of having his picture taken, even if he was standing next to one of the most amazing women he'd ever met. He was clean-shaven tonight, a small attempt to alter his appearance for the cameras. Sienna shifted closer to him, her arm hooked loosely around his waist, his own hand resting on her shoulder.

He wished he could enjoy simply being with her, but he had a job to do, and the constant barrage of people to meet made it difficult to appear casual as he surveyed the other guests. The impromptu photo shoot was one in a long line of interruptions.

After what felt like forever, the photographer gave them a nod of approval. "Thanks so much."

"Are we done now?" Craig whispered to Sienna.

"For the moment."

"I don't know how you do it."

She looked up, curiosity in her eyes. "What?"

"Deal with the constant attention." Craig led her to the side of the room where he could survey the guests more easily. "I don't think there's a single person in this room who hasn't made a point of talking to you tonight."

She tucked her arm through his. "Maybe they all want to meet my handsome boyfriend."

He looked down at her and adopted a wounded expression. "I've been demoted to boyfriend? I thought I was your fiancé."

"That's right. I keep forgetting." She held her left hand up as though examining her new manicure. "I guess that's why men give women engagement rings. To remind them of those promises."

"I don't think your dad is quite ready to see me put a ring on your finger."

"We could have been together for three years and he wouldn't be ready," Sienna countered.

Instinctively Craig did a search of the crowd until he located Sterling. He and Monica stood at the edge of the dais across the room, along with Senator Whitmore and his wife. The large clock mounted on the wall revealed that the time was drawing near for Kendra's and Charlie's families to focus everyone's attention on the real reason they had all gathered together.

A heightened level of activity stirred near the main entrance, a short distance from where the happy couple's parents were standing.

"Wait here," Craig instructed.

"What's wrong?" Sienna asked, but Craig had already walked away.

Craig strode across the room, taking position behind Sienna's parents as a man standing right outside the door called out, "Sterling! Over here!"

"Do you know that man?" Craig asked Sterling.

Sterling's response was more to himself than to Craig. "I didn't know Carter Wells was going to be here."

"Carter Wells? The actor?"

"Yes. We've been in several projects together over the years," Sterling answered. "I haven't seen him in much lately."

Before Craig could ascertain why Sterling's old friend was being denied admittance, William arrived and spoke directly to the security officer at the entrance. "What's going on here?"

"Mr. Wells said he is here with the Blake family, but he isn't on the guest list."

William glanced down at the list and looked up at the new arrival. "No, he isn't. Do you have an invitation?"

"Well, no, actually," Carter said. "I heard through the grapevine that Sterling was going to attend Senator Whitmore's anniversary party. I arrived here today, on my way to Virginia Beach to shoot a movie with his daughter, and thought I would stop in to see the family before Sterling leaves town."

Craig could tell by William's body language that he had every intention of denying the man admittance. He didn't get the chance to open his mouth before Sterling stepped beside him and said, "For heaven's sake, Dad, let him in. Carter has been a friend of the family since before the girls were born."

William's jaw tightened, but he motioned to the security guard. "Let him in, but he has to go through the metal detectors first."

"Yes, sir."

Anticipating that William's next words would likely be directed at him to find out his granddaughter's location, Craig turned to rejoin Sienna only to see her closing the distance between them. Craig lowered his voice. "I thought I told you to wait over there."

"I only wanted to say hi to Carter. I heard he has a part in the movie I'm about to start."

Carter cleared the metal detector and headed their way.

"Sienna Blake!" Carter reached for Sienna's hand and effectively cut off any other objections from Craig and William. "My, how you've grown up. I can hardly believe you're old enough to be a headliner."

"It's so good to see you, Carter. It's been a long time." She put her hand on his arm as he leaned forward to kiss her cheek. "Still as handsome as ever."

"You always have been a charmer." He spared a glance at Craig hovering beside Sienna. "And who is this?"

Sienna offered the introductions, and a moment later, Senator Whitmore stepped onto the portable stage in the front of the room. "Ladies and gentlemen, if we could have your attention."

The murmur of conversation dulled, then slowly came to a stop. Craig waited for Sterling to take his position at the edge of the room once more before he reached into his pocket and pressed a button on the remote, a simple device that would activate the dampening field in the room and ultimately prevent anyone from being able to utilize their cell phones or access the Internet.

Senator Whitmore's wife joined him on the stage, along with Sterling and Monica. The senator continued, slipping his arm around his wife's waist. "I want to thank all of you for coming out tonight to help Katherine and me celebrate our thirty-fifth wedding anniversary."

Applause and cheers sounded from the guests. A grin crossed Senator Whitmore's face, and he waited for the crowd to quiet again. "What most of you don't know is that we're here to celebrate another wedding. Three and a half decades ago, I made the best decision of my life when I managed to convince this lovely woman to take a chance on me. I pray today's newlyweds will be as blessed as Katherine and I have been."

Senator Whitmore handed the microphone to Sterling, who offered his award-winning smile. Faced with the curious stares of his audience, he waited several heartbeats before lifting the microphone and announcing, "The Blake and Whitmore families are pleased to present the bride and groom, married today in the Washington D.C. Temple." He paused, letting the anticipation build for a moment. "Ladies and gentlemen, please put your hands together and welcome the new Mr. and Mrs. Whitmore."

Charlie and Kendra emerged through the door behind the platform. With Kendra's hand in his, Charlie led his new bride up the three steps and onto the stage as the crowd reacted with surprise, delight, and cheers. Kendra and Charlie took center stage. A moment later, the Whitmores' bishop joined them to conduct the brief ceremony during which the newlyweds would exchange their rings in front of their friends and loved ones.

12

A SHIVER RAN THROUGH HIM, his gloved hands trembling as he lifted his rifle and looked through the scope. His cheeks and nose were undoubtedly red from the biting cold, but he was acutely aware of his responsibilities.

His eyes swept over the exterior of the building he knew housed the Whitmore anniversary party. Lights shone brightly from the windows, and people mulled around inside, elegant dresses and tuxedos the obvious choice of apparel for the evening. He considered his possible targets, irritation surfacing when he couldn't easily identify any.

The security team's movement on the grounds had forced him to set up much farther away than he would have liked, and he found he didn't particularly care for working from such distances. His pulse quickened when he caught a glimpse of Sienna Blake through the window, his grip tightening on the barrel of the gun. Before he could take aim, a man approached and pulled her out of view. He lowered the gun barrel slightly, annoyed he had missed the brief opportunity.

He reminded himself that he wasn't in this alone, that he had a job to do. Looking through the sniper scope again, he forced himself to consider what he had to do to finally get what he wanted, what he deserved.

* * *

Craig guided Sienna past the window and escorted her to the front of the room with the rest of her family. Not wanting to intrude, he took a few steps back to where Seth and Vanessa stood. Craig's eyes swept the room, glancing to the front in time to watch Charlie slip a wedding band on Kendra's ring finger.

Brent and Amy stood with the rest of the happy couple's family at the front of the crowd, and Craig was happy to see his commanding officer relaxed and enjoying the ceremony. The notion that Brent was able to forget about any security duties was admirable.

That thought was enough to make Craig scan the room again. His eyes looked over the guests and then the doors leading to the hallway. Damian and Jay stood by the door in the rear of the room, with Tristan positioned beside the door closest to him. Satisfied that everything appeared to be as it should, he did another sweep of the guests before settling back on the bride and groom.

Beside him, he noticed Vanessa nudge Seth with her elbow. She stood on her toes as she whispered to him. "Look out the window. Did you see that?"

"What?" Seth shifted his gaze to where his wife indicated.

Craig turned as well.

A light reflected in the darkness, and his eyes narrowed.

"Is that someone on the security team?" Vanessa asked quietly.

"If it is, they're out of position," Seth said. He reached up and touched the communication device in his ear, activating the microphone. "Can I get a check on quadrant three? I saw movement near the tree line."

Craig heard the response come through his earpiece. "Stand by."

They all watched out the window and saw another flash of light reflecting in the moonlight, followed by movement as the external security team began their search.

Though his view was limited because of the lights shining inside, Craig could see several men outside quicken their steps and break into a run across the open field between the trees and the resort.

"Looks like there was someone out there," Craig muttered as he fought the urge to sprint out of the room and join the chase. He was inside for a reason tonight. Two reasons, actually. He was Sienna Blake's date, and he was one of the people who would make sure they could all leave here safely without incident.

* * *

"Any idea who was out there?" Craig asked after the last of the guests had left.

"None," William answered, having already debriefed the men from the rest of the security team. "They saw someone in the trees, but when they approached, he took off and managed to get to the road before they could catch up with him."

"I gather he had a car waiting there," Seth commented. "Did anyone get a license plate or description of the vehicle?"

"Neither. They saw taillights disappearing around the corner," William said. "Footprints appear to have been a men's size ten or eleven, but the snow was too slushy to identify anything beyond that."

"What about tire tracks?" Craig asked.

"We had more luck with those. The vehicle was likely a Honda CRV." William shook his head. "Unfortunately, that's the most common SUV in the country."

Brent blew out a frustrated breath. "Do Charlie and Kendra know anything about what happened?"

"No, and they don't need to," William said. "They'll be heading out in the morning for their honeymoon. I checked out their accommodations myself to make sure they wouldn't have any trouble."

"Where are they going?"

"A secluded cabin in the mountains. Even if word gets out that Kendra got married, everyone will expect they'll be on a plane to somewhere exotic."

"And they'll be looking for evidence of their travel plans," Tristan agreed. "I gather you think the guy in the woods was a reporter."

"That's my best guess, but I'll feel better when everyone is safely back home." William nodded toward Craig. "Since Sienna is heading for a movie set, I wonder if I could impose on you to check on her from time to time to make sure she's doing okay."

"I'd be happy to, but I doubt anyone is getting past George," Craig said, rather surprised by William's request.

"We can never be too careful when it comes to the people we love."

* * *

Sienna couldn't remember the last time her father had attended church with her. He had said he was coming with her to make sure she stayed safe, but she suspected it had more to do with Craig's presence than his concern for her safety. Surely her grandfather and six members of Craig's squad would be sufficient. Since the five married members were accompanied by their wives, clearly security wasn't expected to be an issue today.

As a group, the Saint Squad and friends were hard to miss when they walked into the chapel, but for once, Sienna didn't stop to see if everyone's eyes were on her. She was too busy wondering how she would feel if she noticed such a large group of visitors walk in together in her home ward.

Brent led the way to a long pew in the center of the chapel. Her father preceded her, followed by her grandparents. Sienna ended up between her grandfather and Craig. When she noticed her father's furrowed brows, she wondered if her grandpa had manipulated their seating arrangement. The memory of how he had orchestrated her sister's relationship with her new husband caused her lips to curve up.

"What?" Craig whispered, apparently noticing her smile.

"I was just thinking how nice it is that my grandpa likes you."

Craig's eyebrows drew together, and he glanced beyond her to look at William before shifting his attention back to her. "I'm not sure I understand."

"I'll explain later."

Her grandpa winked at her, causing her to grin wider. She might have been the one to suggest a pretend engagement to distract her father, but William was enjoying every minute of this fictional relationship.

She reached over and took Craig's hand, beaming up at him when their eyes met. He linked his fingers through hers and rubbed his thumb over the back of her hand. Her stomach fluttered, and on impulse, she reached up and kissed Craig's cheek.

His eyebrows wrinkled in confusion before he shifted beside her and reached his arm across the back of the pew, his hand resting on her shoulder.

She leaned into him, finding warmth and acceptance. Their engagement might be fake, but this relationship was a long way from over.

* * *

Sienna settled into the passenger seat of Craig's car. When she had suggested Craig pretend to be her fiancé as a distraction tactic for her father, she hadn't anticipated that he would be expected to drive her back to Virginia Beach. In fact, she had planned to tell her father the truth right after the wedding.

Realizing emotions were already running high after finding out Kendra had gotten married, she and her grandfather had ultimately decided to wait until there was some distance between them before they announced she had fabricated the whole story.

When Craig started the car, she glanced behind her and offered a wave to her parents, who were standing beside their rented limousine. George was already in her rental car, prepared to follow her on the four-hour drive south.

"I'm sorry you got stuck driving me back," Sienna said as Craig put the car in gear and pulled away from the resort.

Craig shot her a sidelong glance. "You're acting like I mind spending time with you. If I remember correctly, we had planned to keep in touch this weekend even before we found out we were going to the same place." He gave a slight smile. "Of course, that was before we got engaged. I hope you aren't planning on dumping me before I get the chance to take you on a real date."

Her insecurities melted away. "Were you planning on asking me on a real date?"

"I was thinking about it." Craig grinned at her now. "That is, if you have time with your movie starting up."

"I'll make time for you," Sienna said. "Besides, I may need to pick your brain about some of these action scenes again."

"Ah. The truth comes out. You're using me for my martial-arts skills."

"Nah. That's just an added bonus." Sienna shifted and put one foot on the dashboard. She fell silent for a moment and then asked, "How often do you have to travel for work? You were asking about my schedule. What's yours like?"

"I'm honestly not sure. Since I joined my squad, we've spent most of our time training for your sister's wedding."

"That's pretty bad that her wedding was something people had to train for."

"If we weren't training for that, we would have been preparing for something else," Craig said matter-of-factly. He motioned to his backpack behind his seat. "Could you grab my sunglasses out of there for me?"

"Sure." Sienna lifted the backpack into the front seat and onto her lap. She opened it and fished around inside unsuccessfully. "Are you sure they're in here?"

"Yeah. They're in a black case. They probably settled at the bottom again."

Sienna pulled out a sweatshirt and what appeared to be a sketch pad before she found what she was looking for. She opened the case and handed the sunglasses to Craig. "Here you go."

"Thanks." He slid them into place.

"You're welcome." Sienna started to put everything back, pausing at the last item. She held up the sketchpad. "Are you an artist?"

"Not really, but I like to draw." He shrugged. "Just a hobby."

"Do you mind if I look?" Sienna asked, intrigued.

"Go ahead."

She opened the pad and studied the first page. In it, a woman walked along a beach hand in hand with a young boy. It was good. Not hang-in-a-gallery good but good nonetheless. "You have talent."

"Thanks." He seemed to hesitate before he said, "If you flip a few pages back, you'll find a couple of you."

"You drew a picture of me?"

"I didn't know it was you for the first one."

Eager to see his creation, she flipped through several pages until she reached a drawing of her walking along the beach, her hood up, and George walking along behind her. "No wonder you tackled George. He looks menacing."

"I may have exaggerated that aspect a bit."

She turned the page and stared at her portrait. "Wow."

"What?"

"It's just strange to see a picture of myself like this."

"Why? People take pictures of you all the time."

"Not like this." She looked over at him, not sure what to think. She didn't look like a movie star in the sketch, nor had Craig glamorized her features. The drawing was simple and honest, and yet there was a softness about it she couldn't explain. "You really are talented."

"Careful, or you'll make me blush."

She smiled at that. "I didn't think Navy SEALs were capable of blushing."

"Let's not find out," Craig suggested. "Tell me, how long are you going to wait to tell your dad we aren't really engaged?"

"Grandpa is going to tell him tonight. We thought it best to have a couple hundred miles between us before he found out what we were up to."

"Smart."

As they continued their drive, they fell into easy conversation, discussing everything from their childhoods to their favorite movies. When they arrived in Virginia Beach four hours later, Sienna could hardly believe how quickly time seemed to have passed.

Craig took the turn toward her hotel. "Do you want me to drop you off in front?"

"I'm not sure. Let me call George and find out. I know he won't want me going inside without him." Sienna called to check in, worked through a couple possible scenarios, and hung up once a decision was made. "He said he'll meet us by the pool entrance after he parks the car."

"No problem." Craig continued to the parking lot and pulled into a space near the entrance she indicated.

George pulled past them on his way to the covered parking.

"You'll text me tomorrow when you get off work, right?" she asked.

"Yeah, I'll text you." He turned off the car and shifted to face her more fully. "Are you able to have your phone with you when you're working?

"The first day of filming is always crazy, but I try to keep my phone nearby when I'm on set. You never know when you'll have some downtime."

Craig looked around the deserted parking lot before turning his attention back to her.

"What are you looking for?"

"Just making sure we had some privacy before I did this." He leaned forward, and his lips touched hers.

The naturalness of the gesture took her by surprise. This wasn't a staged kiss that she had to pretend she wanted. No, this kiss made her *feel*. Her stomach bounced to her toes before jumping up into her throat. Her skin tingled under his touch when his fingers brushed over her hand, and a shiver ran through her. He drew out the kiss as though memorizing her flavor. When he pulled back, his eyes were dark and mysterious.

A wrinkle of confusion formed on his brow, and she couldn't help but wonder if he had been as shaken by the kiss as she had. He straightened suddenly, and Sienna followed his gaze to see George walking toward them.

Not ready to let the moment pass, Sienna lifted her hand to his cheek to draw his face closer to hers. She pressed her lips to his for another kiss. Though brief, it created the same sense of wonder, confusion, and awe the first one had. "You promise you'll text me tomorrow?"

"I'll text you," Craig said. "And I want to see you if you have the time."

"I've always heard you have to make time for the people who are important in your life." She squeezed his hand. "You're important."

She had expected him to smile, but the intensity of his gaze didn't waver when he said, "The feeling's mutual."

13

WHAT HAD HE GOTTEN HIMSELF into? The question played over and over in Craig's mind on his drive back to base. Kissing Sienna had been an impulse he had been thinking about for days. If he was honest with himself, he could admit he had been a bit star struck their first couple meetings, but that now seemed like a distant memory. He wasn't sure when his perception started to change, but he suspected it had happened somewhere between their first dinner together and ordering dessert.

Never would Craig have thought he would feel so comfortable with any woman, yet the drive from Northern Virginia to Virginia Beach had flown by. He could have talked to Sienna for hours longer, and it still wouldn't have been enough. And the kiss. Adrenaline still pumped through his body.

It wasn't like this was the first time he'd ever kissed a woman. He'd dated plenty in high school and during college. Granted, he hadn't been interested in anyone since he'd broken up with Teresa shortly before he'd started SEAL training, but then, opportunities had been limited.

Still, he couldn't remember a time he'd been flattened by what should have been a simple meeting of lips.

He wondered if it was because of her fame but then dismissed that thought immediately. He hadn't been thinking of her as Sienna Blake when he'd kissed her. She had simply been Sienna, the beautiful woman who loved life, enjoyed the outdoors and its freedom, loved her family, and had a fun and sometimes quirky sense of humor.

The truth was that he preferred her the way she looked today, with her hair pulled back in a ponytail, her face nearly free of makeup. He supposed she felt more real this way, more attainable, more his.

His hands tightened on the steering wheel at that last thought. Now he really was navigating unchartered waters. Terror and shock rocketed through him and mixed with a kind of wonder. Yes, he may have dated in the past, but for the first time, he felt vulnerable to a woman. He wasn't sure he was ready for such a depth of emotion, and he was quite certain he didn't like it.

* * *

Sienna followed George down the hall toward the main elevators, her mind still spinning with thoughts of Craig.

"You're awfully quiet," George commented. "Everything okay?"

"What?" Distracted, she glanced at him and repeated his question in her mind before answering. "Oh, yeah."

"When are you seeing Craig again?" George asked, not quite able to hide the smirk on his face.

"Hopefully tomorrow."

"You really think you'll have time?"

"Aren't you the one who said I need to make time for what's important?"

"I'm just surprised to see you taking my advice," George said. "I'll make sure his name is on the approved list to come on set."

"Thanks."

"You know, it would be a lot easier if you would bring Jane out for this film," George said, referring to her personal assistant.

"I know, but her mom just started chemo, and I didn't want her to have to travel right now. Besides, she has plenty to do dealing with the fan mail and the business side of things."

George let the subject drop. They turned the corner into the main lobby and saw Adam Pratt's entourage enter the hotel. Sienna's opinion of him immediately began forming. She had met so many celebrities over the course of her life. Some made great efforts to keep a low profile in public, while others needed to be noticed everywhere they went. Adam appeared to belong to the latter category.

The desk clerk, a woman in her midtwenties, looked up when they approached. She goggled at Hollywood's poster boy before she recovered enough to signal the nearby bellhop. A gangly teen who barely looked old enough to have graduated high school goggled too before he stepped forward and prepared to load luggage on his cart.

The woman at the desk tapped on computer keys to check the new arrivals in, and Adam stood back while another man in his group took care of the details.

Adam exuded an air of impatience, his fingers playing over his cell phone, his gaze shifting upward frequently as though he was silently asking if this tedious process was over yet. Sienna imagined he thought he had important business to attend to, but with shooting starting in the morning, she didn't know what could be so important unless he hadn't yet memorized his lines.

She reminded herself that his lines were limited in number during the first few scenes they were shooting, the first one an action scene. Her mind immediately shifted to Craig. It made sense now that he knew so much about the training government types would go through. She wished he really could be a consultant on the movie but knew he'd never have that kind of time. The action scenes in his life weren't played out for an audience. They were real.

The memory of his kiss washed over her, though tempered by the reality of her situation. She was falling for a guy who not only didn't understand the limelight but also didn't have any interest in sharing it with her. She reminded herself that Kendra and Charlie had a similar situation and had somehow made it work. They loved each other enough to find a middle ground, even when it meant forging their own way through previously unnavigable waters.

Adam Pratt's gaze swept the lobby, not stopping to linger on anyone in particular. Sienna couldn't help but notice the difference between Adam's presence and Craig's. Besides having a generally friendly demeanor, Craig always seemed to be so aware of everyone. She suspected Adam hadn't even recognized her, even though he undoubtedly knew what she looked like. Granted, with her hair pulled back and her casual attire, many people didn't equate her with the woman they saw on the big screen and online.

The elevator doors slid open, and she and George stepped inside. Her soon-to-be costar now forgotten, Sienna wondered if she would be able to see Craig tomorrow.

* * *

Craig leaned over and put his hands on his knees, his breath coming rapidly. The sprint at the end of the obstacle course wouldn't have been so bad had he not run ten miles before completing it. Footsteps sounded behind him.

Tristan sucked in a deep breath. "What's wrong, Craig?" he asked in his lazy Texan drawl. "Looks like you need to get back in shape after taking it easy the last few days."

"He beat you, didn't he?" Quinn asked Tristan, lacing his fingers behind his head, his own breathing heavy as he too waited for his body to recover from the most recent challenge.

"I didn't want to embarrass him," Tristan responded. "After all, he is new to the squad."

"You never took it easy on me," Jay said.

"Sure I did. Remember when we raced in freestyle? I totally let you win," Tristan said.

"Right." Jay turned his attention to Craig. "It's amazing how every time someone beats him, he says he's taking it easy on them."

When Craig didn't respond, Jay continued. "But on to more important things. You haven't said a word about how your drive home with Sienna Blake was."

Craig made an effort to keep his expression neutral before he straightened. "It was fine."

"Fine? That's it? That's all you're going to tell us?" Jay turned to Brent. "Commander, don't you think now would be a good time to practice our interrogation techniques?"

"Apparently," Brent said straight-faced. "But for now, go hit the showers. We have a briefing with Admiral Mantiquez in an hour."

"Do you know what it's on?" Tristan asked.

Brent shook his head. "Not yet, but we'll all find out soon enough."

* * *

From across the lobby, he casually turned a page of his newspaper, his right foot resting on his left knee. To anyone walking through, he would simply be part of the background scene, a hotel guest waiting for someone. He was most definitely waiting for someone.

Sienna Blake stepped out of the elevator with her bodyguard, and the man lifted the newspaper a little higher to hide his face. The action kept her out of view until she approached the front door to catch the shuttle that would take her to the movie set. Adam Pratt arrived right behind her, barely visible behind his two bodyguards and personal assistant.

The newspaper now lowered so he could peer over the top, he watched, amused when Adam extended his hand to Sienna, apparently introducing himself. Sienna smiled graciously, and it didn't appear that she let her costar know that he had failed to recognize her the night before. Instead, Sienna chatted amiably while they waited for the shuttle.

He had seen Adam's arrival last night; he'd been sitting in this same spot, using the same ploy to blend in. He also knew enough about Sienna to recognize her when she wasn't dressed for attention. The two stars looked good together, he noted. Of course, that wouldn't last. He couldn't let it. This was his golden opportunity, his best chance to step out of the shadows and into the headlines. It was only a matter of picking the right time.

14

CRAIG KNEW HE SHOULD BE excited about his first real mission, but the fact that he was missing out on spending time with Sienna put a huge damper on it.

He still wasn't quite sure what to think of the current status of their relationship. Every time he thought of their time together, he was confused and uncomfortably overwhelmed. When he managed to think of her as simply Sienna, the person he enjoyed spending time with, all he wanted was more—more time, more memories. Then he would remember her last name and her fame, and he would wonder what in the world he was thinking. Her lifestyle would never mesh with his, as was evident from his current position at the edge of an airfield, where he was waiting for their ride.

Several of his teammates were on the phone, talking to their wives, or in Damian's case, his fiancé. The conversations were all similar.

"No, we're not sure yet," Tristan told his wife.

"I'll call you as soon as I can," Quinn said into his phone.

Seth's conversation took more of a practical tone. "Can you see if Brother Howard can cover my Sunday School class until I get back?"

Craig stuck his hand into his pocket and fingered his cell phone. He had texted Sienna as soon as he'd found out he couldn't see her tonight, but she hadn't responded. Now he wondered if he should call her while he still had the chance.

Damian ended his call and took a step toward him. "Have you talked to Sienna yet?"

He started to deny the need to but didn't see the point. These men were quickly becoming like brothers to him, and Damian was the closest to him of them all. "I'm not sure she'd be able to take a call right now. It's her first day of filming."

"There's only one way to find out." Damian motioned to Brent standing a short distance away with his wife, Amy. "Brent once told me to make sure you never leave for a mission with regrets if you can help it." He paused for a moment and added, "It's good advice."

Craig gripped his phone and pulled it free of his pocket. "I guess I'd better try to make a call."

"Good decision."

* * *

Her bones heavy and her muscles aching, Sienna dropped into the canvas director's chair with her name on it. She hadn't actually chosen this particular chair because it had been labeled hers but rather because it was the closest, and she didn't think she could take another step.

Exhaustion was normal after a full day of filming, but these action scenes were taking more of a toll than she had expected. She didn't want to think of how bad it would be if she wasn't used to running a few miles every day. She also didn't want to dwell on how many times they had shot the first scene.

She had expected a few takes, especially since she was so inexperienced with the use of stunt doubles, and she had thought she would be the weak link. She hadn't realized Adam would come into today's filming completely unprepared. Liam Rickman, the other actor in that particular scene, at least knew his lines, but he too clearly hadn't prepared for the physical demands of his part.

Though it wasn't particularly fair, she was a little more understanding of Liam's difficulties. He'd grown up a well-known child actor, and this was only the second adult role he had landed in recent years, and he had never before performed in an action film. Liam's first attempt at transitioning from child to adult actor had been playing the role of a disturbed mental patient. Unfortunately for him, the film hadn't done well at the box office.

Adam, on the other hand, had several action flicks under his belt and should have known what was required to prepare for his role. Unfortunately, their first hour of filming had been little more than a rehearsal. Craig had figured out what the screenwriter had wanted within a minute or two, but Adam had to be told over and over what he was supposed to do.

The thought of Craig was enough to push her muscles into action, at least enough to lean forward and retrieve her cell phone from her bag, which was currently hanging off one side of her chair. She scrolled past the text messages from her mom and dad, two from each, and found one from Craig.

Her heart lifted a little at the prospect of seeing him tonight, but that hope was dashed when she read the short message: *Change of plans for tonight. Call you when I get back in town.*

Her brow furrowed as she read the words a second time. She had heard that people in the military sometimes had to leave town with little notice, but she had always thought those stories were exaggerated. Apparently not.

"Hey, Sienna." Adam approached and lowered himself into the chair beside her. "How about we go grab some dinner?"

"I don't know . . ." Sienna began. She was a little surprised by her knee-jerk reaction to decline the offer. It wasn't like Craig had asked her not to date other people, but the truth was she didn't want to date anyone else.

"Hey, we both have to eat sometime, right?" Adam interrupted before she could continue. "Besides, it will make shooting these scenes together a lot easier if we know each other a little better."

What Adam said made sense, and it wasn't like they would really be alone. Between his bodyguards and George, they had the beginnings of a party.

"I guess that's true." She tried to readjust her mind-set for her evening plans and get over the disappointment Craig's text had caused.

"How about I pick you up at your room in an hour?"

"Why don't we make it half an hour, and I'll meet you in the hotel restaurant," Sienna countered. "We need to make it an early night since we have an early call time tomorrow."

"Don't you want to go out and see the town a bit?"

"Not tonight." Sienna thought of the last fodder she had seen about Adam in the tabloids, a rumor that he had cheated on his longtime girlfriend. Immediately she wondered if he was deliberately trying to be seen with her to get them and their movie noticed. She couldn't blame him if he was. After all, publicity was part of the business, but she didn't have the energy for it today.

Her cell phone rang, and she looked down to see Craig's name light up the screen. Shamelessly, she used the call as a lifeline to reclaim her freedom for the evening. "Sorry. Looks like I'm going to have to take a rain check for tonight." Not waiting for Adam to respond, she stood up and started walking away from him so she would have some privacy. On the fourth ring, she answered the call. "Hello?"

"Hey, Sienna. I just wanted to make sure you got my text."

She continued walking along the far side of the set in search of a quiet spot. "Yeah, I got it. I gather you're still heading out of town?"

"I am. I don't know much about when I'll get back, but the guys in my squad seem to think it might be a couple weeks," Craig told her. "I'm really sorry about the timing. I was looking forward to seeing you tonight."

"Me too," Sienna admitted. "I guess we'll have to postpone until you get back."

"I'd like that," Craig said before changing the subject. "How did your first day of filming go? Did you already shoot that first action scene?"

Sienna's mood lightened when she thought of how happy the director had been with her preparation for that particular scene. "I did. My part went very well, thanks to you."

"You did the work. I just offered a few suggestions."

"That may be, but your suggestions were exactly what the director was looking for."

A rumble sounded in the background. "Sorry, that's my ride. I have to go."

"Your ride? It sounds like a helicopter."

"It is. I'll call or text you as soon as I can, but it may be easier to e-mail. Can you text me your e-mail address?"

"Sure."

"I'll write to you before I leave so you have mine."

"Sounds good." Not sure what else she should say at such a moment, she finally settled on "I'll talk to you later."

"Yeah. Take care."

The call clicked off, and Sienna replayed the conversation in her mind. Where would he have to go for a couple weeks, especially with so little notice? The thought of her current script, of the many dangerous situations her character would go through, made her heartbeat quicken. Craig wasn't living the military version of a terrorist situation, was he?

"Everything okay?"

Sienna startled at Adam's voice, turning to see him standing behind her. "Yeah, everything's fine."

"It sounds like your plans changed again. Maybe we can catch dinner together after all."

"Thanks, but I really am wiped out. I think I'm going to stick with room service tonight. Maybe another time."

"Tomorrow we have a night shoot. What about the night after that? We can make it a working dinner."

"I guess that would be okay," Sienna began, still hesitant over the idea of being out with Adam, even if it was work related.

He didn't give her the chance to reconsider, pouncing on the opening. "Great. I'll see you later."

Sienna watched him turn and walk away, already regretting her decision.

* * *

A helicopter ride to Norfolk, a flight to Italy, and now another flight to take them to their final destination in Abolstan, a country known for its hostilities toward Americans. Craig thought Brent had been joking when he'd told him to catch as much sleep as he could on the flight over the Atlantic, but that had literally been their only downtime since their meeting with Admiral Mantiquez yesterday.

Three missing American doctors had been the catalyst for the briefing. What had started as a goodwill gesture by a group of medical personnel working in Turkey had turned deadly when a band of rebels had crossed the border from Abolstan. A nurse had been killed during the brief skirmish, and two others had been injured. Latest intelligence indicated the missing three doctors were still alive, but no one was sure how long their captors would keep them that way.

The news had barely hit the airways before the navy had devised a plan of action. Craig could hardly believe it had been less than twenty-four hours since they had shipped out, his time in Virginia now feeling like a fading dream. An image of Sienna flashed in his mind, but a signal from Brent forced him to push it aside.

The high-altitude, high-opening parachute jump would take all of his concentration. Now that the two-minute warning had been issued, he and his teammates switched over to their oxygen tanks, checking, double-checking, and triple-checking their equipment. The gear strapped to his back and his weapon at his side made it difficult to get comfortable. Then again, he doubted comfortable was a word many SEALs truly understood after joining the teams. As the seconds ticked down, they all stood in preparation for their jump that would initiate from 28,000 feet.

Craig took his place in the middle of the line. He knew he had been placed there deliberately because he was the least experienced in the group. The first two of his teammates would have the responsibility of guiding them the forty miles to their landing site and ensuring the site was clear of enemy presence. The last two would have the challenge of making sure they were able to follow the rest of their teammates in while also ensuring that no one had any trouble during their descent.

Besides the danger posed by the enemy, he and his squad first had to battle the possibility of hypoxia and decompression sickness that could occur from a potential lack of oxygen or an inability to regulate it during the jump.

One of the crewmen on the plane opened the door, his face also covered by a breathing mask. A blast of cold air filled the compartment, and Craig reminded himself to keep his breathing slow and steady. Seth gave Craig's shoulder a squeeze, a silent signal that he had his back.

Dozens of details ran through his mind, the various instructions that had been drilled into his head while in SEAL training and the anticipation of what would come next. The next signal came, and Tristan stepped out into the darkness of night, followed immediately by Quinn. One by one they jumped, with Craig fourth in line.

He stepped free of the aircraft, counted off five seconds, and popped his parachute open. Instantly the straps jerked hard against his shoulders, and he tried not to think of the soreness that would remain there over the next few days. Instead, he activated his GPS as he joined his teammates on what would be a nearly hour-long descent, a ride that would hopefully allow them to silently insert behind enemy lines while the aircraft that had dropped them would continue on undetected.

15

SIENNA PRESSED HERSELF AGAINST THE outside wall of the office building, the shadows of the nearby streetlight coming within feet of her position. She let herself believe someone inside was really in danger and that their life depended on her.

The director would show clips of the guards inside, most of their efforts focused on the main entrances instead of the window she would use to make her way inside. She looked to the right and then to the left before she crept forward, coming to a stop below a window that was slightly ajar.

Her fingers gripped the sill, and she placed one foot against the side of the building to prepare for her climb. She pulled herself up enough to peer through the pane, holding an expression that revealed both curiosity and concern.

"Cut!" the director called out. To her relief, he added, "And print."

Sienna relaxed her body, letting her foot drop firmly back to the ground. The next scene, beginning with her climbing through the window, wouldn't be shot for a couple more days. After three takes with this scene, she was relieved she could leave it behind and focus on the next one.

"That's it for tonight," Marcus announced. "Make sure you have your call times for tomorrow before you leave."

The woman assigned as Sienna's assistant stepped forward. "I already have that for you, Miss Blake."

"Thank you, Toni." Sienna took the paper Toni offered her and read through the shoot schedule, her emotions mixed when she saw her call time wasn't until nine. She checked Adam's and saw that he would report at the same time.

The idea of sleeping in past five in the morning was appealing, but she hoped Adam wouldn't see the later call time as an excuse to draw out their dinner together.

She saw George approaching and said to Toni, "I'm going to head back to the hotel. I'll see you tomorrow."

"Okay. Let me know if there's anything you need."

"I will. Thanks, Toni." Sienna joined George and started toward their car. What she wouldn't give to be able to go back to her room and fall face-first into bed. She sighed.

"Are you ready for your date tonight?" George asked after they were both in the car.

"Not really, and it's not a date."

George cast her a sidelong glance. "Is something going on between you and that Navy SEAL?"

"Maybe." Sienna's shoulders lifted. "It's hard to know where we stand since he had to ship out."

"How long until he gets back?"

"That's the million-dollar question, and I'd love to know the answer to it."

* * *

Craig stood at the edge of a side street a short distance from the local restaurant. He pretended to ponder the specials scrawled on a board near the entrance as he really watched the foot traffic on the street.

The strip of businesses in downtown Khalar bustled with activity. Women with hijabs and niqabs carried baskets filled with food, fabric, and other goods traded in this part of town. Two businessmen holding briefcases emerged from an office across the street, and some kind of tradesman loaded tools into the back of his truck.

The location they were most interested in was three doors down. That was where intelligence believed local mercenaries were holding the three American hostages.

"What do you see?" Craig asked Quinn through his lightweight headset, unnerved by his lack of visibility of the target.

"Two men guarding the front entrance," Quinn said in his typical no-nonsense tone. "Brent, what does the back look like?"

"One guard in the back. With the way he's staggering, I think he may have spent the afternoon bending his elbow instead of worrying about who else was in the alley."

"An armed drunk can be unpredictable. We might be better off trying for a front-door approach." Seth's Southern drawl sounded through the earpiece.

"Unless I disarm the guy in back first," Damian said.

"You sound like you have a plan," Brent responded. "Care to share?"

"Did I ever mention that one of my uncles was an alcoholic who liked to carry his revolver everywhere he went?"

"I remember the drunk uncle but not the armed part," Seth replied.

"Watch and learn."

"Be careful," Brent cautioned before giving him the go-ahead to follow through with his plans. "Craig, shift to the alley in case he needs backup."

"On it." Craig strolled a few steps to the edge of the sidewalk and turned the corner. He fought the urge to quicken his pace, forcing himself to do the opposite as he reached the back of the building.

He came to a stop and took a quick peek around the corner to identify the guard's current location. "I'm in position," Craig said quietly. "The guard's heading away from me."

Damian's voice sounded through his earpiece once more. "When I tell you, step out into the alleyway and start toward him. Ask him a question or wave at him. Anything to get his attention for a minute."

"Roger that. Standing by."

Craig edged out of sight, his heartbeat quickening. The thought of Damian approaching an armed man out in the open was unnerving, as was his role as the distraction. What if the guard felt threatened and pulled his gun before Damian disarmed him? Craig pushed those doubts aside, reminding himself that they trained for situations like this. He trusted Damian, and he knew Brent and his assault rifle were hidden out of sight on the roof above them.

"Now." Damian's voice was quiet and firm.

Craig rounded the corner, a little surprised at how slow the guard was to notice him. Apparently he *had* been drinking his afternoon away. At the edge of his peripheral vision, Craig saw Damian angling toward him from the other direction. When the guard finally looked up, Craig said one of the few phrases he knew in Arabic: "Excuse me."

The guard staggered a step toward him, his focus now completely on Craig. Damian's pace quickened, and he deliberately bumped into the larger man.

"Sorry," Damian said. Through the earpiece, Craig could hear Brent coaching him in Arabic how to say, "Didn't see you."

The guard grumbled for a minute before brushing off Damian's presence and focusing again on Craig.

"Craig, speak to him in French now. That'll throw him off long enough for you to take him down."

Craig complied, switching to one of the languages he was proficient in. "*Excusez-moi.*"

Sure enough, the man's eyes seemed to blur with confusion. He reached inside his jacket, his confusion increasing when he apparently didn't find what he was looking for.

"Looking for this?" Damian asked from the edge of the alley. He held up the gun he had apparently lifted from the man's pocket.

The man's attention shifted again, and Craig used his close proximity and a right cross to send the man tumbling to the ground. Though he remained conscious, he was too stunned to let out a cry of warning.

Damian rushed forward as Craig clamped a hand over the man's mouth. A moment later, Damian injected a sedative into the guard's arm, and the man slumped to the ground.

"Back is clear," Damian announced.

"Secure the guard," Brent ordered. "Seth and Jay, get into position. Tristan and I will come in through the upstairs windows."

"Almost there," Jay responded.

"Wait for my signal," Brent commanded.

Craig secured the guard's hands, surprised that his own hands were steady. They had bypassed their first obstacle, but the challenges would only become more difficult as they moved closer to their objective.

16

SIENNA CROSSED THE THIRD-FLOOR lobby and headed for the hotel restaurant. She was surprised to see Adam sitting in one of the chairs by the entrance, one leg crossed over the other, his agent seated beside him and his bodyguards hovering nearby. She was ten minutes early and hadn't pegged Adam for the type to be so prompt.

She approached him, noticing the man by a far window with a camera in hand. She had hoped her dinner with Adam would go unnoticed, but apparently that hope wouldn't be fulfilled.

Adam and his agent stood as she approached, George taking his usual position a short distance behind her.

"Sienna, you know Murray, don't you?"

"Yes. He used to represent Carter Wells."

"That was some time ago," Murray said, extending his hand to shake hers. "It's good to see you again."

"You too." She motioned to the restaurant. "Are you joining us for dinner?"

"No, no. I wouldn't want to intrude."

"It wouldn't be an intrusion," Sienna said.

"I was actually hoping to chat with the two of you for a minute before you eat though."

"Oh? About what?"

"The Oscars." He motioned for Sienna to take a seat. She lowered herself into a chair, and Murray and Adam both sat again before Murray continued. "You and Adam are both going to be attending next weekend. I hoped you might be willing to be Adam's date."

"I don't understand."

"Neither of you is involved with anyone at the moment, and it would be good publicity for the movie."

"So it's a publicity stunt."

"In a manner of speaking. Both of you are young, attractive, single. The speculation about you being seen together could go a long way to generate interest in the film."

"I think we're already generating interest." Sienna inclined her head slightly toward the photographer on the other side of the lobby.

"This can work in your favor." Murray stood again. "I'll let you discuss it over dinner. Adam, I'll call you later."

"Sounds good." Adam stood again and signaled the hostess before offering Sienna a hand. "Shall we?"

"I guess we shall." Sienna put her hand in his, feeling very much like she was playing a part. When they started toward their table, she realized she *was* playing a role. Even though she had known Craig only for a week, she wished he was the person holding her hand. It took everything in her to pretend she didn't mind being here with Adam instead.

* * *

Something didn't feel right. Craig approached the now-unguarded back door. Everything about the scene made it look safe to enter, but his gut kept churning a warning.

He took a small flashlight from his combat vest and shined it around the edges of the doorway, looking for any sign of trip wires or booby traps. Nothing.

He reached for the doorknob but stopped short of making contact. The thought surfaced that he couldn't get himself killed doing something stupid, not when he had an amazing woman waiting for him at home. He hoped Sienna was waiting for him at home. He checked the door again.

"What's wrong?" Damian asked. "We're all clear."

"I don't know. Something doesn't feel right."

"It's just nerves," Damian said. "You'll get used to it."

Craig tried to force himself to continue. Before he managed to follow through with his intended action, Brent's voice came over his headset. "Stand by."

"Is something wrong?" Damian asked.

"The guards at the front of the building shifted their positions. Tristan and Seth, they're far enough apart that you should be able to disarm them both without a problem," Brent said. "Taking a couple more guns out of the equation will increase our chances of getting the hostages out alive."

Brent and Quinn talked Tristan and Seth through their steps to help them close in on their targets without being obvious. Craig could imagine the well-timed strike and its choreography as their other teammates gave them a verbal play-by-play. Almost simultaneously, Tristan and Seth announced their tasks' completion.

Craig thought of Sienna's script and the rehearsal they had gone through on a similar scene. Annoyed that he couldn't keep her out of his mind, even in a time like this, he tried to refocus on his task. Flashes of the fictional world Sienna would help create continued to surface, an eerie feeling continuing to flood through him.

"Is this feeling too easy to anyone else?" Craig asked. As soon as the words left his mouth, he regretted speaking them. He was the new guy, the one who was still learning. He should be relying on everyone else's expertise instead of questioning their judgment.

"I was thinking the same thing," Seth said.

"The pedestrian activity on the street has slowed down," Quinn added. "Do you think these guys staged a trap?"

"Make sure the guards are secured. Then I want everyone to move back to a safe distance. Let's see what happens."

Craig and Damian had only taken a couple steps when Jay's voice sounded through their comm gear. "Brent. We may have a problem."

"What's wrong?"

"The heat signatures inside the building are gone."

"Gone as in something is running interference with our equipment, or gone, gone?" Brent asked.

"Gone, gone." Jay took a brief moment before he continued. "We showed six heat signatures when we arrived. Sometime between when Damian disarmed the first guard and now, they all left."

"We know there are a lot of tunnels beneath this part of town," Seth said. "Maybe they took the hostages out that way."

Brent responded with a more pessimistic view. "Or maybe the hostages weren't here in the first place."

"What do you want to do?" Seth asked.

"Fall back."

Craig picked up his pace, putting more distance between himself and their original target. A door to a nearby building creaked open. Fingers gripped the edge of the faded wood. A head slowly emerged, peering through the narrow opening.

"Damian. Eleven o'clock," Craig said, indicating the possible threat. "Third building down from the target location."

The next few seconds flashed by in a series of disjointed images. The ground shook, and a wave of heat blasted through the air. Out of the corner of his eye, Craig saw the building he had nearly entered now engulfed in flames, pieces of debris flying in every direction. He dropped to the ground to avoid getting hit, the smell of burning wood assaulting his senses.

"Shooter!" Damian shouted, his voice nearly lost beneath the sound of a second explosion.

Craig drew his weapon, rolled over, and aimed. And stared down a nightmare. For one terrifying moment, all he saw was a petite woman with dark hair. Then he focused on the eyes—not Sienna's eyes but Renee Merdigall's, the lone female hostage. She stood at the edge of the doorway he had been watching a moment before, terror etched on her face and a gun pointing over her shoulder at him.

"Brent!" Damian's voice carried through Craig's headset, but all he could think was he had to move. Craig rolled over again, a gunshot sounded, and a second followed.

Craig both felt and heard the bullet whiz by his right ear, pieces of the road spraying up from the impact. He sprang to his feet and saw the hostage on the ground, blood splattered on her neck and shirt. It took him a moment to realize Brent must have taken a shot from his position on the roof across the street.

Part of his brain registered the commands Brent was issuing to the rest of the team, instructing Seth and Tristan to rush the front of the building the captors apparently now occupied. Damian had his weapon drawn and was using a car parked in the alley for cover as he worked his way to the far side of the doorway.

Still out in the open, Craig rushed forward until he was against the wall a few yards from the hostage. Now no longer a target, Craig took a split second to assess the situation. He could see now that his would-be assassin was on the ground. Renee Merdigall moaned and tried to sit up.

"I'm going in for the hostage," Craig announced.

"Stay out of the line of fire. We don't know who else is in there," Brent told him.

Craig reached the hostage as another burst of gunfire erupted. Though his heart was pounding, he reminded himself that he had to trust his teammates. He focused on the woman before him. "Are you hurt?"

Her eyes were dazed, and she looked like she was in shock, but she slowly shook her head. That was all Craig needed to know. He grabbed her by the arm and dragged her out of the doorway and up against the side of the building. "I have Merdigall. She's uninjured."

Voices came through the headset but not in response to his words.

"Target down. Second hostage secured," Seth announced.

"Where's the other one?" Brent asked.

Jay immediately responded. "Two heat signatures in the center of the building. Could be a closet."

"Damian, you take the back entrance. Craig, stay with your hostage and cover the back."

"Coming in." Damian emerged from the far side of the alley and headed for the doorway.

Craig stood, peering in the window to his left. Just as Damian reached the entrance, Quinn called out. "Targets moving. Heading toward the rear."

Through the glass, Craig saw an interior door open, one man holding another around the throat, a gun in his hand. Before he could utter a warning, Damian reached the door.

The second Damian came into view, the gunman shifted his aim as well as his body. With the hostage now shifted away from him, Craig didn't think. He reacted.

His gun hand came up, took aim through the window, and fired.

17

"Seth and Damian, sweep the building," Brent ordered. "Quinn, cover us while we secure the hostages."

Craig knelt next to the two men and the woman who now sat at the edge of the alley and tried not to think about the other man lying a short distance away, the man he had killed.

"Thank you," the man beside him whispered. "Thank you for saving my life."

Craig didn't turn to look at him. He didn't want to see the blood spatter his shot had left on the man or the reminder that if he had missed, the hostage could have died instead of the captor. The sickness in his stomach threatened to rise up in his throat. He swallowed hard, desperate to maintain his composure.

"We're clear," Seth announced.

"Let's move," Brent commanded.

Within moments, six of the seven SEALs were visible in the alley. They formed a wide diamond, with Craig and Tristan taking the center and the hostages walking between them.

Craig knew they were fortunate that all three hostages were mobile. They had come in prepared to take them out on stretchers if necessary, but now they could keep their focus on any potential threats.

Half a mile later, they reached an open field beside an abandoned school. Quinn finally appeared behind them when their helicopter approached.

Two minutes after the chopper touched down, they were loaded and on their way again. Craig looked at the ground below, his mind still trying to process that he had killed and nearly been killed in the space of four minutes. He had survived, he reminded himself. They all had.

He glanced at the hostages, again struck by Renee Merdigall's resemblance to Sienna. Grateful that Sienna was safely in Virginia, Craig closed his eyes and tried to focus on the future in the hope of blocking out the recent past.

* * *

Sienna didn't know what she had been thinking when she'd agreed to dinner with Adam. Her first instinct to decline had been right on. The whole meal had been awkward and filled with long pauses and stilted conversation. Adam apparently had had a different experience in their time together. He had asked her out for the past three days straight since that first night.

She was running out of excuses, and he wasn't giving up. Agreeing to be his date to the Oscars was supposed to be a publicity stunt, but apparently Adam thought dating for real was in their future. What she wouldn't give to have Craig show up right about now. Unfortunately, she hadn't heard from him since her first day of filming.

"Have you figured out what you're going to tell Adam when he asks you out today?" George asked, both hands on the steering wheel of their rental car.

"He might not ask me out again," Sienna said from the passenger seat. "Maybe three refusals in a row will clue him in that I'm not interested."

George glanced sideways at her. "I don't think he's getting a clue."

"I hate to say it, but I'm really not looking forward to the Oscars this year."

"It'll be fine. Your dad already made arrangements for you all to sit together. That will keep it from getting too awkward."

Sienna let her head fall back against the headrest, her eyes wandering to stare out at the ocean. She watched the waves rise and fall. They were much smaller than those she was accustomed to seeing in the Pacific.

It was odd, she mused, how oceans could look so much the same and still have their own unique shades of blue, their own rhythm. She supposed it was a lot like people. Adam looked a lot like Craig. They were both tall and toned; both had dark hair and were attractive in their own way.

Admittedly Adam had more of a pretty-boy look, while Craig's features were more chiseled, but all in all, if they were standing next to each another in a crowd, they would both be noticed. And if she had to choose one to talk to, there was no contest. Quite simply, Adam bored her.

When Sienna didn't respond, George asked, "Do I need to run some interference?"

"I'm not sure. Maybe," she said. "I guess I don't have much choice at this point but to be direct and tell him I'm not interested."

"I get the feeling this may be a new experience for him. I think he actually believed you yesterday when you said you had to wash your hair."

A chuckle escaped her. "He really is clueless, isn't he?"

"It's the same thing we see all the time. Sometimes people in the spotlight start believing the hype and forget they're human."

"I have no delusions about my humanity. I'm starving."

"You ate an orange twenty minutes ago."

"Key words: 'twenty minutes ago.'" Sienna pointed at the upcoming intersection. "That smoothie bar we found is right up there."

"What happened to wanting to get to the set early today?"

"I forgot to consult my stomach."

"Craft services will be ready for us when we get there."

"Yeah, but they won't have smoothies." She batted her eyelashes at him dramatically. "Please?"

George huffed out a breath. "Fine, but call it in so we don't have to wait."

Sienna smiled, then pressed call on the number she had saved in her phone two days before. She put in her order, pausing to ask George, "Do you want your usual?"

"We found the place three days ago, and we already have a usual? This is so wrong," George muttered. Then he shrugged and said, "Might as well."

Sienna chuckled and passed on the rest of their order.

George made the turn into the parking lot. "You know the drill."

Sienna nodded and pulled the hood of her sweatshirt up over her hair, her sunglasses already shading her eyes. She handed him cash and settled back to wait for him to retrieve the order.

Two minutes later, he reemerged with a smoothie in one hand and a breakfast sandwich in the other. He took a bite of his food before opening the door and handing the smoothie and a straw to her.

She took her first sip. "See? Wasn't this worth it?"

"Maybe," George said. "But don't blame me when makeup gets mad that you aren't early."

"Are you kidding? They'll be thrilled that I'm not trying to eat a donut while they're putting on my lipstick."

"Oh, the challenges of being a big star."

Sienna smirked at him. "Yeah, like you'd be willing to let someone put lipstick on you."

"Somehow I don't think your makeup artist has my color," he said wryly.

Sienna laughed. "Come on. Let's go see how many people you can catch trying to sneak onto our set today."

"You can laugh." George started the car. "I'm the one your dad lectures every time someone tries. Three different attempts yesterday, and not once did the studio's security guards catch them."

"What can I say, George? You're the best."

"If they don't get me some help soon, I'm going to be exhausted."

"Sounds like they'd better get you some help, then."

* * *

"You look exhausted. Did you manage to get any sleep?"

Craig looked up from his food and saw Damian standing in front of him, a tray from the ship's mess hall in his hand. "Not really."

"You okay?" Damian set his tray down at Craig's table and took the seat across from him.

"I guess."

"Did you already talk to the ship's shrink?"

"Yeah. Passed through that okay." Craig's mood lightened slightly when he thought of that particular interview. "The doc did think I might be a bit delusional though."

"What made him think that?"

"He had read through Brent's after-action report, and he asked why I had hesitated to go inside the building the hostages were being held in."

"That's a pretty normal question. What did you say?"

"I told him the whole situation felt like it was right out of Sienna's movie script."

"And?"

"He's not buying the idea of me going out with Sienna Blake."

Damian chuckled. "Okay, I have to admit that if I hadn't seen you with her, I wouldn't have believed it myself."

"I can understand that. When I think of her last name, even I have a hard time reconciling my Sienna with the person in the movies."

Damian's eyebrows lifted. "So she's *your* Sienna now, is she?"

"That's not what I mean. The Sienna we know is a real person."

Damian steered the conversation away from Sienna and back to the heart of Craig's sleepless night. "Sienna isn't what's keeping you up at night. What's bothering you? Still freaked out by your near-death experience?"

"I guess that's part of it. No amount of training prepares you for someone trying to kill you, but it's more than that. I still can't believe I took the shot when that guy aimed at you."

"If you hadn't, I wouldn't be here."

"If I'd missed, one of the hostages would be dead right now." Craig drew a deep breath and let it out fast. "I let instinct take over, but I keep wondering if it was the training that helped me hit the target or if it was pure luck."

"The rest of the guys will tell you God's hand was probably involved." Damian smeared strawberry jam on a piece of toast before looking back up at him. "Whether you believe that stuff or not, I like to think if we trust our training and trust our team, everything will turn out the way it's supposed to."

Damian crunched into his piece of toast. "Of course, what do I know? I've only been doing this six weeks longer than you have."

"Thanks a lot," Craig said sarcastically.

"Anytime. So tell me. What's really going on with you and Sienna?"

"That's a question I need a little more time to answer. I'm hoping we get stateside again soon though. I hate not being able to talk to her."

Damian looked up from his food and studied Craig for a brief moment. "Yeah, that's what I thought."

"What?"

"You're already sunk." Damian grinned. "I hope she feels the same way."

"That makes two of us."

18

"SIENNA!" ADAM WAVED AT HER from across the enormous living room in the beach house they were using as their set. Inwardly she cringed at the thought of letting the guy down gently. If this didn't stop soon, she was going to have to be more direct, something she'd rather not do since they would be working together for the next three months.

"Sienna!" Someone else called her name. This time it was Carter's voice carrying across the room.

Happy to use her father's old friend and colleague as a distraction, she passed under the bank of lights strung overhead and moved across the room to embrace him. "I was wondering when you were going to show up. I thought you were going to be here on our first day."

"Directors don't worry much about old-timers like me being here for rehearsals. My first scene won't shoot until tomorrow."

"Coming by to get a lay of the land?"

"Exactly." He shifted his attention when Adam approached. Carter extended his hand. "You must be Sienna's new leading man."

"That's right," Adam said with a hint of possessiveness.

Sienna managed to keep her smile in place. "Adam Pratt, this is Carter Wells. Carter, Adam."

"Good to meet you," Carter said with his typical charm. "I've been looking forward to working with you. Your career has certainly been fun to watch so far."

"Thanks."

Carter turned his attention back to Sienna. "Sienna, do you have the shoot schedule for today? I haven't received my copy yet."

"My assistant should have it." Sienna looked around. As if on cue, Toni crossed the room toward her. "Toni, this is Carter. He needs a copy of today's shoot schedule. Could you get one for him?"

"Of course. I'll take care of that right now," Toni said. "Miss Blake, can I get you some breakfast or anything?"

"I'm fine for now. Thanks."

Toni nodded and spoke to Carter. "I'll get that schedule for you."

"Thank you." Carter watched her cross the room once more to search out the desired information. "It looks like you trained her well."

"Actually, she came that way," Sienna said. "My regular assistant had to stay behind in California for some family issues. The studio hired Toni to fill in."

"The studio does like to take care of its stars."

Sienna gave him a wry smile. "You should know."

Her phone chimed, indicating a new e-mail. Though she didn't have any reason to think it might be from Craig, she excused herself anyway. She had been trying since he left not to worry, but her efforts had yet to be successful. "I'm going to leave you two to get better acquainted. I believe you have a scene together tomorrow."

Sienna headed for a chair by the wide bank of windows overlooking the Atlantic and pulled her phone out of her purse. She opened her e-mail, her heartbeat quickening when she saw Craig's name illuminated on her screen. She clicked on the message and read the short note:

Sienna,

Sorry this is the first time I've been able to send a message out. I hope everything is going okay with you. Not sure yet when we're heading back home, but it should be soon. Looking forward to seeing you. Don't eat too much apple pie without me.

Craig

Sienna's smile bloomed. The message was simple enough, but the most important thing she wanted to hear was in front of her in black and white. He was planning on coming home soon, and he wanted to see her again.

"Miss Blake, they're ready for you in makeup."

"Thanks, Toni." Sienna followed her assistant toward the makeup room and wondered how she was going to manage to stop smiling long enough to let the makeup artists do their work.

* * *

He saw that private smile of hers that made him know she was keeping secrets again. He knew her so well. So much better than she could ever understand.

Adam Pratt took the seat beside her as the makeup artists prepared them for their first scene of the day. Adam put his hand on her arm, a brief show of affection. So that was how things were now. It was too bad, really. A developing relationship between Adam and Sienna could cause complications, but there was nothing he could do about that now. If he was lucky, he might even be able to use this new tidbit in his favor.

His plan was in place, and nothing was going to hold him back. Today was another new beginning, another step toward reclaiming the past he had worked so hard to earn.

* * *

Sienna kept her smile in place even though she was cringing inside when Adam ran his hand down her arm. She really had to find a time to talk to him. Maybe once he realized she had no romantic interest in him, they could get past this touchy-feely thing he had with her and could become friends.

The makeup artists had completed their tasks, and she and Adam would have a few minutes before the cameras were ready to roll, but they already had their microphones on, and Sienna did everything she could to keep her personal business private. Any number of people could hear anything she said right now, and unfortunately, there was always someone around who was ready to trade a story to the tabloids for a few bucks.

"You know, we really need to figure out a way to get our schedules to work. I feel like I hardly see you when we're away from the set," Adam said.

"That's because we don't see each other away from the set. Why don't we talk about this later?"

"It looks like we're going to have a long lunch break today while they shoot some of the extra scenes. We can talk then."

"Maybe," Sienna said noncommittally. Feeling a bit claustrophobic, she took a step toward the window.

"Everyone on their marks," Marcus called out.

Though she was normally quick to take direction, Sienna hesitated, needing a moment to clear her head. Adam had already reached his mark and had turned back toward her.

"Come on, Sienna." Adam stepped closer to her, reaching out his hand.

A creak sounded above them, and a split second later, metal and glass crashed to the floor right where Adam had been standing. Adam yelled out. Sienna gasped. The rest of the cast and crew had reactions varying between the two.

Sienna barely had time to register that one of the huge overhead lights had nearly hit them before Carter rushed forward a step ahead of George. He grabbed Sienna by both arms. "Are you okay?"

Sienna's hand came up to rest over her pounding heart. "Yeah."

"Are you sure you're okay?" George asked.

"I think so." Her eyes lifted to the heavy cable that had supported the light until just a moment before. The cable vibrated but appeared to still be intact. Yet somehow, whatever held the light in place had failed to do its job. "That was scary. A second later and Adam and I would have been standing right under that."

"Very scary," Carter agreed. "You're shaking. Come on. Let's go sit down for a minute."

A tremble worked through her, and she felt like her head was spinning a foot off her shoulders. "Yeah. That's a good idea."

"What in the world happened?" Marcus asked.

"I don't know," one of the crew members responded. "We check the equipment every night. Everything looked fine."

"I want it all checked again," Marcus demanded. "Now."

"Yes, sir."

Sienna lowered herself onto the sofa that was part of the living room set. She looked over at the crew members who were scrambling to check the remaining lighting and Adam, who was now sitting in a chair on the other side of the room, apparently also unharmed. Sienna took a deep breath. "I've never seen anything like that happen before."

"Me neither. And I've been around the business a lot longer than you," Carter said. "I can tell you one thing though."

"What's that?"

"I don't think either of us has to imagine what it feels like to be scared to death now."

"Isn't that the truth."

* * *

Craig checked his e-mail, hoping for a response to the last one he had sent Sienna. They had been writing back and forth since the communications blackout was lifted onboard the USS *Enterprise* almost a week ago, each letter growing longer than the last. They had progressed beyond chatting about their previous time spent together. Now they were telling each other about their families and friends and even sometimes daring to share their dreams for the future.

For so many years, Craig had aspired to become a Navy SEAL. Now he pondered what else he wanted in life. When Sienna had opened the door into her dating struggles, specifically about how hard it was to be in the spotlight while also holding on to her LDS standards, Craig wondered if they could make this relationship work. He didn't have any answers except a resolve that he wanted to try.

He was disappointed but not surprised when he saw she hadn't written back yet. With the time difference, she had likely been sleeping since he had last e-mailed her. After spending three days on board an aircraft carrier in the Mediterranean, they had finally arrived in port in Naples. That was four days ago.

Debriefings, skills training, PT. The days had passed in a blur, and each night he had closed his eyes and tried to guide his dreams away from the memories of Abolstan and toward happier times when he had been with Sienna. He opened his sketchbook and flipped past his recent drawings of the Italian countryside until he reached one of Sienna. He stared at it, a warm rush of emotion flowing through him.

How was it possible that he could feel so much closer to her now even though they were thousands of miles away? Maybe the shrink was right. Maybe he was delusional.

Craig stared at the sketch a moment longer before putting his pad away, then dressed for morning PT and headed for the weight room, where he was supposed to meet his squad. When he arrived, he glanced at his watch to see he was ten minutes early. Only Brent had arrived before him.

Craig closed the distance between them, lowering himself onto the weight bench beside where Brent was currently stretching his arms above his head to loosen his shoulders. "Do you know how much longer we're staying in Italy?"

Brent let his arms drop back to his sides and looked down at him. "Are you in a hurry to get home?"

Craig started to deny it but didn't see the point. "A little."

"Me too." Brent crossed his left arm over his chest and continued his stretching routine. "That's why I put in our transport request yesterday. We're waiting to see when they can get us out of here, but it looks like they're sending us home tomorrow or the next day."

"What's the plan until then?"

"We're going to spend some time in the Italian countryside."

Brent's tone told Craig the commander wasn't talking about sightseeing. "And what are we going to do in the Italian countryside?"

"Run," Brent told him. "I figure after we hit the fifteen-mile mark, we'll all be ready to sit on a plane for eight hours."

"Makes sense to me."

The rest of the squad filtered into the room.

Quinn was the first to speak. "Is it time to go home yet?"

"Quinn, you aren't going to believe this, but you weren't the first person to ask this time." Brent jerked a thumb at Craig. "He was."

"Yeah, you're going to fit in here just fine."

"Glad to hear it," Craig said, though he wasn't nearly as glad as he had been to hear they were heading back to Virginia.

19

"WOULDN'T YOU KNOW IT? CRAIG said he's headed back any day, and I have to leave for California," Sienna complained over the phone to her sister, flopping onto the bed in her hotel room.

"It's only for the weekend," Kendra reminded her. "And I'm glad you're coming to California. It will be good to see you."

"You saw me a couple weeks ago at your wedding."

"Yeah, but we spent most of that time trying to keep secrets. This weekend we'll be able to spend some time together."

"Kendra, I fly in on Saturday afternoon, go to the awards show on Sunday, and fly back on Monday morning. Not exactly a lot of time to spare."

"We're getting our nails done together on Saturday night," Kendra said.

"I guess that's better than nothing." Sienna kicked her shoes off and debated whether she had the energy to change into her pajamas or if she was going to sleep in her clothes. Again. "And I am glad you're going to be there, especially since I got cornered into being Adam Pratt's date."

"What's the deal with you two? I've seen a couple shots of you together holding hands. For you, that usually means the guy is boyfriend material."

"Adam is definitely not boyfriend material," Sienna insisted. "Craig, on the other hand . . ."

"I see," Kendra said. "Charlie and I were thinking about coming to Virginia to surprise his mom on Mothers' Day weekend. Maybe we can all get together then. I'd love to get to know Craig better."

"That makes two of us."

* * *

Craig texted Sienna the moment the plane touched down in Virginia Beach. He looked at his watch for the fifth time in less than ten minutes, confirming that it wasn't quite nine o'clock on Sunday night.

He hadn't received any e-mails from Sienna since yesterday. She had said something about going out of town for a couple days, and he remembered her mentioning something about Sunday. He hoped she was back by now.

He felt a little foolish making a woman his top priority after returning home from his first mission, but when he glanced at the rest of his teammates, he saw he wasn't the only one.

Just as when they had departed, everyone had their phones up to their ears, speaking quietly to the people most important to them.

Craig looked at his watch again, checked the blank screen on his phone, and gave up on waiting. He dialed Sienna's number.

Her phone rang only once before it went to voice mail. He let out a frustrated sigh and waited for the beep. "Sienna, it's Craig. I'm back in town. Give me a call when you have a minute."

He hung up and stared at his phone again. Where could she be on a Sunday night?

* * *

Cameras flashed, gowns sparkled, and stars abounded. Fans of all ages lined the red carpet leading into the Oscars, a scene that would make it onto any number of news and social-media sites before the night was out.

Best dressed. Worst dressed. Who arrived with whom. Reporters would write all of those articles, many of them overshadowing why everyone was here in the first place: to find out who would win the many awards presented tonight.

Sienna had a single nomination tonight for her supporting role in a romantic comedy. Predictions were already running against her, but her agent and her parents had all told her she needed to make an appearance.

Adam stepped out of their limousine first and held a hand out to her. She pasted on her best smile, anticipating the increased attention they would get by arriving together, and forced herself to put her hand in his.

The questions were instant, "How long have you been dating?" being the most common.

They stopped together for one of several prearranged interviews as they made their way toward the entrance of the Staples Center, where the awards ceremony was being held tonight.

A reporter in her late twenties spoke into the microphone she held. "Sienna, this new project is a departure for you. How different is it filming an action movie?"

"The rehearsals are a lot more physically demanding, but I'm enjoying the new challenge," Sienna responded with a smile.

The reporter shifted her attention to Adam. "Adam, you've played opposite so many of Hollywood's top stars. How is the chemistry between Sienna and you? Is it as strong on-screen as it is off?"

Adam flashed his most charming smile, and for a brief moment, Sienna could almost believe he was someone she would consider dating. "Working with Sienna is everything I'd hoped it would be. Dating her is a dream come true."

The reporter turned to the camera, her own smile beaming. "You heard it here first, everyone. Adam Pratt and Sienna Blake: a couple off screen as well as on."

Only her years of media training prevented Sienna from disputing Adam's claim, but immediately her mind started spinning.

Normally she wouldn't care if rumors started, especially if it meant garnering more interest in her movie, but now that she had someone else she cared about, she was charting new territory.

What would Craig think if he saw the news clip? Could she explain that publicity was part of the job, a part she wished she could do without?

She forced herself to keep moving forward to the next prearranged interview. What was she worrying about? Craig was still overseas somewhere, and it was doubtful he would see anything about this. As soon as she got back to her parents' house tonight, she would e-mail Craig and tell him exactly what had happened and why the headlines were so far from the truth.

* * *

Craig stared at his computer screen, a ball of lead in his stomach. Up until ten seconds ago, he had liked Adam Pratt as an actor. Now that the image of him with his arm around Sienna was staring him in the face, Craig couldn't stand the guy. So much for the idea of Sienna Blake dating someone outside the social circles of Hollywood.

What had he been thinking, that someone like her would really want to spend her free time with someone like him? Obviously she chose her friends from people who were easily available to her, who wouldn't have to worry about the government sending them out at a moment's notice every time a crisis occurred.

His room in the barracks suddenly felt too small. He closed his laptop, locked it in his lockbox, and stuffed his cell phone in his pocket. He was halfway down the hall when his phone rang.

He wanted to ignore it, not feeling able to deal with anyone right now, but in this career, he didn't have that luxury. He pulled it free of his pocket and saw his mom's name illuminated on the screen. Concerned that she was calling him at seven in the morning, he pressed the talk button and prepared to test his own acting abilities.

"Hi, Mom."

His mother's voice came over the line, bright and cheerful. "Hi, sweetie. What's wrong?"

Craig rolled his eyes. How was it that mothers could sense something wrong from a thousand miles away? "Nothing. Just tired. I got to bed later than I should have last night."

"I've been worried about you. I haven't talked to you in a couple weeks. Is everything going okay?"

The image of gunshots hitting inches from him popped into his mind with a clarity he wished he could forget, but he wasn't about to tell his mother about that. "Everything's fine. How is old man Standen's new foal doing?"

"He's a beauty."

Craig stepped outside into the cool morning air. When a gust of wind whipped through him, he wished he had remembered to grab a jacket. Without a specific location in mind, he started toward the mess hall, even though his appetite had been squashed the moment he'd seen the image of Adam and Sienna. Dutifully, Craig asked his mom about her friends and neighbors, prepared to give her a few minutes before apologizing for being out of reach over the past two weeks.

After talking about her closest friends, she said, "By the way, I wanted to ask you something."

"What's that?"

"Do you know the actress Sienna Blake?"

Craig swallowed. "What? Why do you ask that?"

"Oh, Maggie was telling me about some photos she saw online from Kendra Blake's wedding. You know, the singer."

"Yeah, I know who Kendra Blake is," Craig said.

"Anyway, Maggie said she saw a photo of Sienna Blake with a handsome young man who looked just like you. Said he was the spitting image."

Craig stopped walking, torn about what to say. He didn't want to lie to his mother, but he certainly didn't want his name associated with Sienna's, especially now that she was dating someone else.

He attempted to dance the line between truth and fabrication. "This isn't something I really want you telling people, but I did meet her. It wasn't a big deal. She was just at a party where I was helping with security."

His mother's pitch went up an octave. "You met Sienna Blake and didn't tell me?"

Craig held the phone away from his ear for a moment, hoping there wasn't any permanent damage to his eardrum. "Mom, you just screamed in my ear. Can you blame me for not mentioning it? Besides, I don't want to be the local gossip. It isn't good for my career."

"Oh, honey. That's not what I meant. It's just, she's one of my favorite actresses. And of course I've watched just about everything her dad has ever starred in."

Craig let her ramble for a moment. When she finally came up for air, he asked, "Mom, can I trust you to keep this to yourself?"

"Surely I can tell your aunt Jessie."

"If you tell Aunt Jessie, you might as well take out an ad in the newspaper and announce it."

He heard his mother sigh. "You're taking all the fun out of this, you know."

"Yeah, I know." Craig managed a small smile. "I'm a terrible son. I don't know how you put up with me."

"Let me tell you. It's a challenge."

"So you keep saying." Craig reached the door to the mess hall. "Hey, Mom. I've gotta get going. I'll talk to you later, okay?"

"Okay. Love you."

"Love you too." Craig hung up the phone and stepped in out of the cold, his mood lighter after bantering with his mom.

He breathed in the scent of pancakes, scrambled eggs, and sausage. His stomach growled, but he wasn't sure if it was from hunger or protest at the thought of eating. He hoped it was the former.

After loading his tray, he found Damian at a table with Kevin, one of the guys who lived in their barracks. Damian gave Craig a pitying look.

"I'm really sorry, Craig."

Craig straightened his shoulders. "I gather you've been surfing the Internet this morning."

"It was kind of hard to miss it."

"Miss what?" Kevin asked.

"Nothing," Craig said before Damian could air his personal business in front of anyone else. "There's nothing to talk about, okay?"

"Sorry," Damian mumbled and took another bite of his eggs.

Craig scooped some eggs onto one of his pancakes, rolled it up, and took a bite. When he found both the pancake and eggs colder than he liked, he dropped it back onto his plate and stood. "I think I'm going to head over to the office. I'll see you later."

"Aren't you going to eat more than that?"

"Not hungry." Craig took a step back. Before Damian could make the assumption that Sienna had caused his lack of appetite, he added, "I must not have adjusted to this time zone yet."

Damian simply nodded. "I'll see you later."

Craig started to walk away but heard Kevin ask, "What's going on?"

"Nothing. Just a rough morning," Damian said.

Craig looked behind him to see Damian stand and prepare to follow him. Craig was only a few steps out of the mess hall when Damian caught up.

"Hey, man. I'm really sorry about that. I didn't mean to say anything in front of Kevin." Damian fell into step with him. "Did Sienna say anything about what she was doing with Pratt?"

"She doesn't owe me an explanation. We only hung out a few times."

Damian gave him a meaningful look. "You might have only hung out a few times, but she looked just as interested in you as you were in her."

"I guess she was giving us an up-close look at her acting talent," Craig said, fighting the bitter taste in his mouth. "Come on. Let's get to work. I'm ready to think about something else for a while."

20

It was torture, pure and simple. Five hours, confined in a small space with Adam. For all of his appeal on-screen, the man had the personality of a doorknob. To make matters worse, George had ended up in a seat several rows back. Since the flight had been full, Sienna hadn't been given the option to switch seats.

If she didn't love her publicist, she would seriously consider firing her over coordinating her flight with Adam's and subjecting her to his mindless conversation.

Had she heard about Bethanie's latest shopping spree to Milan? Like she cared. Had she noticed Angelina's new tattoo? Did she think it would look bad if he bought another Mercedes? After all, he already owned two. Along with the Ferrari, the classic '64 Corvette, and a Lexus SUV for when he wanted to blend in. She had listened to him talk about the cars and had somehow managed to ooh and aah over the photographs he had shown her of each and every one.

What would he be like if he ever got married and had children? Heaven help the poor soul who had to fly with him then!

She had tried to escape the constant chatter with sleep, but Adam hadn't stopped, even when she'd forced herself to keep her eyes closed for twenty minutes straight.

Then and there she resolved to never travel with Adam again. She wondered if her publicist could spin a good breakup story for the media in which Sienna was forced to avoid Adam at all times except when they were working.

When their plane touched down, Sienna could have kissed the ground . . . and the elderly lady who managed to step between Adam and her as they were deplaning.

She knew the studio would send one car to pick both of them up from the airport. In anticipation of that ride, she put her earbuds in and turned on the music on her iPhone. She had tried the same ploy on the airplane, but he'd kept talking so loudly to get her attention she'd taken pity on their fellow travelers and given up. At this point, with her nerves frazzled, all bets were off.

As soon as they were up the Jetway and in the airport, Adam sidestepped the woman walking between them and came up beside Sienna again. George followed behind them, but he wouldn't associate himself with them unless he detected a problem. Sienna expected Adam's bodyguards would follow similar protocol, except they would use their own transportation to follow them back to the hotel.

As a defensive measure to keep Adam from more PDA, Sienna put her free hand in her jacket pocket and gripped the handle of her carry on bag with the other. When they exited past security, they found their chauffeur, a man around forty, holding a white card with their last names on it.

"Let me take that for you, Miss Blake," her driver said, taking her suitcase from her.

"Thank you." Now she shoved both hands into her pockets. "I'm sorry. I didn't catch your name."

"I'm Ron."

"It's good to meet you." Sienna walked alongside Ron, leaving Adam to bring up the rear.

After waiting twenty minutes for Adam's checked luggage and introducing Ron to George, they finally got underway. With this limited opportunity to speak to him privately, she pressed the button to raise the window between the front and back seats of the limousine.

Once Ron and George could no longer hear them, Sienna shifted to face Adam. "Adam, I think we need to talk."

"About what?"

"Our breakup."

"Breakup?" Adam repeated, clearly confused. "What breakup?"

"The one that's about to happen." Sienna sighed. "Look, you're a great guy, but the truth is, I'm seeing someone else. He should be back in Virginia any day now, and I don't want our fake relationship to cause problems for my reputation or yours."

"But I thought . . ."

"You thought I would want to date you if you showed interest in me," Sienna finished for him. "And that would help our movie sell and keep us in the press."

"Well, yeah," Adam admitted.

"I appreciate your honesty, but that doesn't work for me. I'm sure we can find any number of ways to stay in the news when it's time to promote our movie." Sienna thought for a minute. "In fact, we can spin a story about how we both worked through our personal differences to deliver such a great product."

"I guess that could work."

"I appreciate your understanding. Craig isn't in the business, and the last thing I need is for him to believe the hype."

The partition window began to lower, and Sienna looked forward, surprised to see it going down.

"Hold on!" George shouted.

Sienna gripped the edge of the door and looked through the window. "What's wrong?"

George didn't answer, but Sienna felt the limo skid sideways. Then it did a complete 180. Cars wove and swerved to try to miss them.

Her heart was racing, and everything seemed to slow down, but that didn't change the inevitable. They were going to crash. More tires squealed. Someone honked.

"No!" The word came out in a whisper, the only word she managed before the back of the car slammed into the barrier on the side of the highway.

The impact jarred her body, the seat belt jerking her back against the leather seat. Her head, shoulders, and back throbbed, but she couldn't quite process the pain.

For several seconds, no one spoke. Then George managed to turn around to face her. "Are you okay?"

"I think so."

"Adam?"

He pressed his hand against his forehead as though pushing against some pain centered there. "Yeah, I'm okay. What happened?"

"There were a couple tires in the road. Ron did some fancy driving to keep us from hitting anything besides the guard rail."

Someone knocked on the window, and Ron rolled it down. A concerned driver stood on the other side, a man in his twenties.

"Are you all okay?"

"I think so," Ron said.

"I called 9-1-1. They should be here any minute."

"Thanks." George turned to Sienna. "Are you sure you're okay?"

"Just sore."

"We should probably have you taken to the hospital to get checked out." George motioned to Adam. "You too."

Still stunned, Sienna tried to visualize what would happen next. A trip to the hospital didn't sound terribly appealing, regardless of how sore her back was. "I'm sure I'll be fine."

"Better safe than sorry."

She watched as one car after another passed them, picking up speed as they did so. Seeing the cars reaching highway speeds, she sent up a prayer of gratitude that no one had been seriously hurt.

A policeman arrived first, followed immediately by an ambulance. One of the ambulance attendants opened the back door and started asking her simple questions to make sure she was still coherent. Realizing she was suffering only from stiffness, the attendant shifted his attention to Adam.

No longer distracted by the EMT, Sienna listened to the policeman questioning their driver.

"I don't know where the other car came from. One minute we were driving along with the flow of traffic, and the next, this big pickup truck jumps out in front of us, and a couple of large tires fly into the road right in our path."

"Sounds like someone didn't tie down their load."

"I don't think so," George countered.

"What do you mean you don't think so?" the officer asked.

"Someone was in the back of that pickup truck. The tires in our path weren't an accident. They were deliberate."

"Why would anyone do that?" Sienna asked, leaning forward.

"I have no idea, but I know what I saw." George's eyes met hers. "Makes me wonder if that accident on set last week was really an accident."

"You think someone's out to get one of us?"

"I don't know, but like it or not, your security force is about to get bigger." George gave her a sympathetic look. "Sorry, Sienna, but you know we have to."

"Just do me a favor. If we have to bring on some more help, can you organize it through Grandpa instead of my dad? I don't want to feel like I'm under a microscope again."

"Fair enough," George agreed. "But no arguing when I insist you go to the hospital to get checked out."

"I will if you will."

George pressed his lips together before muttering, "Fine."

21

CRAIG WASN'T SURE WHETHER TO thank Brent or beg for mercy. They'd spent all day Monday on the ocean. Swimming, boating, running on the beach. If any of the other squad members had planned to ask Craig about the situation with Sienna, they hadn't had the chance with the rigorous training Brent had put them through.

With that in mind, Craig approached the weight room skeptically on Tuesday morning. As soon as he arrived where the rest of his squad had assembled for their morning PT, Brent said, "Craig, you're with me." Brent then motioned to Seth. "Seth has the training schedule for the rest of the day."

"Where are you two off to?" Quinn asked.

"To do a favor for a friend." Brent didn't elaborate. Instead, he motioned for everyone to gather around so they could offer their morning prayer. As soon as the amens were said, Brent left the room, expecting Craig to follow.

Craig fell into step beside him, not sure why he had been singled out to come with the commander over everyone else. He wanted to ask where they were going, but after Brent evaded Quinn's question, he opted for a different question and motioned to his BDUs. "Is it okay to be in uniform where we're going?"

"I have a feeling we'll blend in just fine." Brent led the way to his car, and Craig got into the passenger seat. Brent put the car in gear. "Did you pay any attention to the news yesterday or today?"

"Not since yesterday morning," Craig said. "I've been kind of avoiding it since then."

"Late yesterday afternoon, there was a car accident on I-64. Someone threw a couple of semi retreads out of the back of a pickup truck and caused a car to crash."

"That's too bad . . . What does it have to do with us?"

"Directly, it doesn't have anything to do with us." Brent started toward the base exit. "Sienna Blake was in the car that crashed."

Craig straightened in his seat. "Is she okay?"

"A little sore, but luckily she and everyone else in the car were wearing their seat belts."

"Everyone else in the car," Craig repeated. "I gather that included Adam Pratt."

"It did. My brother-in-law asked me if we could look over the security on set. Apparently there was also an accident last week. Sienna and Adam narrowly missed being hit by some overhead lighting that came undone."

Craig tried to push his personal feelings aside and concentrate on Sienna's safety. "Do you think the two incidents are related?"

"I don't know, but Sienna's bodyguard is worried."

"That's understandable."

"I know the situation with Adam must make things uncomfortable for you, but Sienna and George both know you, and I thought it would be easier for you to help me nose around than any of the others." Brent turned toward the ocean. "We bring in a bunch of Navy SEALs onto a Hollywood set, we not only run the risk of garnering bad press, but we also could very well end up in a spotlight we'd best be avoiding."

"It might be a little late for me on that."

"What do you mean?"

"Apparently some of the photos of me and Sienna at her sister's wedding leaked onto the Internet. One of my mom's friends saw them."

"Sorry about that, but we knew it might happen. As long as you don't go around announcing you're a SEAL, I don't think anyone will take notice for long," Brent said. "Even if they did, no one from the press is going to follow you around unless you want them to. You're one of the best at concealment in the unit."

"Really?"

"I saw your scores coming out of BUD/S," Brent said. "That was one of the things that brought you to our attention."

"I figured it was because I'm LDS."

"That didn't hurt either," Brent said. "We like keeping the Mormon standards within our unit, but in our line of work, the mission comes first. Had your aptitude scores not been high enough, you would have gone somewhere else."

Craig repeated Brent's words in his mind and tried to focus on the reasons he had been assigned to the elite Saint Squad instead of focusing on Brent's earlier comment about Adam being with Sienna at the time of the accident.

* * *

Sienna thought she must be crazy to be working today. The hospital had released her and the others who had been in the accident yesterday after making sure that, indeed, nothing had been broken.

Their director had decided to use the accident to their advantage, right down to their stiffness and bruises. Instead of following the schedule planned for today, he had altered the schedule to shoot several scenes that would come after a fictional car crash. Sienna now stood with Adam and Carter, waiting for the action to start.

"I didn't think we had any scenes with extras today." Adam motioned toward the barriers down the street.

"We don't," Carter responded. "Wait a minute. I've seen those guys before. Sienna, weren't they at Kendra's wedding?"

Sienna looked where they indicated, delighted to see Craig coming toward them. As he and Brent came closer, she realized Craig wasn't nearly as happy to see her as she was to see him.

"Places!" Marcus demanded.

"Great," Sienna mumbled under her breath.

"What?" Adam asked.

"It looks like Craig believed the stories from last weekend."

"That's Craig?" Adam asked. "He's the guy you're dumping me for?"

"He's the guy who thinks I dumped him for you," Sienna corrected.

"Well, that's awkward." Adam must have seen the crestfallen look on her face. "Relax. When we break, we can go explain the whole thing."

"You'd do that?"

"Yeah. It's no big deal." Adam took his place at the edge of the sidewalk. "Like you said, we can spin the press in our favor when we announce our breakup."

Sienna looked over at Craig again. "The sooner, the better."

* * *

Craig tried to keep his attention on the security aspects of the current movie set, but every time he heard Sienna's voice, he felt his attention being pulled. It was fascinating actually, watching each scene being shot multiple times from various angles until the director decided he had what he needed for the final product.

Two police cars were parked on either end of the street where the traffic was being diverted. The studio had been granted exclusive access to the three blocks they needed to shoot these particular scenes of the movie.

Additional barricades had been erected a block inland to keep cross traffic out of the area but still remain out of sight of the cameras. Security guards were posted at various locations, and they appeared to have been successful thus far in keeping unauthorized personnel out of the area.

Brent appeared from one of the cross streets and moved to stand beside him. "What do you think?"

"Security is tight. The paparazzi seem to be everywhere, but they're all behind the barricades so they don't pose any real threat. I don't see where anyone could get in, unless . . ."

"Unless they were already here before the barricades went up," Brent finished for him.

"Exactly," Craig agreed. "The good news is that the director switched up the schedule. The city had to scramble to change the shoot dates ahead a week."

"Do you know how much longer they're shooting on location?"

"From what Sienna told me when we were looking over her script, the studio rented one of those big beach houses to use for their main set. They also have a warehouse they'll use for a second set and their green-screen shots, whatever that means."

"Beats me."

Craig noticed a flatbed tow truck pull up at one of the barricades. Security cleared the entrance, and the truck backed into the street, a classic Ford Mustang strapped to the back. The director called a break, and Craig looked over to see Sienna motioning toward him, Adam at her side.

He immediately shifted his attention back to the car. "What year do you think it is? Seventy-four?"

"That would be my guess," Brent said as several crew members joined the driver to help unload the Mustang.

"Should we give them a hand?" Craig asked, all too aware that Sienna was now heading in his direction.

"You're going to have to talk to her eventually," Brent said with entirely too much understanding. "It'll probably be easier on both of you if you get it over with now."

"I think I'd prefer avoidance in this particular scenario."

"Talk to her," Brent insisted. "I'm going to talk to the director to see if I can get an updated schedule."

"I thought my teammates were supposed to have my back, not throw me into the line of fire," Craig complained.

"And sometimes you have to trust the experience of your commander to know what's best for you."

"Thanks a lot."

Brent ignored Craig's sarcasm and was too cheerful when he said, "You're welcome."

Brent lifted a hand in greeting to Sienna as he passed her. Sienna waved in return and continued forward.

Craig squared his shoulders and braced for what he expected would be a difficult encounter. His jaw clenched in anticipation.

"Craig, I'm so glad you made it back okay."

Craig shifted his gaze to Adam.

Sienna motioned to Adam. "Craig, this is Adam Pratt. Adam, this is the friend I was telling you about, Craig Simmons."

"Good to meet you, Craig." Adam extended his hand.

Craig hesitated briefly before shaking the other man's hand. "Yeah, you too."

"Hey, I'm really sorry about the whole publicity thing. I didn't realize Sienna was in a relationship when we planned it out."

Craig's eyes narrowed. "Planned what out?"

"Our date to the Oscars. My publicist and I thought it would be great hype for the movie if we made people think we had a thing going while working together."

"A thing," Craig repeated, not sure he was understanding Adam correctly. Was Adam really standing here telling him his relationship with Sienna that had been blasted all over the news was completely fake?

The expression on Sienna's face made him think that was exactly what Adam was telling him. "I was going to e-mail you when we got back from California, but then we got into an accident, and everything got crazy."

Not sure how he felt about Sienna and Adam's revelation, Craig remembered why he was really here. "What did happen with the car accident?"

"We were sitting in the back, so we didn't see anything, but George said someone deliberately threw a couple old tires in our path so we would crash," Sienna told him.

Adam's attention shifted to where the crew was unloading the car. He looked back to Craig. "Are we good?"

"Yeah, we're good."

"I'll catch you later." Adam went over to check out the car and talk to some of the crew members.

Craig watched him go, and when he looked back at Sienna, he found her staring up at him, looking vulnerable. "I'm really sorry about all the hype surrounding me and Adam."

"What I don't understand is why you would put yourself in that position in the first place," Craig said. "And why you didn't tell me about it in one of your e-mails."

"Honestly, I didn't think it was that big a deal. Publicity is part of the job description," Sienna said. "I didn't realize Adam and his publicist had decided to say we were really dating until we were standing in front of the cameras. By then, I was trapped."

"Whether that's true or not, the fact remains that the whole world thinks you're dating Adam Pratt." Craig folded his arms across his chest.

"You're the one I want to go out with." Sienna waved toward Adam. "I told you, everything that happened with Adam while you were gone was an act for the cameras. Nothing more."

"That doesn't change the world's perception." Craig didn't want to admit how much it had hurt when he'd thought Sienna was dating someone else, but he could explain why it still bothered him. "The last thing I need right now is to get caught up in a media circus and some love-triangle story."

She jutted her chin up in a challenge. "If you kiss me here, with Adam in the background, the rumors will stop right now. Everyone will know last weekend was just for show."

Craig stepped closer, and he saw an awareness on Sienna's face, that look he had seen the moment before he had kissed her the first time. He was tempted and annoyed at himself for it. He surprised both of them when he shifted to stand beside her. He leaned down slightly and lowered his voice so only she would hear his words. "What happens between us is not for public viewing."

Without another word, he stepped past her and tried to ignore the tangle of emotions he didn't want to feel and the regret he was certain would dominate before the day was over.

22

REGRET, ANNOYANCE, FRUSTRATION. EACH EMOTION flooded through her. Craig's presence only magnified their intensity. She closed her eyes, harnessing her feelings and turning them outward to be seen by millions.

"Keep the cameras rolling," Marcus told his cameramen, indicating he wanted them to continue filming after he stopped the action so they had more film to edit from. He shifted his attention back to the set and called out, "And action!"

Sienna turned to face the car speeding toward her and lifted the gun in her hand. She squeezed the trigger three times, the blanks producing corresponding sounds. Bullet holes would be added to the Mustang's windshield during editing, but she pretended she saw them now.

She held her pose, counted to three like she'd rehearsed, then shifted to her right and shot two more times. After another second, the director yelled, "Cut!"

Sienna relaxed, even though the car was still speeding toward her. For the next take, they would back the car up again and shoot from behind so her stunt double could stand in for her when she was supposed to get hit and roll off the hood of the car.

"Sienna! Watch out!" The combination of Craig's voice and hearing her real name startled her.

She turned, saw the car hadn't slowed down, and froze. An instant before the car reached her, someone grabbed her arm and yanked her out of the way.

A fraction of a second later, the car crashed into the barricade at the end of the street, finally coming to a stop.

Sienna's throat closed up, and she couldn't breathe. Her shoulder throbbed from the sudden jerking motion of her arm, and the soreness from yesterday's accident resurfaced. She turned her head to see Carter had been the one who had grabbed her.

"Are you okay?" he asked, his eyes wide.

"What happened?" Sienna managed. She stared down the street at the totaled Mustang.

"I don't know. The driver wasn't slowing down, and he was heading right for you."

"I know that's how it's scripted, but my stunt double was supposed to take the hit, and I don't remember a crash in the script."

"There wasn't a crash in the script."

Craig reached her side, with George right behind him. Craig put his hand gently on her arm. "Are you okay?"

"My shoulder's sore, but I think I'm all right." Sienna looked once more at the car. "I wonder if the driver is okay."

"Brent and the cops are checking him out." Craig looked over at Carter. "Sienna was lucky you reacted so quickly. That was a close call."

Looking a little startled himself, Carter blew out a breath. "I guess all those years of working action flicks have paid off."

"Thank you, Carter," Sienna said. "Seriously. You probably saved my life."

"Just in the right place at the right time," he said. "I'm going to see what's going on over there."

"I'll come with you," George said. He turned to Craig. "You'll stay with Sienna?"

"Yeah."

Sienna watched George and Carter head toward the accident. The whole scene truly did look like it belonged on a movie screen.

She replayed the incident in her mind and focused on Craig. "You yelled out. How did you know there was something wrong?"

"The director had already yelled 'cut,' but the car didn't slow down. It was obvious the car wasn't supposed to hit you, especially once the action had stopped." He motioned to her injured arm. "Let me take a look at that shoulder."

She held still while he prodded around her shoulder joint. When he hit a particularly sensitive spot, she moaned in pain.

Craig released the pressure he had put there but continued to gently knead the area. "The good news is that it's not dislocated. You might want to get an MRI to make sure there isn't any tissue damage."

"I think the soreness is mostly from the accident yesterday. When Carter grabbed my arm, it aggravated it." She turned her head and shifted so she was facing him. "How do you know so much about injuries?"

"Everyone in my job goes through advanced medical training, but most of what I know is from firsthand knowledge. Ten years in martial arts leaves you with a few bumps and bruises."

"I bet." She stared up at him, pleased he seemed to have forgotten his earlier frustration with her. "Have you decided to forgive me yet?"

He pondered for a moment. "I'm still thinking about it."

"While you're thinking about it, do you think we could go find someplace to talk that isn't in front of the cameras?"

"Maybe."

They both looked up when Brent and George approached them. "Well?" Craig asked.

"Brake lines were cut, and the steering wheel had locked in place," Brent said. "The driver couldn't stop, and he couldn't steer."

"Sabotage." Craig said distastefully. "How is the driver?"

"He has a concussion and a possible broken ankle. The ambulance is on the way."

George motioned across the set. "I'm going to talk to the director. I want to get Sienna out of here. We're done for the day."

"I agree." Sienna looked over at the far end of the street, where George had parked their car. "I hate to ask it, but what are the chances you guys could look over our car before we go back to the hotel?"

"I'll take care of it." Brent fished his car keys out of his pocket and held them out to Craig. "Craig, why don't you take Sienna back to the hotel? George can drive me back, and we can talk strategy then."

Craig reached out a hand. "Are you sure?"

"Yeah. I think the sooner we get Sienna out of here, the better."

* * *

"Craig, the hotel is that way."

Craig didn't have to look to know she was pointing in the opposite direction. "I know. I want to make sure no one is following us before we head back over there."

"It's not like everyone doesn't already know where we're staying. The whole cast and most of the crew is staying there too."

"Have you considered changing your accommodations?" Craig asked. George had briefed Brent and him on the car accident the day before and the lighting mishap. Both sounded a little fishy, but seeing that car heading straight for Sienna had put Craig's protective instincts into overdrive.

"Not really. I haven't had any trouble at the hotel."

"If someone can manage to get past security on the set, I'm worried they might try to get to you at the hotel."

Sienna's face paled. "Do you honestly think someone is trying to hurt me?"

"Until that car almost ran you down, I thought it might have been Adam who was the target. He was closer to the light that fell." Craig glanced over at her.

"But why? Why would anyone want to hurt me?"

Craig turned inland. "I was hoping you could shed some light on that. Has anything like this ever happened to you before?"

"Not to me." Her voice trailed off.

Craig guessed where her thoughts had wandered. "But this kind of stuff has happened to your sister."

"Yeah." She shuddered and fell quiet. A minute passed before she spoke again. "I don't think it was like this with Kendra."

"What do you mean?"

"The guy who was after her was on our security team. He set an explosive at one of her concerts to freak her out. The FBI thinks he believed Kendra would turn to him for help and fall for him."

Craig's fingers tightened on the steering wheel. "And when that didn't happen, he stalked her until he found her."

"Yeah." Sienna let the word out on a sigh.

Craig considered her comments, choosing a random turn and starting to backtrack toward her hotel. "You're right. It is different. All of the incidents with you could have left you injured or worse. The question is why would someone want you out of the way?"

"Out of the way of what?"

"That's exactly the question we need to answer. It could be someone else believed the story about you and Adam dating— maybe an old girlfriend who wants him back." Craig considered. "Or another actress who thought she deserved your role."

"If you're talking about Adam's old girlfriends, I'm afraid the list is long, and the list of people who want to date him is even longer."

"We don't have to consider everyone. Just people who have access to the set."

"Actually, there were a couple of break-ins at the beach house right before we started shooting. George was really frustrated because the security company that was supposed to be monitoring it wasn't doing a good enough job."

"How did George know there had been break-ins?"

"He stopped several of the attempts himself, and he figures there were probably at least a couple that got by him."

"I'm sure the cops will look into that angle."

"What have I gotten myself into?" Sienna asked.

"We'll find a way to tighten security so you won't have to worry anymore. If it is someone who isn't on the cast or crew, we should be able to catch them if they make another attempt."

"And if it is someone on the cast or crew? What then?" Sienna asked. "That would mean whoever is doing this is someone I know."

"Which is why we're also going to run background checks on everyone working on this project. People don't do things like this without a motive. Something will pop up eventually."

"I don't want to wait for eventually. I'm ready for this to be over now."

"You and me both."

23

SIENNA COULD FEEL THE TEARS welling up in her eyes, and she blinked hard against them. She didn't want to cry. She didn't want Craig to see her cry.

For the past several minutes he hadn't said a word. He had driven silently, taking one turn after another until she had no idea where they were. She stared blindly out the window, barely noticing when the ocean came into view in patches between tall hotel buildings.

Craig pulled into a parking lot and turned off the engine. "Come on."

Sienna looked around. "Where are we?"

"About a mile from the hotel. I thought we could both use a walk on the beach."

Emotionally exhausted, Sienna blinked hard again, willing her tears to subside.

Craig circled the car and opened the door for her. She shifted to climb out, unnerved when she stood and saw the quiet understanding in Craig's eyes. A tremble worked through her body, and she folded her arms tightly to prevent the sensation from repeating. "I can't do this anymore."

"It's going to be okay," Craig said automatically, but Sienna could tell he was trying to believe his own words.

"No, it's not. This is twice. Twice I should have ended up in the hospital." Sienna paced three steps away before turning back to him. "If you hadn't shouted and Carter hadn't been close enough to pull me out of the way, I'd probably be dead right now."

A tear spilled over, and Craig reached for her, pulling her into his arms. "It's okay," he said again soothingly.

Those two words were all it took for all of her pent-up fears and emotions to spill over. Her tears flowed freely, and her body trembled as she sobbed. All the while, Craig held her, running his hand over her hair, speaking softly to her.

Sienna linked her hands around his waist and held on tightly as though she could hide from the world right there in his embrace. Minutes passed, her tears finally slowing. She felt Craig's lips press against her forehead, and she shifted to look up at him.

His eyes met hers. The compassion reflected there quickly turned to something else. He lifted his hands and used his thumbs to brush away her tears. She could only stare at him when his hands came to rest along her jaw, holding her in place as he lowered his lips to hers. A thrill danced up her spine, and she let herself get swept away in the moment.

She could smell the salt, hear the rumble of the water rushing up over the sand. The wind coming off the ocean should have made her cold, but all she could feel was a warm sense of belonging.

Craig changed the angle of the kiss, and Sienna was surprised her bones didn't melt into a puddle right there in the parking lot. When he pulled back, he lowered his hands to run them down her arms. "I missed you."

"I missed you too."

"Come on." He took her hand and locked the car door. "Let's take that walk."

* * *

Craig walked along the beach, Sienna's hand in his, and wondered how his life could change so completely in such a short period of time. This morning he hadn't wanted to think about Sienna, hadn't wanted to ever hear her name again for the pain it had caused. Now he didn't want to think about anything else.

Her vulnerability ate at him, especially knowing how much she craved normalcy. He supposed that was why the rumors about her and Adam had hit so hard. Never had he considered the rumors not only to be false but to be scripted as well. The fact that Sienna hadn't told him about her date with her costar and that she had subjected herself to the rumors of a relationship with Adam still grated on Craig.

Water under the bridge, he reminded himself. As much as that situation hurt, Sienna's safety was his top priority now.

"Should we head back?" Sienna asked after ten minutes.

"Actually, I thought we could walk the rest of the way to your hotel. We're over halfway there."

"What about Brent's car?"

"I can jog back and get it later. I figure we'll have an easier time getting into the hotel unnoticed if we arrive on foot and go in the side entrance."

"It's a great idea, but the paparazzi tend to cover all the entrances, especially when they know there's a story to go with their photos."

Sienna rubbed her arm with her free hand.

Craig studied her clothes, the same ones she had been wearing when the car had nearly hit her. Jeans, some kind of knit top, and a blue hooded jacket. "Hold on a minute." He let go of her hand and motioned to her. "Take off your jacket."

"Are you serious? It's freezing!"

"Trust me."

She pulled the jacket off, and he took it from her, pleased to see the lining was white. He turned the jacket inside out and handed it back to her. "Here, put it back on."

"Do you really think changing the color of my jacket is going to help me go unnoticed?"

"Can't hurt." Craig pulled her hood up over her hair. "This should help."

She pursed her lips, considering. "Actually, that might work." She pushed the hood off long enough to tuck her hair behind her ears so it was no longer visible. "I don't suppose you have any sunglasses, do you?"

Craig pulled his sunglasses out of his vest pocket and handed them to her.

She slid them into place. "Aren't you just a Boy Scout?"

"Hey, Eagle Scout all the way."

"I should have known."

He put his hand on her back and nudged her toward the hotel. "Come on. Let's see how well you blend in."

"Shouldn't we wait until after dark or something?"

"We could, but I doubt you want to stand out in the cold that long." Craig pointed at the lowering sun. "Besides, twilight can be a great time to sneak in. The photographers will be looking right into the glare on the water."

"If you say so."

"Watch and learn." Craig gave her a cocky grin and continued toward the hotel. By the time they reached the edge of the grounds, the sun was burning low in the sky, its rays reflecting off the water.

Craig kept his hand on her back and gauged the best angle to get lost in the fading sunlight and shadows. He chose the door at the back of the hotel that led to a beach café. He imagined during the summer the café would be filled to capacity this time of night, but in the off-season, like many other beachside businesses, it was closed.

They entered the rear doors, and Craig turned to the left, guessing he would find a stairwell somewhere near the corner of the building. He kept his voice low. "What floor are you on?"

"Fifteenth."

"Hope you're ready for a workout."

"Not really."

Craig looked at her, surprised, then noticed her holding her side. "Are you okay?"

"Still a bit sore from the accident."

"Today's accident or yesterday's?"

"It's so wrong that I have to clarify," she said. "Both, I guess."

"Come on. We can go up a couple flights, and then we'll catch the elevator from there."

"Okay."

Craig found the stairwell door and opened it for her. Once they were inside, he asked, "Do you want me to carry you? I can give you a piggyback ride."

"That's sweet, but I think I'll be okay."

Sienna took the first few steps slowly, and Craig shook his head. "Have you been hurting this whole time? I never would have had us walk so far had I known."

"George had me take some pain meds earlier today. They must be wearing off."

Craig waited until they reached the first landing before he reached out and put a hand around her back. "Hold on. There's no reason for you to make it worse." He leaned down and scooped her feet out from under her.

She let out a little squeak of surprise. "Craig! I'm fine, really."

"Great. Let's keep you that way." Craig climbed up the first few flights of stairs, debating briefly when he reached the fourth floor. He imagined the guest rooms would start somewhere around the fourth or fifth floor, but he decided not to take a chance of exiting into a common area and kept going.

"I feel ridiculous," Sienna said as he continued upward.

"Why?"

"Hmmm. Let me see." She tapped a finger to her chin. "I'm wearing sunglasses indoors, my jacket is inside out, and you're carrying me up an obscene number of stairs."

"Fifteen flights isn't bad. Now, if we were talking about more than twenty, we might be in trouble."

"I thought we were going to take the elevator partway up."

"No need. I was only going to do that so you wouldn't have to walk so far."

They were nearing the tenth floor. "Aren't you tired of carrying me yet?"

Craig considered for a minute and decided she'd given him an opening he couldn't pass up. "Maybe I do need a break."

He stopped at the landing between the ninth and tenth floors and set her down, one hand remaining firmly on her back. He saw the surprise in her eyes when he caged her against the wall and lowered his lips to hers.

The kiss was brief, but it sent his pulse racing. He tried to keep the mood light. "Yeah, I feel much better now."

Sienna rolled her eyes, but he saw the humor dancing there. "You know, I can probably walk the rest of the way."

"Probably," Craig agreed and promptly picked her back up.

"You do realize George isn't going to be happy if he comes back and finds you in my room."

"I'm not coming in unless he's there anyway, but my guess is that he and Brent are already here."

A few minutes later, Sienna unlocked her door, and Craig's guess was confirmed. Brent and George both sat in the dining room area, a laptop open in front of them displaying the latest news.

24

SIENNA WENT STRAIGHT TO HER bedroom to retrieve her bottle of extra-strength Tylenol while the men started talking about how to proceed. She was pretty sure she could have made it up a couple flights of stairs, but she was extremely grateful she hadn't needed to.

With every heartbeat, another streak of pain shot through her, the stiffness in her back also causing her discomfort. She swallowed her medicine and took a few moments to change into a pair of sweats. Once she was more comfortable, she headed back into the dining room.

Her suite really was a bit excessive for one person, but for the moment, she appreciated the convenience of having a living room and a dining area because George, Brent, and Craig were now using the dining area as an office. The second bedroom remained untouched since George was currently staying in the room across the hall, but she wasn't going to complain to the studio about having too much space. Many times over the years she had stayed in economy hotels where she would have considered a chair a luxury.

Though she had hardly made any sound, Craig looked up the moment she entered the room. His eyes narrowed. "Maybe we should take you to urgent care and see if we can get you some pain medicine. It also wouldn't hurt to have them check out that shoulder."

"You already looked at my shoulder," Sienna reminded him.

"Yeah, but I'm not a doctor."

"I'll be fine. I took some Tylenol a minute ago."

Craig didn't look convinced, but he stood and pulled out the chair next to him. Stiffly, she lowered herself into it.

"I talked to your director before we came back over here," George told her.

"And?"

"He's going to redo the schedule to give you a couple days off."

"How is he going to manage that?"

"They'll focus on the scenes with Adam and Carter."

Brent slid a piece of paper across the table to her. "In the meantime, can you give Craig and me a rundown of the cast and crew?"

"What do you want to know?"

"Anything that might give us a clue as to who might want to cause you harm."

"I can't think of anyone."

"What about Liam?" George asked.

Craig shifted beside her. "Who is Liam?"

"Liam Rickman," Sienna said. "He's playing a supporting role."

"He's playing a supporting role now," George clarified. "Rumor had it that Liam was up for the lead until Marcus found out Sienna was interested. Liam wasn't too happy to be demoted."

"Yeah, but that kind of thing happens all the time," Sienna said. "And besides, he's always been really friendly to me."

"I'm confused. How is it possible that a man and woman would compete for the same role?" Craig asked.

"It's not very common, actually," Sienna said. "This movie was originally written for two male leads, a mentor and his rookie partner."

"But Liam and Adam are around the same age."

"Yeah, but apparently Marcus was looking for more of a draw for the younger viewers. When he found out I was interested in the movie, they changed it to make it a man and woman so they could introduce a romantic element that would appeal to a wider audience."

"The screenwriter couldn't have been too happy with that," Craig mused.

"It's hard to say. Screenwriters go through changes all the time, sometimes daily. It's part of the job."

"Let me ask you this," Brent began. "If you were unable to complete the film, especially at this stage, what would happen?"

Sienna didn't like where this was going. "Marcus would have to replace me."

"Would he go with Liam or someone else?"

"This early on, with the scenes we've shot, he'd probably go with Liam because they wouldn't have any lag time on their production schedule." Sienna thought through the script as a whole. "Most of our scenes so far have been from the early part of the movie. If they had to, they would kill off my character and beef up the role of another character or change the ending story line altogether."

"Sounds to me like Liam is a suspect," Brent said.

"But you said the brake lines were cut on the car that almost hit me. I don't think that's something Liam would know how to do," Sienna said. "He's not exactly known for being into cars or anything, and he wouldn't have had access to the car before it was brought here today."

"Maybe not, but it doesn't mean he couldn't have paid someone to do it for him."

"This sounds so farfetched." Sienna leaned back in her chair and instantly straightened when a muscle spasmed in her neck. She reached up and started kneading it.

"You okay?" Craig asked.

"Just stiff."

"Here. Let me do that." Craig stood and pressed firmly on the spot she had been holding.

Pain and pleasure mixed, the first fading as the muscle loosened. Craig continued to massage her neck and shoulders, all the while analyzing her coworkers with George and Brent.

Sienna was starting to think she might slide bonelessly to the floor when Craig finally gave her shoulders a final squeeze. "How's that?"

"Much better. Thanks." She looked up at him, proving her statement to be true when she didn't wince with the movement.

"Are you up for going through this right now?"

"Yeah. Tell me what you want to know."

"Everything. You never know what might be important in figuring out who is behind this string of accidents."

* * *

He surfed one website, then another, each mention of the accidents plaguing Sienna Blake giving him a brief sense of satisfaction. The attention was like a drug. The moment he finished devouring an article, he craved more.

The latest accident had been beautifully scripted, if he did say so himself. The players hadn't been exactly who he had planned, but everything had worked out in the end. Most importantly, no one would ever think he was anything besides what he appeared to be.

He read one article, searching for familiar names, delighting when he found the ones he wanted to see. His mind churned with possibilities, the doors that would undoubtedly open with the new publicity.

If an almost accident could bring this much attention, he could only imagine what a real tragedy might do for him. His mind spinning, he let himself consider. His day was coming. Soon he would be able to achieve his destiny.

* * *

"What do you think?" Craig asked Brent as they walked down the beach toward his car.

"I think you have good reason to be worried," Brent said. "George said the car hadn't been driven for several days, so it could have been sabotaged anytime."

"I'm having a hard time wrapping my mind around a motive."

"That's what worries me the most. From what Charlie told me, when a stalker was after Kendra, it took some serious resources to figure out who it was."

"Great," Craig muttered.

"Hey, at least their suspect list is primarily limited to those who are authorized to be on the set. George will call in some help to work through those names. If we get lucky, this will all be over before she has to go back to work."

"Let's hope so." Craig replayed Brent's words in his mind, a little surge of jealousy surfacing. "What kind of help is George calling in?"

"Don't worry. I think you'll approve."

* * *

Sienna woke to a throbbing sensation in her shoulder and neck. She moaned, struggling to sit up so she could reach the Tylenol and the water glass on the night table.

"Sienna, honey? Are you okay?"

Sienna thought she must be dreaming. Why else would she hear her grandmother's voice?

Her bedroom door opened, and she saw light spill into the room from the hall. To her disbelief, her grandmother stood in the doorway.

"Grandma? What are you doing here?"

"We were visiting friends in Boston when we heard what happened. Your grandpa and I drove down to make sure you're okay," she said. "I assume you don't mind if we stay in your spare room."

"Of course I don't mind. I'm glad you're here." Sienna grunted as she sat up straighter.

"Here, let me get that for you." Hannah hurried into the room and turned on the bedside lamp. She handed Sienna the half-full glass, then uncapped the medicine bottle and handed Sienna two pills.

As soon as Sienna downed the pills, Hannah took the glass from her and sat on the edge of the bed. "You try to get some rest now. Your grandpa and I will be in the next room."

Gingerly Sienna settled back onto her pillow, grateful when her grandma pulled the covers up for her so she didn't have to reach for them herself.

When her grandma stood and started for the door, Sienna called after her. "Grandma?"

"Yes, dear?"

"Thanks for coming."

"You're welcome, sweetheart. Try to get some sleep."

Sienna closed her eyes and tried to think of something besides the pain—like what an incredibly good kisser Craig was. She smiled slightly at the thought, the memories of him carrying her up the stairs making her smile more fully. As she started to drift back to sleep, thoughts of Craig overshadowed the terror of the day, and she miraculously found peace.

25

CRAIG WALKED DOWN THE HALL toward Sienna's room and considered how much had changed in the past few weeks. Instead of enduring George's glaring looks like he had after their first encounter, Craig now had the man's cell phone number programmed into his phone. He reached Sienna's door and lifted his hand to knock. That was another unexpected development: George's willingness to let him come to Sienna's suite—supervised, of course.

Craig expected George to answer, but instead, Sienna's grandfather stood across the threshold when the door swung open.

"Mr. Blake. I didn't realize you were in town."

"Please, call me William. Mr. Blake makes me sound old."

"William it is, then." Craig followed him into the living area, where Sienna's grandmother was sitting on the couch. He greeted her and asked, "Where's Sienna?"

"She's in her room." Hannah stood. "I'll let her know you're here."

"Thanks." Craig watched her walk across the room toward one of the bedroom doors and became aware of William staring at him. He turned to face the older man.

"Craig, I have to say I'm disappointed in you."

"Sir?"

"I noticed my granddaughter still doesn't have a ring on her finger. You've been engaged for weeks now, and still no ring."

Craig tried to read the older man's serious tone, certain there must be some underlying humor there. Or maybe he was going senile and didn't remember the engagement was fictional.

"Sir, I thought you were aware that the engagement wasn't real," Craig said tentatively.

"That was then." William crossed his arms over his chest. "My son may have been relieved when he found out Sienna's engagement wasn't real, but I don't share his sentiment."

Craig knew Sienna's parents were going to be told the engagement was staged, but he hadn't heard anything since. He still wasn't sure where this conversation was going. "I'm not sure I understand."

William's stare didn't waver. "I heard the two of you have been seeing each other since Kendra's wedding."

Sienna walked in, moving more slowly than Craig expected. "Grandpa, leave him alone." She came farther into the room. "Craig, ignore him. He's obsessed with finding me a husband."

"I'm confused," Craig said.

"So is he." Sienna motioned to William. "He keeps forgetting arranged marriages went out of style a long time ago."

"Just trying to make sure my favorite granddaughter is taken care of."

"I've been taking care of myself for some time now, thanks. Besides, last time I saw you, you said Kendra was your favorite."

"The girl was days from her wedding. I had to dote on her a bit, didn't I?"

"If you say so." Sienna didn't take a seat on the couch. Rather, she chose a straight-back chair by the dining room table.

Craig's eyes narrowed suspiciously. "Have you seen a doctor yet? You're obviously still in pain."

"Actually, Grandpa insisted on having a doctor come in this morning." Sienna shifted back in the chair, taking care not to move too quickly. "He said the same thing you did."

Craig looked at her skeptically. "Are you really going to be able to work tomorrow?"

"They're rewriting the script to put me in a sling after the accident. That way it won't look odd when I'm stiff."

"I guess that's one way to deal with the problem, but I'd like it better if they would give you a few more days off."

Sienna looked at her grandfather. "He's starting to sound like you."

"I like this kid," William said. "Even if he is being too slow getting that ring on your finger."

Sienna rolled her eyes before turning to Craig. "Take it as a compliment. He doesn't try to marry me off to just anyone."

Craig leaned closer. "Does he do this a lot?"

"Not really," Sienna whispered back. "He usually just lectures me about dating people who aren't Mormon."

"You know," William stated, "my hearing is perfectly fine."

"Good to know," Craig said, feeling more comfortable now that he was starting to recognize William's dry sense of humor.

"I know you came to visit my granddaughter, but I assume you also want the latest on our possible suspects."

"Actually, yes."

"Have a seat, and I'll show you what we have."

* * *

Sienna listened to the discussion about who could be trying to hurt her. As her grandfather, George, and Craig spoke, she vacillated between feeling like she was in a read-through for another action film and feeling utter disbelief that someone would really go to such lengths to get to her.

"The police are looking at the surveillance video from the garage at the beach house where the Mustang was parked until the truck picked it up and brought it to the set. Unfortunately, they haven't found anything except a couple shadows," William said.

"Was there anything on the other surveillance cameras?" George asked.

William shook his head. "Nothing they could identify."

"I think the most likely suspects are Liam and the screenwriter, Devin Radford," Craig said. "No one seems to have anything personal against Sienna, so it comes down to who would have the most to gain."

"I have a hard time believing either of them could be involved," Sienna insisted. "Devin has written almost a dozen action films. I'm sure this isn't the first time he's undergone a major rewrite."

"If Devin isn't involved, then everything points back to Liam," George said.

"I also want to know what Bruce Parsons and Joseph Hurst have been up to lately," William added.

"I remember Bruce. He's the one who was at Kendra's concert, but who is Joseph Hurst?" Craig asked.

"Sienna's last boyfriend," George said, not giving Sienna the chance to answer.

Craig shifted his gaze to her, concern and something else Sienna couldn't define in his eyes. "Is there any reason to think this Joseph guy might resort to violence?"

"I seriously doubt it." Sienna shook her head. "He wasn't happy when we broke up, but it was more because he wanted the publicity he could generate from us being a couple than any real hurt about us going our separate ways."

"It's still not a bad idea to make sure he hasn't been around Virginia Beach lately," Craig said, apparently jumping on the overprotective bandwagon with George and her grandfather.

Overwhelmed, Sienna lifted a hand and ran her fingers through her hair. "Maybe I should quit this movie. If that's why someone keeps doing this stuff, if I'm not around anymore, all of this should stop, right?"

The room fell silent.

Craig was the first to speak. "Do you want to quit?"

"Of course not. I've never quit anything before in my life."

"Sweetheart, we'll find a way to keep you safe," William promised. "The truth is, everything we've said is still speculation.

We don't want to take a chance that whoever is behind this is someone like Kendra's stalker."

"What do you mean?" Craig asked.

"The man who obsessed over Sienna's sister set off a bomb at her concert to get her to leave the safety of her normal routine. That was how he managed to get to her."

"You think someone might be doing the same thing to Sienna?"

"I don't know, but knowing that Bruce was here in Virginia a few weeks ago makes me nervous. We also have to face the reality that many of Kendra's struggles were described in the press."

George straightened now, concerned. "You're worried about a copycat?"

"Not a copycat, per se, but it is possible someone might try to use the same ploy," William said.

Sienna pushed out of her chair and crossed to the window. Again, the room fell silent. A prayer ran through her mind, questions tumbling along with it. Should she stay with the movie? Should she go into hiding like her sister when she found herself in a similar situation? Answers eluded her, and she turned to face everyone again. "What do you suggest I do?"

Her grandpa rubbed his thumb along his jaw the way he always did when contemplating a serious decision. "I feel like we have more control over your safety here. With the extra help we're bringing in, we also have a better chance of figuring out who is behind the trouble."

"Okay. I'll stick with this, but I do have a favor to ask."

"What's that?"

"I really could use a blessing." She shifted her gaze to Craig. "Would you be willing to give me one?"

A brief flash of surprise crossed his face. Then his whole demeanor seemed to melt into acceptance, and a sense of peace settled over the room. "I'd be honored."

Her grandfather pulled a chair out, and Sienna took a seat. William and Craig laid their hands on her head, and Craig offered her a blessing of comfort and peace.

The peace he spoke of rested gently on her shoulders after he concluded the blessing. She stood and gave her grandfather a hug. When she turned to Craig, she did the same, finding comfort when he drew her close.

She couldn't say why tears welled up in her eyes, but she held on to Craig, blinking rapidly and trying to get her emotions under control.

Craig ran a hand down the length of her hair. "It'll be okay. We'll be here for you."

She closed her eyes and tried to find the strength to believe his words. After several minutes, she stepped back and noticed her grandfather quietly watching them. She wasn't sure what to think of what she could only describe as acceptance in his expression.

26

CRAIG WAS NEARLY TO THE barracks when his phone rang. He looked down at it, at first disappointed not to see Sienna's name on the screen. Then curiosity took over with the 480 area code.

"Hello?"

"Craig, this is William Blake."

"William, what can I do for you?" He walked the last few steps to his building and pulled open the door.

"Just thought you would appreciate an update," William said matter-of-factly. "I had a friend of mine do some research on the suspect list we came up with yesterday."

Craig halted his step. "Did they find anything?"

"It's what we didn't find that has me concerned."

Craig's own concern heightened. "What do you mean?"

"Bruce Parsons hasn't been seen or heard from since Kendra's concert."

"Any credit card or cell phone activity?" Craig resumed his forward progress toward his room. "I assume you FBI types can look up that sort of thing."

"Actually, I had my FBI guys do exactly that. Bruce's phone is turned off, his car is still parked at his house in California, and the only credit card activity since the concert was an automatic payment to his electric company." William paused before adding, "We also found that Bruce's credit card balances have been climbing steadily since he lost his job working for my son."

"Could something have happened to him?"

"Something has definitely happened to him. The question is whether something is wrong or if his lack of electronic signature is deliberate," William said. "He isn't the type of guy who would easily be taken by surprise."

"He acted like he was giving a warning when he was at Kendra's concert," Craig said, considering.

"Exactly. It makes me wonder if he's involved."

"Do you seriously think he might be the one behind all this?"

"It was his son who went after Kendra. For all we know, this could be some sort of revenge. Maybe when he realized he couldn't get to Kendra, he decided to go after Sienna."

"That's sick."

"It is."

Craig unlocked his door and walked into his room. He waited until he was inside with the door closed before he asked, "Did you find anything on any of the other names we talked about?"

"A little bit. Sienna's instincts on the screenwriter appear to be accurate. Not only has he written several movies, he is known for his ability to do quick rewrites and adapt easily. He's not one of these prima donnas who can be so difficult."

"What about the old boyfriend?"

"If you believe the latest press, he's in Hawaii with his new girlfriend," William told him.

"If he has a new girlfriend, I find it unlikely he would bother Sienna."

"I agree."

"That narrows your list to Liam Rickman and Bruce Parsons," Craig surmised.

"Exactly. I'll let you know if I hear anything else, but at least now we know where we need to focus our search."

"I appreciate the call."

"And, Craig?"

"Yes?"

"You make sure you keep my granddaughter happy."

The corners of his lips curved. "I'll do what I can, sir."

* * *

He looked at the rewrites, his jaw clenching with each line he scanned. This wasn't supposed to happen. How could the director not see the obvious solution to how this story should go? It was right there in front of him, but Marcus seemed determined to look past him, as though he was invisible.

His hand tightened on the page, the paper crumpling. This was his movie, his chance for his name to rise to the top in the industry. This was his comeback.

He thought of the other actors he had worked with over the past few years, people everything came so easily for. They didn't appreciate what they had. He might have been like that once, but he knew better now. Now he was ready to take his place at the top, ready to appreciate everything Hollywood could offer.

And if Hollywood wouldn't offer it to him, he was determined to take it by force if necessary. He would be famous. Someday soon, everyone would know his name.

He stood, and his script fell to the floor. It was time for action.

* * *

Sienna donned her sunglasses and pulled the hood of her sweatshirt up. She followed George to a side door of her hotel. Experience told her the paparazzi would be everywhere, but George helped her time her exit to when the rest of the cast would be wrapping up for the day and the photographers would be clustered near the main entrance.

George pushed open the door, and she braced for the cold, surprised to find the weather had warmed significantly since the day before.

She walked toward the beach, only going a few yards before she saw Craig waiting for her near the edge of the sand. She was surprised and disappointed when she reached him and his greeting didn't include a hug or kiss.

He must have seen the concern on her face. "We have company. I didn't think either of us would want to be in the news." Craig's words didn't match his casual demeanor. "There's a photographer at your ten o'clock."

Sienna turned away from the direction he had indicated so only the back of her head would be visible to the camera lens. "You know I'm really not used to this."

"What's that?" Craig asked, starting to walk toward the beach.

She fell into step with him. "It seems like every other guy I've dated has liked the press attention that comes with my name."

"It sounds like you haven't had the best track record with guys."

Sienna laughed, much of her tension disappearing. "You're absolutely right. My grandfather has been lecturing me for years about my poor choices."

"Oh, really? Anyone I should know about?" he asked. "Anyone serious?"

"Not since Jimmy Mickelson in the seventh grade."

"Jimmy Mickelson, huh? Should I be jealous?"

"He did look quite handsome in his football uniform."

"A football player? I was more into baseball myself."

"We may have to catch a game sometime. Kendra's brother-in-law plays for the Marlins."

"That would be fun. We'll have to check the schedule and see if there are any games in DC before you leave Virginia." The words left Craig's mouth, and he immediately stopped walking, waiting for her to look up at him. "How long are you in Virginia?"

"The current shoot schedule has us here for a few more months, until the end of May."

"Then what? Do you have another movie already lined up?"

"My agent said he's had a couple directors express interest in having me read for some upcoming movies, but I haven't had time to look over the scripts."

"That must be hard, always going from one movie set to the next. Do you ever get to take a break?"

"I like to take a couple months between projects, but sometimes it depends on the timing of what comes my way."

"Selfishly, I hope the timing works out well after this one. It would be nice to spend some time together when you aren't working so much."

Sienna smiled up at him. "I think I might be persuaded."

"That's what I wanted to hear."

* * *

Craig sent a quick response to Sienna's latest text before following Quinn and Damian toward the helicopter pad.

"I gather you and Sienna made up," Quinn commented.

"What?"

"For the past two days, every time I look at you, you've got your cell phone in your hand."

"That's not true. I wasn't holding it when we were at the shooting range or when we did the obstacle course—"

"But you did have it when we had breakfast," Damian cut him off before he could come up with any other times his phone had been out of his hand. "And when we did our five-mile run this morning and lunch and . . ."

"Okay, fine. So I'm worried about her. She's supposed to go back to work this afternoon, and we still don't have any idea who was behind the accidents that keep happening."

"You know, I've always wanted to check out a movie set up close," Quinn said.

"Me too," Damian agreed.

"Did I hear someone say we're going to the movies?" Tristan walked up behind them.

"In a manner of speaking." Quinn nodded. "We thought we could go check out Craig's girlfriend's place of business. You know, just to make sure everything is safe for her there."

"Cool. I wouldn't mind a field trip."

"Load up," Brent told them, bringing up the rear of the group. "For now, you have another movie role."

"What are you talking about?" Craig asked.

"The navy authorized Sienna's movie crew to film our training exercise today. Looks like you all get to pretend to be movie stars."

Quinn looked at Brent skeptically. "Is the navy really going to let them film us?"

"The navy agreed months ago, but the higher-ups waited to assign a squad until they knew who would be available."

"I wouldn't think they would want to take the chance of us being identified," Damian said.

"It's all from long range. They won't be able to see our faces, but while we're doing our preliminary overflight of their set, I thought we could take a look at what they're all up to."

"Break out the binoculars, boys," Quinn said. "It's time to do some spying."

27

"Are you ready for this?" George asked when they pulled up in front of the beach house.

Sienna drew a deep breath and let it out in a *whoosh*. "I think so."

She had hoped to talk to Craig before going back on set, but his last text had told her he was heading out to work and wouldn't be able to call or text for a couple hours.

George motioned to the sling on her arm, a reminder to keep her from overdoing it with her sore shoulder. "Are you sure you're okay doing these scenes while you're still so sore?"

"The screenwriter was kind enough to redo the script to allow for the injury. The least I can do is play along."

"I don't know that Devin has ever had this many rewrites," George said wryly. "First adding a car crash he hadn't planned and now giving a main character a new injury. He's earning his money."

"Definitely." Sienna waited for George to circle the car and help her out. They walked in together, and immediately she noticed her grandfather talking to the director. "Looks like Grandpa is already hard at work."

"Can't blame him for worrying." George walked her to her chair before motioning to William. "I'm going to check in with him. I'll be right back."

"Okay." Sienna took another deep breath. What did it say, she wondered, when George felt the need to explain where he was going to be when he was only walking five yards away?

She saw Liam approaching, and it took all of her willpower not to turn and walk the other direction. All this talk about him being involved with the accidents had her second-guessing herself.

She studied him objectively. She knew this was only his second significant role in the past several years. Like many other famous child actors, he had struggled to transition into adult roles, but this film would most certainly help change that image. He had already started on his transformation, his sandy-colored hair now short and styled rather than all straggly, as it had been when he'd hit his late teenage years. Like Adam, he also spent a decent amount of time in the gym. Since he recently signed with a new agent, he clearly wasn't happy with his lack of professional opportunities over the past few years.

Could his need for validation as an adult actor cause him to resort to extreme measures? She didn't think so, but she still had to remind herself to relax when he approached.

"Sienna, so good to see you back on set," Liam said. "We've all been worried about you. How are you feeling?"

"A little stiff, but better than I was. Thanks for asking." Sienna glanced at the cameramen nearby setting up for the first scene of the day. "How has everything been here?"

"A little different without you around, but other than that, it's the same old stuff. We did several scenes with the extras yesterday, and, of course, there's a lot more security."

"That makes sense after having two accidents." She noticed the cameramen had their equipment facing the beach. "What scene are they shooting first? I thought we were doing the interrogation scene this morning."

"Apparently someone convinced the navy to give us some live footage for the movie. They're getting ready to film one of their training exercises," Liam told her. "They'll do the close-ups of us right afterward so the lighting is the same."

"Sounds like we'd better get to makeup."

Sienna heard the helicopter overhead, her attention immediately diverted. She looked up and decided she could wait and watch. After all, it wouldn't hurt to see what her character was supposedly doing before she had to stand in front of the camera and try to pretend it was her.

* * *

Craig sat on the floor of the helicopter, his legs hanging into the open space above the landing skid. Through his binoculars, he could see the beach house as well as the cameras already pointed their way. Brent had given the pilot orders to make two wide circles around the property before heading back over the water, where they would make today's jump.

"Looks like we're about to become famous," Quinn said, motioning to the cameras.

"The best you can hope for is notorious," Tristan quipped back.

"Anyone see anything suspicious?" Brent asked.

Seth was the first to respond. "Nothing on the perimeter of the house."

Craig focused on the people gathered below. It didn't take him long to identify Sienna's dark hair, her head tilted upward to watch them. His hands tightened on the binoculars when he saw who was standing beside her. "I see Sienna. Liam Rickman is standing right next to her."

"Jealous?" Damian asked.

"Worried," Craig corrected. "He's one of the people on her grandfather's suspect list."

Jay pointed below as they completed their first circle. "Take a look at the beach north of the house. I see some tracks."

"Could be from a jogger," Tristan suggested.

Craig focused on the beach where Jay had indicated. He was still trying to process what he was seeing when Brent spoke. "I don't think so. They don't continue past the house." Brent addressed the pilot. "This time swing wider to the north."

"Yes, sir," the pilot answered. He did as requested, giving the squad the chance to see where the tracks started.

Brent pointed again. "Looks like they start on that side street over there."

Craig studied the area. Several beach houses lined the street, and a long pier sat a short distance away, along with what appeared to be a public parking lot. "Anyone could have parked in that lot over there and made their way up to the house."

"Not exactly the best place for security," Tristan agreed.

"Sounds like William is going to have his work cut out for him," Brent said. He signaled to everyone. "Get ready. Time to go to work."

Craig put his binoculars in his pack, checked the straps, and prepared to jump out of a helicopter moving at twenty knots per hour.

* * *

Sienna's eyes widened with disbelief when she saw the first person jump out of the helicopter. "Are they really jumping without parachutes?"

"That's what it looks like," Liam said in awe. "Boy, am I glad we don't have to do that for real. Who would do such a thing?"

"Navy SEALs," William announced from behind them.

Sienna turned to look at her grandfather, her eyes questioning. "That isn't . . ."

William nodded, and Sienna's head whipped around again as she watched with renewed interest. When Craig had said he wouldn't be able to talk for a couple of hours, she figured he had a meeting or something. Was this really what he did during the day?

She counted the number of bodies that jumped into the water below. Seven. She thought of the men who had been at her sister's wedding. Brent, Craig, Damian, Seth, Jay, Tristan, and Quinn. Seven men. "Wow."

"It's something to see, isn't it?" William said, putting his hand on her good shoulder.

Liam looked from William to Sienna. "Do you know those guys?"

"I met them briefly when I was preparing for this role," Sienna said, downplaying her friendship with the squad. "They're great guys."

"Looks to me like they're on the crazy side."

"Oh, they are," William answered. "But they're the kind of crazy you want to have on your side."

28

"I NEED A COUPLE VOLUNTEERS tonight," Brent said when he walked into the hangar bay where the squad was checking their chutes in preparation for the next exercise.

Before Craig could process the request and the possible conflict volunteering would create with his planned date with Sienna, Quinn spoke up. "I'm in. What am I volunteering for?"

Tristan stood beside him and shook his head. "How is it you're always the first to volunteer *and* the first to complain about whatever you volunteered for?"

Quinn grinned at him. "That's one of the many complexities of the universe. Besides, complaining is an art form I'm trying to master."

"Right, Quinn." Tristan shook his head. "I'm happy to help too. What do you need?"

"William asked if we would be willing to do security sweeps of Sienna Blake's movie set for a few nights," Brent said. "He wants to make sure no one else can cause Sienna or the movie any more trouble."

Brent passed the papers he held to everyone. "Here's an updated training schedule. Amy was able to adjust our plans for this week so we could use a couple security sweeps for training, but there are a few gaps I'd like to have volunteers fill in, starting with tonight."

"I'm game too," Damian said, followed by similar comments by the rest of the squad.

"I'll take tomorrow night," Craig offered, aware that Sienna would be working late.

"Do you have a particular time you want us to do these sweeps?" Quinn asked.

"The set security team will do their last sweep at twenty-two hundred. We'll take over then," Brent said. "I'd like to send an extra sweep in around oh two hundred. As part of our training the next night, we'll give our new guys some practice reading heat signatures while we set up motion detectors."

"Will we have to retrieve the motion sensors before morning?" Seth asked.

"No. It's a private beach." Brent gave him a wicked grin. "In fact, I thought we could have a little game of laser tag one night after we make sure the area is clear."

"I'm always up for some target practice." Quinn grinned back.

"Of that I have no doubt."

* * *

Sienna looked skeptically at the car parked a short distance away. The basic black sedan looked harmless enough, but she couldn't stop thinking about the last time she had tried a stunt with a car in it. Why did this one have to happen on her first day back?

"Are you okay?" George asked.

"Honestly, I'm not sure about this."

Marcus put a hand on her shoulder. "We've taken every precaution. The car was checked out completely before they brought it out. We even had the stunt guys take it for a test drive this morning to make sure there weren't any problems."

"Okay." Sienna took a deep breath. "I'm supposed to look terrified anyway, right?"

"Actually, yeah." Marcus nodded. "You'll see the car coming toward you, and you'll dive to the left."

"Let's get this over with." Sienna forced herself to stand and walk across the pavement to her mark. This would be her last scene for the day, and then she would be able to spend some time with Craig. That thought put a smile on her face despite her pounding heart.

"Sienna, terrified, remember?" Marcus called out to her. "Not happy."

"Right." Sienna tried to push her personal life aside and turned to look at the car again. She closed her eyes, letting herself remember the terror of the car heading straight for her before. Her breathing quickened, and she opened her eyes to focus on the perceived threat.

"Better," Marcus said. "And action!"

As Marcus had promised, this time when the car came racing toward her, everything followed as outlined in the script. They shot the scene from several angles until finally Marcus gave them the words they all wanted to hear. "Okay, that's it for tonight."

Adam approached when Sienna started toward wardrobe. "Hey, Sienna. Do you want to grab some dinner?"

"No, thanks, Adam. I already have plans."

His eyebrows drew together. "Same guy?"

"Yes, with the same guy." Sienna breezed past him and called over her shoulder. "See you tomorrow."

"Yeah. See you then."

* * *

Craig waited by the entrance to the restaurant Sienna had chosen for dessert. Her shoot schedule had taken her work day well past the dinner hour, but neither of them had wanted to miss the opportunity to spend time together.

A text message from George alerted Craig to their arrival, and he approached the hostess to ask for a table for two. She picked up their menus, the door opened, and Sienna entered.

Her hair was tied back in a ponytail, and he could see her fatigue in how she carried herself. "Hey, there."

"Perfect timing. She was just about to seat us." He motioned for Sienna to follow their hostess, who led the way to the booth Craig had requested in the back of the restaurant without any sign of recognition.

"How was your day?" Craig asked as soon as they were both seated.

Her eyebrows arched up. "Enlightening."

"How so?"

"You never said you were going to jump out of a helicopter today."

Craig stared at her with disbelief and a sense of uneasiness. "How did you know that was me?"

"Grandpa told me." She seemed to sense his concern and added, "Don't worry. He didn't tell anyone else."

"It's not that big a deal, but we don't usually go around announcing who we are to people. Sometimes we have security issues we have to deal with."

"Do you do this sort of thing often?"

"We're always training for something." His shoulders lifted. "Physical training and target practice are usually part of our daily routine. Other skills we rotate through pretty regularly."

"Like jumping out of helicopters."

"Helicopters, planes, boats. If it moves, we probably jump out of it."

She leaned forward and lowered her voice. "Let's not add cars to that list, okay?"

"Okay," Craig agreed amiably. "Tell me about your day. I gather everything went all right."

"Yeah. It was hard working with Liam, though, after everything Grandpa was talking about. And I felt like I was looking over my shoulder to see if Bruce might be anywhere around."

"It's normal to feel paranoid, especially after what happened." Craig thought of his earlier conversation with his squad and decided it couldn't hurt to give her an extra sense of security. "Your grandfather is pulling in a lot of favors to make sure your set is secure. I don't think you'll have any more problems."

"I hope not. I almost didn't survive the first two."

"Then you don't have a choice but to stay safe."

She ran a finger along the edge of the menu she had yet to look at. "You make it sound so easy."

"The simplest things in life usually are. They only get complicated when people think about them too much."

"Now you sound like a philosopher."

"Nah. Just someone who has listened to that lecture dozens of times from my mother."

Sienna smiled, and some of her weariness seemed to fade. "Sounds like a smart woman."

"She is." Craig imagined for a moment what it would be like to see his mother and Sienna in the same room, and his lips twitched at the thought. "She'd like you."

"You think so?"

He smiled fully. "Yeah."

"Does this mean you want me to meet her?"

"I don't know when we would find the time with our crazy schedules, but yeah, I'd like that."

"I'd like that too." Sienna hesitated and then added, "She's not anything like my dad, is she?"

"Not at all."

She let out a sigh. "Good. I haven't been trained to withstand interrogations like you have."

"Believe me, I've never had better practice than I did when I met your dad."

"Oh, I believe you."

* * *

Bruce stared at the man across from him with disbelief. What had begun as a publicity stunt and a ploy for him to gain employment had taken a complete left turn and was going in a direction he didn't want anything to do with. "You realize I can't let you go through with this."

"What are you going to do? Stop me?"

"Yes." Bruce squared off against the other man. "I may not be working for the Blake family now, but they'll listen if I tell them what you've been up to."

"You aren't going to tell the Blakes or anyone else. If you do, I'll tell everyone you're the one who tried to recruit me to help you sabotage Sienna's movie."

"I did no such thing!"

"My word against yours. In fact, I'll likely come out as the hero when I explain how I found out you were the one planning everything."

"And I'll make sure the authorities know you're just trying to cast suspicion elsewhere."

"You forget I've been acting my whole life. I can make people believe anything." He looked Bruce dead in the eye. "And I'm not the one who has a criminal for a son." He took a step closer, the greed in his eyes now more evident than ever. "Don't think for a minute you can stop me."

"You're insane."

"I've played that character before, but I'm perfectly sane. I know what I want, and I'm going to get it."

29

CRAIG ACTIVATED THE SCREEN IN front of him, identifying two of his teammates moving along the beach from the south and three others converging from the north.

"You see them?" Damian asked from his position behind him. They had been given the boring task of standing watch on the street side of the house while monitoring for heat signatures.

"Yeah."

Brent's voice came over their communication headsets. "What do you see?"

"Two from the south; three from the north." Craig estimated their speed and added, "You should intercept in three minutes."

"Tristan and Quinn, fan out. Place your motion detectors along the base of the deck," Brent instructed. "Jay and Seth, you take care of the front yard and parking lot."

"What about us?" Damian asked.

"Keep track of everyone's movement. It's good practice."

Craig looked back at his screen, counting out his team members. Now that Brent had given orders to everyone, he could identify Seth and Jay moving up the hill along the side of the house.

When he looked back to the beach side, he saw two clustered together beneath the deck, another heading toward them, and one more on the side of the house opposite where Jay and Seth were climbing up the slope.

"Brent, where are you?"

"You should see me heading toward you."

"We may have a problem. I'm showing six heat signatures, not five. Repeat, we have a visitor."

"Where?"

"He's heading toward Tristan and Quinn."

"Tristan and Quinn, go silent and disappear. Let's see what this guy wants."

Craig heard both of them click into their microphones to confirm they received his orders.

"Craig, call out their distance."

"Fifty yards," Craig began, calling out the mystery figure's progress at ten-yard increments. "He's angling toward the northeast side of the deck. Ten yards . . . five yards."

Craig fell silent, waiting impatiently. Could this be Bruce or Liam? Was there someone else involved whom they hadn't managed to identify? Or was this some random fan who had the bad sense to try to sneak onto a movie set?

Quinn's voice was the first to break the silence. "Hold it right there."

Craig could see the newcomer freeze momentarily. A split second later, he took off the way he had come.

Both Quinn and Tristan pursued him, catching up to him within thirty yards. One of them dove after the man, forcing them both onto the ground.

"I'm heading down there," Craig announced to Damian.

Craig half expected Damian to insist he remain on surveillance with him, but he nodded in agreement. "Go ahead. I'll keep an eye on things here and make sure we don't have any other unexpected visitors."

"Thanks."

Craig took off at a jog down the sloping side yard and onto the beach where Tristan, Quinn, and now Brent were leaning over a prone figure. Quinn had his hand on the man's head, and Craig could see a flash of white in the moonlight. He took several more steps before he identified the white as a bandage.

"What happened?" Craig asked when he reached them.

"Our friend here hit his head on a rock when I tackled him," Tristan said.

"Is he okay?"

"He's unconscious, but his breathing is steady."

Brent motioned to Quinn. "Call for an ambulance."

Quinn did so while Craig moved closer and shined his flashlight on the man. "That's Bruce Parsons."

"He's the one from the concert, isn't he?" Tristan asked.

"He is," Craig confirmed. "He's also one of William's top suspects. According to William, Bruce dropped out of sight right after Kendra's concert."

"Looks like we may have found the source of Sienna's troubles."

"I'll feel better after we get the chance to talk to him," Craig said. "I can't tell you how happy I'll be when we're sure this is all over."

Brent exchanged glances with Tristan and Quinn. "Oh, we have an idea."

* * *

Sienna woke to the sound of her grandfather's voice in the living room of her hotel suite. She started to roll over, assuming he was talking on the phone. Then she heard Craig's voice as well.

She climbed out of bed and debated whether she should get dressed before investigating. She looked down at her T-shirt and Hello Kitty pajama pants and pulled on a sweatshirt, deciding that was all she had the energy for.

She was two steps out of her room before she thought to run her fingers through her hair. "What's going on?"

"Sorry. Did we wake you?" Craig asked.

Sienna decided he deserved serious points for not commenting on her choice of sleeping attire. She answered his question with one of her own. "What time is it?"

"Almost six o'clock," her grandfather answered. "Craig came by with some news."

"What kind of news?"

"Mostly good." William motioned to Craig. "You tell her."

Craig took a step closer. "We did surveillance at the beach house tonight."

"And?"

"Bruce Parsons was there. We have him in custody."

"Bruce? It was Bruce who caused the accidents?" Sienna thought of her father's longtime head of security and tried to wrap her mind around the possibility of his involvement.

"We think so," William offered tentatively.

"Did he say why?"

"That's the bad news," Craig told her. "He's unconscious. He hit his head when he tried to run away, and the injury was worse than we originally thought. He came to a couple times, but he hasn't been coherent enough for the police to question him."

"Is he going to be okay?"

"The doctors seem to think so. The hospital will let us know when he's well enough to answer questions," Craig told her.

"Like why he would try to hurt me?" Sienna asked.

"Exactly."

Her grandfather took a step toward his bedroom door. "I'm going to get dressed and go down to the hospital myself. Not that I don't trust the local cops, but I'd rather be the one to question him."

Sienna watched him go, replaying the conversation in her mind. Finally she managed to ask Craig, "Is this really over?"

"I think so."

The tears that sprang to her eyes were born of relief. She tried to rein them in, but when Craig pulled her into his arms, she let her emotions take over.

He didn't offer any words of comfort or assurance. He simply held her, one hand rubbing lightly up and down her back.

The quiet acceptance undid her. How had he known that was what she needed? His unconditional support said so much more than he realized and reinforced what she had already come to understand. Craig knew the real her. More surprising was her realization that he was the first man besides her father and grandfather she had allowed to get this close.

She reached up and swiped at the tears on her cheek before looking up at him. Her voice raspy, she managed to say, "I'm sorry. I hardly ever cry."

"Everyone needs a good cry now and then."

Sienna tried to imagine what it would be like to go to work today without worrying about another near-death experience. "I know it sounds silly, but is there any way you could come with me to the set today? I think I still need some time to feel safe."

"I have to check in with my squad at oh seven hundred, but Brent said after our morning briefing he was giving us the rest of the day off."

"It sounds like you already worked all night."

"Most of it," Craig admitted.

"I'll understand if you need to go home and get some sleep," Sienna said, though she didn't mean what she was saying.

He leaned down and kissed her, drawing her closer as he did so. "I'll be there."

30

WILLIAM BLAKE SAT IN THE hospital room staring at the man who held the answers he so desperately needed. Why had he been on the beach last night, and what was his motivation behind going after Sienna?

The idea that he was out for revenge against the family was possible, but something wasn't sitting right, and William couldn't put his finger on what it was.

One thing he had learned after more than thirty years with the FBI was to keep digging until that feeling in his gut either panned out or went away. Three hours sitting in a hospital room hadn't helped it go away.

His cell phone rang, and he answered it to find Charlie Whitmore on the other end. "William, I e-mailed you the link and access code so you can see those surveillance videos you wanted."

"Thanks, Charlie."

"You're welcome, but I don't know what you expect to find. The police went over it several times. They said they saw some shadows near the Mustang around midnight two nights before the accident."

"I'll start there," William said. "Thanks for your help."

"Not a problem. How's Sienna doing?"

"She's still rattled, but she's feeling a lot better now that we have a suspect in custody."

"I'll feel a lot better when we know why he was there in the first place," Charlie said. "It's hard to believe two people in the same family could fall from a status of trust so quickly."

"That it is," William agreed, already pulling Charlie's e-mail up on his tablet and accessing the link. "I'll let you know when I have any updates."

"I appreciate it."

After ending the call and pocketing his phone, William focused his attention on the screen in front of him, expanding the images so he could focus on different areas around the car.

The garage area was dimly lit, and the video feed wasn't the best quality. He fast-forwarded to the time Charlie had mentioned, waiting impatiently for something to flash before him, anything that would help him prove Bruce had really been the culprit behind this personal reign of terror.

He glanced over at Bruce where he lay in a stark, white hospital bed. The bandage on his head covered his six stitches, but William could see where part of his hair had been shaved away to make it easier for the medical personnel to treat him.

He turned his attention back to the screen, the minutes ticking by as he studied the same image, feeling like the moment could be standing still in time.

A brief shadow cut across the screen. William refocused the picture to discover the shadow was the garage door opening.

His eyes narrowed when no other shadows appeared. Logically he should have seen some interruption in the light when the saboteur entered the building. Unless . . .

William scrolled lower, focusing not on the car but on the base of the doorway. It was barely visible from behind the Mustang, but after several minutes of manipulating the image, William found the spot he was looking for.

The surveillance tape had a nearly undetectable interruption in the video feed.

William's phone rang, and he looked down to see his son's name on his screen. "Sterling, I was about to call you."

"I just heard. Is it true that Bruce has been stalking my little girl?"

"It looks that way, but I wanted to ask you, what kind of electronics skills does Bruce have?"

"He's a whiz at security systems, surveillance, all that kind of stuff. That's one of the reasons I hired him in the first place. Why?"

"The classic Mustang that nearly ran over Sienna was parked in a locked garage for several days before it was loaded up and brought to the movie location," William told him. "Except for one glimpse of a shadow from a door opening, the video surveillance doesn't show any sign of anyone entering the garage. That makes me think our culprit must have tapped into the video feed and created a loop while he was inside tampering with the car."

"Maybe the shadow you saw was when he opened the door to access the security system."

A chill ran through him. "Let me get back to you."

William hung up the phone and called Charlie. "Charlie, do you have access to the full police report on the car incident?"

"Yeah, I have it right here," Charlie said. "What do you need?"

"Where was the security access panel located?"

"In the main house. There's a security room near the kitchen. Why?"

"Because I think Bruce created a loop in the video feed." William took a deep breath before he added, "The shadow we saw could very well be from his accomplice."

"Accomplice?"

"My son said Bruce is skilled with electronics and security systems. If that's the case, he had the skills needed to make sure we never knew he was there."

"But there was that brief shadow," Charlie said.

"Which makes me think he had someone else working with him."

"The question is who."

Beside him, Bruce shifted slightly. "Pray our friend here wakes up soon so he can answer that question for us."

"Definitely sending prayers your way."

* * *

Craig headed down the hall toward Brent's office, his mind crowded with thoughts. At the center of them all was Sienna. The memory of holding her that morning, of the simplicity of that moment, haunted him. It wasn't the way she had cried on his shoulder and let him see her sensitive side again. Or perhaps that was part of it. More than anything, though, it was the warmth he'd found as they'd stood together.

His heart squeezed in his chest, a tightness that was nearly unbearable when he remembered Sienna would leave when this movie was over. Even if they did try to keep a long-distance relationship going, how long could he expect it to last? He had seen for himself through the many headlines with her name in them that she rarely lasted with anyone for more than a few months. Why should he be any different?

Could he be different? That thought was still forming in his mind when he walked inside to find Brent, Tristan, and Quinn already sitting in the office.

"How is Sienna doing?" Tristan asked.

"A little emotional, but overall I guess she's okay." Craig took the seat beside Tristan and then looked at him quizzically. "How did you know I saw Sienna this morning?"

"Duh." Tristan rolled his eyes. "You said you would let William know what had happened, and you don't look like an idiot to me."

"Thanks, I think, but that doesn't answer my question. I could have called William."

"An idiot would make a phone call," Tristan clarified. "A man with any brains doesn't miss out on a chance to see the woman he's head over heels in love with."

Craig jerked back in his seat, Tristan's words striking him. "I never said I was in love with her."

Quinn gave him a pitying look before speaking to Tristan. "Maybe he is an idiot."

The thoughts that had crowded Craig's mind all morning scrambled and somehow refocused on Tristan's and Quinn's assumptions. Could he have fallen in love with Sienna so quickly? They had known each other for only six weeks, and for part of that, he had been on assignment.

"Good morning." Seth walked in, followed by Jay and Damian. He took a look around and focused on Craig. "What's with you, Craig? You look like you got hit by a truck."

"Don't mind him. He's just coming to grips with reality," Quinn said.

"What reality?" Damian asked.

"That he's in love with Sienna."

"Oh, that." Damian dropped into the chair beside Craig. "Terrifying, huh?"

Craig shook his head in denial. "I've only known her a few weeks."

Damian's voice held entirely too much understanding when he spoke. "Like I said. Terrifying."

Craig let out a shuddering breath. "Yeah."

31

His eyelids felt like they had lead weights in them. He tried to struggle against the heaviness, at first not sure why he felt the need. Then his clarity of thought returned in a swift bolt.

A moan escaped him, his hands gripping at the bed as he tried to push himself into full consciousness.

"Bruce? Can you hear me?"

He heard the man's voice. He recognized the urgency and felt the same urgency himself.

Mustering all of his willpower, he forced his eyes open and managed to focus on the man beside his bed, a man who could be trusted as Bruce had once been. "Have . . ." Bruce began, struggling to get the single word out. He took a breath and tried again. "Stop . . . him."

"Who?" William asked. "Bruce, who were you working with?"

The name wouldn't come. He could see it floating just out of reach, the word begging to get out but still not willing to be said. He tried another tactic. "Deck. Broken."

"What deck?"

He tried again to speak, but his energy failed him, and he felt himself sinking back into the darkness.

* * *

Sienna looked up into Adam's eyes, adoration on her face as he pulled her into his arms. She imagined it was Craig holding her, and she let those warm feelings flow through her for the camera to see, as well as the millions of people who would view this scene in the theaters and their homes. She tried not to think about how grateful she was that this particular scene didn't include a kiss, instead keeping her expression in place until Marcus yelled cut.

Adam released her and stepped back. "That boyfriend of yours must be something."

Sienna's eyebrows drew together. "What do you mean?"

"You almost had me convinced you were in love with me. Only way someone can be that good is if they're feeling the emotion for real."

Sienna stared, speechless. People couldn't fall in love this quickly, could they?

Adam rolled his shoulders. "I'm going to go find the masseuse. My back is killing me."

Sienna managed to regain her composure and looked at her watch. "I don't think you have time. As soon as they get the cameras set, we're supposed to shoot the scene on the deck."

"I thought they were doing the stunt doubles first."

"Nope. Marcus wants us first so he knows where to position the stunt doubles."

Adam let out an exasperated sigh. "It's times like these I wish I'd let Carter get his way."

"What are you talking about?"

"In the original script, Carter had my role, I had yours, and Liam's character had twice as many scenes. After they decided to add the romantic element, it all got switched around."

"I thought it was Liam who originally had the other lead role."

"Maybe before they signed me." Adam pointed at the deck, which was three stories from the beach below. "Personally, I'd love for Carter to be the one who has to hang suspended in air for the next hour."

"Don't worry." Sienna smiled sweetly. "I promise to rescue you."

"Thanks."

Sienna laughed. "I'm sure the masseuse will be happy to give you that massage as soon as we break for lunch. You will have earned it by then."

"You're darn right."

* * *

Craig watched Sienna laughing with Adam. He didn't know which was worse, the easy way they seemed to be getting along now or seeing her in his arms a moment ago. He fought back the surge of jealousy. This was her job, he reminded himself. She was supposed to portray whatever feelings the director demanded. He just wished she hadn't been quite so convincing in that last scene.

He crossed the lawn in front of the beach house and walked to where the cameras were currently being adjusted to point toward the deck and the ocean beyond. His insecurities scattered when Sienna noticed him and lifted a hand in greeting. She headed toward him, leaving Adam behind.

"Hey, there. I'm glad you made it."

To Craig's surprise, she reached up and gave him a quick kiss. He looked around, noticing how many people were milling around. "Why are so many people here?"

"They're setting up for one of the big action scenes. It takes a lot of people to pull them off, and they put an extra camera or two on so they don't have to shoot it so many times."

Craig looked over at Adam and noticed the director watching them. Marcus raised a hand and motioned for Sienna and Adam to join him. "It looks like your director wants you."

"What else is new?" Sienna took a step back the way she had come. "Come on. You can hang out over here."

"How long will it be before they're ready to start again?"

"A few minutes. I have to go make a quick wardrobe change, but I'll be right back."

"I'll be here."

* * *

William picked up the phone to call Craig and pass along what little information Bruce had shared. He wasn't sure what Bruce had meant by the deck being broken, but he had to imagine it had something to do with the movie set. He pulled up Craig's contact information and was about to initiate the call when he noticed Bruce stirring again.

He lowered his phone and sat beside the hospital bed once more. Bruce's eyes were clearer this time, and William waited a moment until he woke up completely. "Bruce, tell me who is after Sienna. I need to know."

"It's not Sienna. It's Adam."

"What?" William asked, not sure he was hearing Bruce correctly. He thought of the various incidents that had threatened Sienna's safety. All had been when she was with Adam except one.

"Adam wasn't around when the car almost ran over Sienna."

"The director changed the schedule. They were supposed to do the scene with Adam driving the car first. Without any brakes or steering, he would have crashed right into the ocean."

"And you helped with this?"

"I didn't know he was going to sabotage the brakes. I only told him how to mess with the steering," Bruce insisted. "I promise. I didn't know."

"Who is it? Who were you helping?"

"Carter Wells." Bruce tried to shift himself up in the bed. "You have to stop him before someone gets killed. He was going to sabotage the deck at the beach house."

"How?"

"I'm not sure. I refused to help him." He winced in pain when he shifted again. "That's why I was there last night, to find what he did and try to fix it."

William unlocked his phone once more and made his call.

32

CRAIG CONSIDERED THE SCENE THAT was about to be shot,
listening to Sienna and Adam discussing the format with their
director. They had chosen to have this particular conversation
in the living area overlooking the third-floor deck. Two sets of
french doors led to the deck, and the doors of the set on the right
were pulled open wide for the cameras to film through. Cameras
were now in place outside to capture the action from below, and
several members of the cast and crew were gathered beneath the
shade tent that had been set up where the lawn gave way to sand.

Craig still couldn't quite wrap his head around the number
of people it took to create a movie or how long it could take
to complete a single scene. He had glanced at the scene with
Sienna last night and had had to bite his tongue more than once.
Objectively, with his training, he could find all sorts of holes
in the scenario, but he supposed it all came down to what the
public would believe.

As he understood it, Adam and Sienna would pretend
someone was trying to infiltrate the beach house where they had
supposedly taken refuge from their enemies. He wasn't quite
sure what the deal was with the fictional biological weapon in

the story, nor was he about to point out how many breakdowns in national security would have had to occur for the scenario to be plausible.

He tuned back into the conversation when Sienna spoke. "Let me make sure I have this right. I take my mark on the left side of the deck until Adam comes out the other door."

"That's right. Dalton and Kent will appear between you. You'll engage Dalton, and Adam will fight Kent. As soon as you trip over the rope on the deck, we'll cut for close-ups."

Craig looked up at where the stage would be set. Why someone would have heavy-duty rope on a deck that was used primarily for sunbathing and water watching he didn't know, but, hey, he wasn't the guy writing the story.

Props littered the side of the room cluttered with cameras and sound and lighting equipment. A folding table held guns, pieces of wardrobe, and a second coil of rope. An A-frame ladder stood beside the wall, several extension cords stacked beneath it.

George stepped up beside Craig. "Are you going to stay up here for a few minutes?"

"Yeah. Why?"

"I want to check out the lower levels. Lots of people on set today, and I'm feeling more paranoid than usual."

Craig understood the sentiment. "Go for it. I'll be here."

"Keep a good eye on her."

"Will do."

George headed for the stairwell near the french doors, and Craig listened to the director's last-minute instructions to Sienna and Adam.

"Okay, let's make this happen," Marcus said.

Sienna and Adam headed for their starting positions. Marcus took his seat in his director's chair and said to the cameraman beside him, "I want you to keep rolling on this one."

Craig's phone rang, and he quickly silenced it.

Marcus turned and gave him a hard stare. "And no phones on my set."

"Sorry."

Craig looked down to see it had been William calling. He walked across the room, away from where the action was being shot, missing the call by the time he was out of range of the cameras. Before he could call William back, his phone rang again.

"Hello?"

"Craig, where are you?"

"At the beach house with Sienna."

"Bruce woke up. It's Carter. He's the one who's been behind the accidents."

Craig turned quickly to look back toward the set. "I think I saw him outside in the yard when I got here. Do you want me to track him down and detain him, or should I wait for the cops?"

"I'm on my way right now. Just make sure no one goes on the deck. It may have been sabotaged."

Craig whipped around at the sound of Marcus's voice. "Action!"

Adam took three steps out onto the deck, a pistol in his hand. Sienna followed him, and Craig heard a faint crack of wood beneath their weight.

"No!" Craig threw his phone down and shouted, "Sienna!"

Marcus stood in a rage and yelled out, "Cut!"

Craig's focus was entirely on Sienna. He waved at her, motioning for her to stay back. The urgency in his voice had the opposite effect. Instead of moving back into the house, she stepped farther onto the deck. "No! Come back!"

Craig sprinted toward the french doors as voices rose in confusion. Sienna started back toward him but only managed to take one step before an explosion sounded, followed by a loud crack.

Time slowed, every second passing in excruciating slow motion. The wood beneath Sienna's and Adam's feet gave way, leaving them both suspended in midair for a brief moment. All of the voices unified in an audible gasp, and Craig prayed he could react fast enough.

* * *

Sienna felt like she was standing on a boat in a stormy sea. One minute the wooden planking beneath her was firm against her feet. The next minute it was gone.

She tried to make a sound, but nothing came. Shock, pure and simple, took over, along with an overriding sense of disbelief.

Beside her, she heard Adam cry out and throw his body toward the open doorway. She felt herself falling millisecond by precious millisecond.

Her brain absorbed every detail: the wood beneath her splintering, shards of wood embedding in her left arm, the coil of rope that had moments ago been something to trip over now hovering above her head, apparently exploding upward when the deck burst into pieces.

Instinctively, she grabbed for it, gripping it for dear life, even though, like her, it had nothing to keep it from falling. In her peripheral vision, she could see the ground more than thirty feet below her.

She heard Craig shout her name and then heard the thump of Adam's body impacting the floor of the beach house five feet above her.

She looked up, saw Adam's feet dangling from where he was sprawled in the open doorway, then her palms burned when the rope jerked hard beneath her hands.

* * *

Craig reached Adam first, gripping the back of his shirt and hauling him up over the doorway threshold and out of his way. Then he looked down, terrified of what he would find.

Twin emotions of relief and fear pulsed through him when he saw Sienna wasn't lying broken on the ground below but was dangling from the rope he had been mocking a few minutes ago. The thick strands of one end had caught in the jagged boards that now jutted six inches from the side of the house. Sienna clung to the rope several feet below.

"Hold on!" Craig called out.

He did a quick assessment. Only a few inches of rope protruded above the boards they were caught in. The splintered wood held flush with the side of the house several feet to his right. The nails holding the wood in place were already groaning under the strain, the end of the rope fraying dangerously.

"Someone call 9-1-1!" Marcus called out to the room, and Craig was vaguely aware of someone tending to Adam while others tried to push to the doorway to determine Sienna's fate.

"Everyone get back," Craig barked, and everyone obeyed.

Sienna tried to put one hand above the other, causing the wood to pull away from the house another fraction of an inch.

"Stop. Don't move." Craig struggled to stay calm. He looked around, searching for anything he could use for rescue equipment. He thought of the other rope across the room, but it was too thick to use easily. His eyes landed on the extension cords, and he raced the few feet to retrieve them.

He put a hand on the banister post located six feet inside the door and gave it a good push to test it for sturdiness. Deciding it was the best he could do for the moment, he looped two extension cords around the base and tied them off. He then stepped to the edge of the doorway and tested his weight against it.

He could almost hear Brent telling him not to push his luck, but he knew he didn't have a choice. It was only a matter of seconds before the rope holding Sienna broke free. He wasn't going to wait. He simply couldn't gamble on whether she would survive the fall, and by the time the fire department got here, it would be too late.

"What can I do?" George appeared at his side.

"Hold on to the end of these cords to help support my weight. I don't know how long the banister will hold."

George gripped the cords, lowering himself onto the ground so he could use his weight to counteract the pressure Craig was about to put on him. "Ready."

Normally he would have looped the cord around his waist and through his legs, but he didn't want to get caught trying to untangle himself. Instead, he took a firm grip on the cords and prepared to climb down hand over hand. Rappelling without a harness wasn't the smartest idea, but he could see no other option. He wished briefly for a pair of gloves but pushed that thought aside as quickly as it had appeared. Right now, all that mattered was getting to Sienna.

33

SIENNA REALIZED THAT WHAT HAD felt like a gentle breeze before was actually enough of a gust to sway her back and forth, her breathing becoming short and shallow as she envisioned the moment when the rope would pull free.

The hint of panic in Craig's voice made her wonder how much worse the situation could get. She searched above her and could see it now—the rope's threads and their tentative hold between the jagged deck planks, the nails under those planks bending slowing toward her.

Any minute she was going to plunge the three stories to the ground below. Any minute she was going to die.

Blood seeped from her hands and into the fibers of the rope, making it increasingly difficult to hold firm. Even if the rope did hold, she wasn't sure *she* would be able to for much longer.

She still couldn't understand what had happened. Why would the deck simply cease to exist while she was standing on it? She could see the second-story deck below her, but it was several yards to her left, staggered with the other decks on the beach house to create a more aesthetic curb appeal. Right now all she wanted was something solid beneath her feet.

She clenched her knees together around the rope below her and closed her eyes against reality. Surely her life wasn't supposed to end this way. She had so much to live for, so much more than she had thought possible.

No longer did everything center around her career. Now she had Craig too, someone she cared about enough to make changes in her life, someone worth sacrificing for.

No sooner had the errant thought entered her mind than she heard movement above her. Then Craig descended beside her, three feet of space between them.

"What . . . ? What are you doing?" she asked.

"We're going to get you out of here," Craig said, his voice confident even if his eyes still illuminated his concern.

Tears stung her eyes, so many emotions blending together, from hope to utter terror. She also felt Craig's sense of urgency. "What do you want me to do?"

He didn't answer her, but he swung himself to the side of the house, now six feet below the doorway and four feet to Sienna's left. His feet found purchase in the grooves between the pieces of siding, and somehow his fingers managed to do the same. Had she not known better, she would have sworn he was climbing up one of those rock walls instead of hanging on to the side of a house.

To her horror, he eased his grip on the cords he was previously using to keep him steady and pulled up several feet of slack. "I'm going to swing this to you. I want you to grab on when it gets in reach."

"I can't," Sienna said, her heart lodging in her throat at the thought. "I'll fall."

"No, you won't. Keep your grip on the rope with one hand and with your knees. Use the other hand to grab the cords."

"I don't know if I can do this."

"Sienna, you can do this." His eyes met hers. "Trust me."

"I do trust you."

"Okay, here we go."

* * *

Craig wished he was as confident as he sounded. He uttered a silent prayer for Sienna's safety before he counted to three and swung the cords in her direction.

She reached for them like he had instructed her, but her adrenaline threw her timing off, and she only succeeded in putting more pressure on the rope she was currently clinging to.

If he could just get her weight shifted to the extension cords, he could help her climb back up, or he could guide her through a climb down to the second-floor balcony.

He knew the cords wouldn't support both of them at the same time, and he was willing to take his chances with his own free-climbing skills if it meant getting her to safety sooner. A piece of siding bent slightly beneath his right hand, and he adjusted his grip to the next strip down, praying it would hold his weight.

"Let's try it again. You can do it." Craig tried to believe his own words, willing Sienna to gain the confidence she needed to trust herself. "Pretend this is all a stunt for the movie. When I say three, I want you to reach for the cord I'm sending to you."

She gritted her teeth for a moment before taking a shaky breath. "Okay. I'm ready."

Deciding to keep things simple, this time he only sent one cord. "One. Two." He pulled his hand back and sent the cord toward her. "Three!"

This time, Sienna's instincts took over, and she reached out and grabbed the cord.

"Great. Now I'm going to send you the second one." Craig followed the same procedure.

Like with the first try, she reached too quickly and missed. A quick pop followed a short groaning sound, and the thick rope that had kept Sienna from plummeting to the ground went slack in her hand.

A scream escaped her, and her grip tightened on the extension cord. Still, she didn't loosen her hold on the thick rope, and the weight of it pulled her downward.

"Let go of the rope!" Craig commanded.

He could almost see her go through the quick thought process of figuring out which hand to relax and which one to grip tighter with.

A fraction of a second later, the rope fell free of her hand and tangled between her legs, pulling her down another six inches.

Her breathing was quick and shallow, and Craig saw the panic on her face. "Relax. Take a deep breath."

He knew his words were contrary to every instinct running through both of them, but somehow he managed to keep his voice calm and firm.

He could see the blood on her hands now, and his concern heightened, suddenly understanding why she was having such a hard time maintaining her grip. He also realized that he might have to readjust his original plan of having George help pull her up.

He looked at where the rope was caught on her left foot. "Try not to move any more than you have to, but I want you to point your toes on your left foot."

She squeezed her eyes shut and did as he asked, but instead of falling free, the rope caught on the tongue of her tennis shoe.

For a brief moment, Craig considered whether it was really necessary to free her from the rope. Then he saw her slip a little more.

She was out of his reach by several feet, and he couldn't use the cord he still held to support his weight without jeopardizing both of them.

"We're going to try something else," Craig said, his mind racing. "I want you to lift your left leg and reach it toward me. I'm going to try to get that rope off you. When you do, I'll loop this cord around your leg so you can grab it."

Sienna remained silent, except for her rapid breathing.

"Do you understand?"

Again, she didn't respond.

Recognizing the signs of shock, he put some authority behind his words. "Sienna, reach your leg toward me."

Again, no response.

Trying a different tack, he let his heart guide him. His words became soothing and persuasive. "Come on, honey. You can do this."

She opened her eyes and looked at him but still didn't seem to be able to send the command for movement from her brain to her leg.

He continued. "I love you. I don't want to lose you like this." He saw surprise in her eyes and wasn't sure if that was a good thing or a bad thing. Deciding any change in her expression was good, he continued. "Now, I need you to reach out your leg."

She gave a subtle nod and strained against the weight of the rope to follow his instructions. Slowly she managed to extend her leg to him, and he reached his hand out as far as he could.

His fingertips made contact with the rope. "A little more."

He could see her leg tremble as she complied.

Craig finally managed to wedge two fingers beneath the rope and lift it the fraction of an inch needed to free it. "Okay, tighten your grip and try lowering your leg."

She did, her body jerking when the rope fell free and hurtled through the air below her.

* * *

Sienna felt the extension cord sway, her body now liberated from the extra weight. She tried to listen to Craig and managed to follow his instructions when he had her lift her leg again.

She felt like she was watching a movie when he looped the second extension cord he had around her leg and then had her lower her leg to bring the cord within her reach.

His plan worked, allowing her to adjust her grip so she was holding on to both extension cords firmly, or as firmly as her bleeding hands would allow.

It took her a moment before she realized Craig no longer had anything to hold on to except the end of the second cord he had given her.

She didn't dare speak, but the thought that he must be crazy implanted in her brain. Who would risk himself like that?

George called from above him. "Are you ready for me to pull her up?"

She slipped down an inch and couldn't hide her panic. "I'm losing my grip."

As an exclamation point to her words, she slipped yet again, this time not stopping.

* * *

Craig gauged the distance to the third floor, nearly six feet up now, versus the distance to the second-floor balcony, four feet to Sienna's left. Seeing her sliding downward, he knew she wouldn't last much longer. Beneath one of his clenched hands, he was still holding the second extension cord, a four-foot length stretched between him and where Sienna clung to it. Praying the siding would hold, he let go of the house with his right hand and pulled the cord toward him in the hopes that he could draw her past him to the balcony. Realizing he didn't have the right angle to do it on his own, he called up to George.

"Swing her to the left!"

He didn't know if George understood his plan or if he simply trusted him, but a second later, Craig saw the lines swing into motion.

Sienna squeaked in alarm when she started moving, her momentum sending her back and forth.

Craig tensed and prepared to do either the bravest thing he had ever done or the stupidest. He watched Sienna's movement, counted down the timing, then pushed himself away from the wall and toward the second-floor balcony.

His left foot landed first on the railing, the pressure causing a loud crack from the wood. He could feel the railing pulling loose beneath him, and he threw his weight forward while he used the extension cord as a tether to bring Sienna closer.

He landed with a thud and heard Sienna scream his name. Then she was crashing into the side of the balcony railing and tumbling on top of him.

Craig grabbed on to her, not taking the time to process what had just happened. He scrambled up, pulled her up beside him, and bolted for the balcony door. If Carter had sabotaged one deck, he could have done it to a second one as well.

Craig found the french doors leading inside locked, but he didn't let that stop him. He threw his shoulder into it, and the doors burst open.

The moment he and Sienna were both on solid flooring, he pulled her into his arms and simply held on.

34

"ARE YOU GUYS ALL RIGHT?" George asked the moment he reached them.

Sienna shuddered, still clinging to Craig. It dawned on her that she was probably getting blood all over Craig's shirt, but she couldn't bring herself to let him go.

"I think we're okay," Craig answered. "Where's Carter?"

"Carter?" George asked. "Why?"

"He's the one who rigged the deck. Where is he?"

Sienna shifted now so she could see Craig's face. He must be mistaken. "I thought you said Bruce was the one causing all the trouble. How could Carter be involved?"

"Bruce didn't have access to the set. Carter did."

Still not able to wrap her mind around the possibilities, Sienna shook her head. "But George said there had been a few break-ins. I thought that was when Bruce tampered with the lights and the car."

"He didn't have any way of knowing the lights wouldn't get you. Besides, for the lights to fall at the right time, they had to have been triggered by someone in the room."

"Someone like Carter," George said. "The last time I saw him, he was outside by the exterior cameras."

"Stay with her." Craig stepped back. "I mean it. Don't let her out of your sight."

Sienna thought George would take offense to the commanding tone, but he seemed to take it in stride. "I promise I won't let anything else happen to her."

Craig gave him a nod before looking back down at her. He leaned down and kissed her, a brief meeting of the lips. His eyes took on a new intensity. "I meant what I said before. I do love you."

She opened her mouth to respond, not sure what she wanted to say. Before she could say anything, he stepped out of her arms. "Stay with George. I'll be back as soon as I'm sure Carter is in custody."

* * *

Craig sprinted down the stairs to the main level of the beach house, slowing to a jog when he reached the open door. He scanned the area by the cameras but found it difficult to distinguish one face from another.

The excitement had brought everyone out en masse, and the grounds were buzzing with activity. The sirens of a fire truck blared, and Craig winced against the sound.

A plain sedan made the turn into the driveway mere seconds before the fire truck came into view. Craig turned away from the new arrivals and looked toward the crowd again.

He didn't have to look long before he found Carter standing near the shade tent as though posing for the nearby paparazzi.

Fury built up inside Craig, and he nearly shouted out the man's name. Realizing that by doing so he would alert Carter unnecessarily, he held his tongue and strode across the lawn.

Emergency personnel poured out of the fire truck, and Craig wondered if a police car was also en route. Selfishly he hoped he got the chance to confront Carter first. His hands balled into fists, the only outward sign of his churning emotions. "Did you enjoy the show, Carter?"

Carter turned to face him and gave him a haughty look. "Do I know you?"

"You're about to." The muscles in his right arm flexed, but a hand reached out and held his fist in place. Craig turned to see William standing behind him.

"He's not worth it," William said coldly.

"Maybe not, but it would make me feel a heck of a lot better."

"You may have a point." With speed that surprised Craig, William's fist shot out and connected with Carter's previously perfect nose.

Carter cried out, his hands coming up to stem the flow of blood now gushing down his face.

Craig considered the older man before giving him an approving look. "I guess it's only fair you take the punch since you're family."

"I thought so," William conceded. "Of course, I still think if you have more than two brain cells in that thick skull of yours, you'll be family too before I see too many more birthdays."

Craig didn't know how it was possible to smile at a time like this, but he couldn't help it when faced with William's dry humor. "I'd like to think I have a few more brain cells than that."

"Glad to hear it."

* * *

Sienna snuggled next to Craig on the couch in the living room of her hotel suite, the news droning on the television that they hadn't bothered to turn off.

Her grandmother had retired to her bedroom a few minutes earlier, her grandfather still at the police station where Carter was being questioned. Sienna considered it a huge vote of trust that her grandma felt comfortable with them being alone. She also realized her grandfather hadn't been joking when he kept teasing Craig about making their fake engagement real.

She looked up at him. As much as she didn't want to replay the terrifying moments when she had hung suspended in midair, the memory of Craig professing his love warmed her.

She wanted to say it back to him, if nothing else as an expression of her gratitude. She also realized he didn't want the words unless she meant them. Was that why he had left her so quickly to go after Carter?

Did she love him? She couldn't remember ever being more comfortable with anyone before, nor could she think of a time she had let someone consume her thoughts so completely. Even when he had been out of town, in the back of her mind, she had always been wondering if she would hear from him soon and what he would say.

Was that love? She studied his profile, the firm jawline and the stubble on his cheeks. A sweeping sensation rushed over her, part pain, part wonder. In only a few weeks, this man had become the most important part of her life. The recognition of what she wanted and the depth of love she felt for Craig swept through her, a pure and piercing sensation she had never before experienced.

Craig looked down at her curiously. "What?"

Still trying to come to terms with her newfound feelings, she chose a different topic of conversation. "You know, the whole showdown with you and Carter was pretty anticlimactic."

"What do you mean?"

"I mean, in the movies there would have been a good chase scene, maybe some people shooting at each other. Instead it was a single punch."

"I know." He scowled. "And your grandfather didn't even let me have that."

"It was nice of you to give him that little gift." She reached up and kissed Craig's cheek.

"I thought so." He turned his head and found her lips.

When she pulled back, she found herself pinned by his stare. "You know, there's something I forgot to tell you earlier."

Craig shook his head. "You already thanked me a dozen times."

"That's not what I was talking about." She shifted and lifted both hands to his cheeks. "I didn't tell you I love you too."

He shifted so his body was facing her more fully, his hands now gripping her arms gently. She could see the questions in his expression and waited for him to make the next move. Finally he asked, "You aren't telling me that because I saved your life, are you?"

"No." She leaned forward until her lips pressed against his. For a fraction of a second, he didn't move. Then he drew her closer, his fingers tangling in her hair and sending shivers through her. She smiled when she pulled back. "I said I love you because it's the truth."

A slow smile spread across his face. "Then I am definitely the luckiest man alive."

"I hope you always think that."

"I plan to." He slid his arm around her shoulders again, and they settled back against the couch cushions.

Sienna shifted her gaze back to the TV, a sense of wonder settling over her. The image of the beach house filled the screen, an insert of her photo covering the bottom corner.

"Big news from the set where Sienna Blake has been shooting her next movie. Everything was caught on film in this incredible scene. And don't think this was staged, folks. It's a little long, but this is what really happened."

The image cut to the moment right before the deck collapsed, and Craig tightened his grip around Sienna's shoulders when the initial sounds of the deck collapsing began.

She saw the small burst of light from where the explosive device detonated to make sure the deck collapsed completely, followed by the miraculous way she was able to grab the rope and Adam succeeded in diving for the doorway. Seeing it all on-screen, she could almost pretend the whole thing had been scripted, but there was nothing fake about the sheer terror that had consumed her when the deck had fallen out from under her feet.

The clip continued to roll, revealing the rest of the rescue and even including close-ups of Craig and Sienna when they finally reached the second-floor balcony.

When the newscaster continued to talk about the incident, Sienna looked up at Craig. "I hate to break it to you, but I think you just started your fifteen minutes of fame."

"I'll settle for fifteen seconds and call it good."

"You might have been able to fly under the radar if the cameras hadn't kept rolling. Marcus will probably give that cameraman a big bonus for thinking to keep filming and for doing the close-ups."

"He told the cameramen to keep rolling." Craig shifted, then looked down at her. "Does Marcus tell the cameramen to keep rolling very often?"

"No, actually. I think the only time I've heard him tell them to was right before that car almost ran me over."

"He knew."

"Who knew what?"

"Marcus knew what Carter was up to."

"How could he possibly know that?" Sienna asked, bewildered.

"I don't know, but can you explain why the only two times he told the cameras to keep rolling was when an accident was about to occur on set?"

"It could have been coincidence. Both of them were action scenes that are difficult to recreate for the different angles," Sienna said. "Besides, what would he have to gain from his movie being sabotaged?"

"I don't know. What would he have to gain?" Craig asked. "If none of this had happened, what would be different?"

She shrugged. "By now the paparazzi probably would have moved on to something else. There are always a few that linger, but we wouldn't have stayed in the press this much. Other than that, I can't think of anything that would be significantly different."

"Answer me this. What would have happened to the film if you hadn't survived today? Would they have kept going with the movie or would they have scrapped it?"

"This is a multimillion-dollar project. I have to think they would have kept going." She shuddered. "It's a pretty sobering thought that my death would have made this movie an icon."

"So a potential blockbuster movie would have elevated into something everyone would want to see because of the tragic demise of actress Sienna Blake."

"The actress Sienna Blake, daughter of actor Sterling Blake."

The hotel room door opened, and her grandpa walked in. Craig stood up. "Did he confess?"

"He lawyered up," William said. "I'm hoping we'll be able to check the surveillance tapes at the house to show him messing with the lights before that first accident. I'm going to meet with the director over there first thing in the morning."

Now Sienna's suspicions started humming, and she stood as well. "Why do you need to meet with Marcus?"

"He's staying in one of the rooms at the beach house, so the owner gave him the key to the room with all of the surveillance equipment in it."

Craig crossed his arms. "Didn't the police already go over all the video feed for that?"

"Everyone thought the light falling was an accident. It wasn't until the car almost hit Sienna that they looked into surveillance at the house." He motioned for them to take their seats and lowered himself into the armchair beside the couch.

"They should have looked at those tapes then," Craig said, irritated.

"I agree, but you know how it goes. No one reported the lighting accident, so it wasn't on the police's radar." William leaned forward and rested his elbows on his thighs. "There's another thing I thought you'd be interested in knowing."

"What's that?"

"Bruce has been driving a Honda CRV since the day before we saw him at Kendra's concert."

"You think he was the one in the woods at the party?"

"He admitted as much. The police also searched his house in California. They found letters threatening the Blake family, including Sienna."

Sienna looked at him, confused. "I never received any threats."

"From what I've gathered, Bruce planned to create a fake threat against you in an attempt to get rehired by your father," William said. "That all changed when Carter approached him about helping sabotage the movie to get rid of Adam. When Carter asked about the Blake family to make sure Sienna's security wouldn't get in the way, we think Bruce decided he could kill two birds with one stone: help Carter get the lead role he wanted while also making it look like Sienna was in danger so he could get back on her security detail."

"That's crazy," Sienna said.

"Yes, it is. That's also why the staged accidents were typically when you were around too."

"I'm starting to think there may be more to these accidents than we thought, but I'm not sure how to prove it," Craig said.

William leaned forward and rested his elbows on his knees. "It just so happens I'm an expert at proving things. Tell me what you've got, and let's see what we can do."

Sienna sat amazed as the two men who held such a huge piece of her heart schemed together in a way that made her head spin.

35

CRAIG CLIMBED UP THE SIDE of the beach house, the memory of his last time in this position fresh in his mind. To his right, Brent followed a parallel path, and they reached the opposite sides of the second-floor balcony at the same time. The doors Craig had kicked in earlier had not yet been repaired and had been tied closed with some kind of twine.

Even though it appeared the alarm couldn't be fully activated with the damaged doors, Brent checked it before giving Craig the signal to proceed. Craig pulled his knife out, cut through the twine, and opened the doors. Eventually someone would notice the doors hanging open, but by then, Craig hoped they would have their man.

Through hand signals, Brent and Craig continued their parallel movements, circling through the game room, past the kitchen, and into the narrow hallway that led to their objective. They found the door to the video room locked, and Brent picked it as though he was holding a key rather than a lock pick.

The door swung open, and Craig retrieved a modified flash drive from his pocket and plugged it into what appeared to be the main computer system. The light on the drive turned on, indicating the download was in progress. Brent stood guard at the door while Craig counted off the seconds. A minute later, the light switched off, and Craig unplugged it.

He signaled to Brent that they were good to go, and they moved on to the next phase of their plan: to inspect everything in the house and plant their own surveillance equipment.

* * *

"I swear, if I get another interview request today, I'm going to scream." Sienna set her cell phone down on the coffee table and moved to sit at the dining room table with her grandparents.

William didn't look up from buttering his toast. "It's tough being popular."

"So I've heard," Sienna said dryly.

"Is Craig coming to church with us this morning?" Hannah asked.

"Yeah. He should be here any minute." Sienna popped a grape into her mouth.

"I think he has enjoyed having you off the past two weeks."

"It was nice for the studio to let us take a hiatus while the repair work is being done to the beach house," Sienna said. "And I really appreciate you both staying for my break."

"We've enjoyed every minute." Hannah patted her hand. "Though I think your grandfather may be spending too much time interrogating your boyfriend."

"I haven't been interrogating him. I've been asking questions. There's a difference."

"Right, Grandpa."

A knock sounded on the door, and Sienna stood. "I'll get it."

Diligently she looked through the peephole before unlocking the door. Craig stood on the other side. "Hey, there." She leaned forward for a good-morning kiss. "How are you?"

"Great, actually."

A little surprised by his response, she smiled. "Well, that's good."

"Better than good." He continued into the room and closed the door before speaking to her grandfather. "He took the bait. We got what we needed."

A kind of dark excitement and anticipation exuded from both men. Her grandfather stood. "When are we springing the trap?"

"Tomorrow." Craig slid his arm around Sienna and looked down at her. "How would you feel about taking another day off?"

"Another day off? Tomorrow is our first day back."

"Yes, and it will be one to remember."

* * *

Craig trailed behind William as they approached the center of the action: the director's chair. Marcus was chatting with one of his cameramen, and the screenwriter sat a short distance away.

Marcus looked up and keyed in on Craig. He must have read the latest gossip articles about Craig dating Sienna because the first question out of his mouth was, "Where's Sienna?"

"Sorry. She overslept," Craig lied. "She really wasn't feeling well, and I'm not sure she can make it in today."

"You've got to be kidding me. She just had two weeks off to rest." Flustered, he picked up a copy of the script, stared at it a moment, and threw it back down. "Now what am I supposed to do? Everything hinges on this next scene."

"Sienna thought you could have her stunt double stand in for her this morning. Since it's a gun battle, she figured you could do without her until it's time for close-ups. With any luck, she'll feel better by tonight."

"That won't work," Marcus said.

"Oh, really?" William stepped forward. "And why won't it work?"

Marcus turned on William and scowled. "What are you doing on my set?"

"Sienna's grandfather had some concerns about her safety." Craig snatched a copy of the script sitting on Sienna's chair. It didn't take him long to find what he was looking for. "Hey, William. You were right."

"Right about what?" Marcus asked.

"Adam's character uses a different kind of gun than everyone else in the scene." Craig tapped the script against the palm of his hand. "Interesting."

"What's so interesting about it?"

"Oh, we were just wondering how you were going to know which gun to give Adam to make sure he killed Sienna," William answered for him. He stepped closer. "It must have been so frustrating that she kept surviving all of the accidents you helped stage."

"I didn't stage any accidents. You were the one who said it was Carter."

"Carter started all of this craziness, but he wasn't trying to hurt Sienna. He wanted Adam out of the way so he could take his role," Craig said. "You were the one who kept changing their positions to put Sienna in danger instead. You figured if Sienna died on this set, it would put you on the map. You'd forever be known as the director who overcame great tragedy, the man who managed to record her demise from three different angles."

"You're insane."

"I hoped I was wrong," Craig said. "The last few days, I thought maybe I was being paranoid. Then I saw you put real bullets in Adam's gun."

Marcus blustered. "I did no such thing."

"You did. You may have figured out how to get around the house's security cameras, but the owner of the house gave us permission to install a little extra protection. This is what we found." Craig retrieved his phone from his pocket and hit the play button to show a video. In it, Marcus could clearly be seen at the prop table switching real bullets for the blanks that had already been loaded.

As soon as Marcus saw the image, he stumbled back several steps. "This isn't happening." He looked around wildly, his hand reaching for the loaded gun on the prop table right beside him.

Craig didn't wait for him to decide where to aim. He kicked his leg out, knocking the gun to the ground before Marcus could get a good grip on it.

Marcus scrambled after it, surprising both Craig and William with how quickly he recovered it. He took a step back as he straightened, the gun now aimed at Craig. "Don't think your little karate tricks are going to work on me. Four years in the army working demolition taught me a thing or two."

"I've never been a fan of the army," Craig said, looking for any opening. Out of the corner of his eye, he could see people scrambling out of the room. He thought he heard someone calling 9-1-1, but that didn't matter now. What mattered was getting this man under control without causing anyone harm. "Of course your plan was brilliant."

"Did you really call him brilliant?" William asked.

"Well, yeah." Craig nodded. "He saw on the house surveillance tapes that Carter had messed with the studio lights, and he must have figured Carter was also behind the car accident when Sienna and Adam were on their way back from LA. Instead of turning Carter in, he decided to use him. Sienna, she's been famous since the day she was born. Her death would cause people to take notice. And certainly her father and sister would make sure no one forgot her."

William chimed in. "Which would mean no one would forget Marcus either, the man who filmed the movie when she died, a movie that included actual footage of her demise."

"I didn't do anything wrong," Marcus insisted. "It was all Carter and that friend of his. I didn't do anything wrong."

"Then why are you pointing a gun at us?" Craig asked, drawing the director's attention again as William moved once more. "This isn't the kind of fame you want. You want to be known for your talent as a director."

"It'll never be the same again."

Craig heard the change in the man's voice, the odd calm that came before the storm. Marcus waved the gun as though trying to pick his target. He finally settled on Craig again. "I never should have let you on my set."

"It is my fault," Craig agreed, his heartbeat now quickening as he saw the sanity draining from the man before him. "I didn't let Sienna die. I couldn't."

William shifted one last time and pounced. He reached his hand out and grabbed the gun barrel, twisting it free of Marcus's hand in one fluid motion.

Craig followed up with a right hook, connecting with the man's jaw and dropping him to the ground.

William's eyebrows lifted. "You didn't have to hit the guy. I had him under control."

"I know," Craig said. "But you didn't let me hit the last guy."

"True." William slapped a hand on his back. "I knew I liked you."

36

CRAIG GLANCED UP FROM HIS desk at the television mounted in the corner of the room, the next segment of news about to begin. Normally the sound was simply background noise. If something popped up that might relate to an area of intelligence they were working with, he would pay attention; otherwise the television was just there.

When the newscaster for the eight o'clock news began speaking and the first segment included Sienna's name, Craig's focus heightened. He had seen plenty of news clips after the deck collapse and, more recently, a good number of segments on Marcus and his manipulation of Carter's sabotage attempts.

"And we caught another glimpse of Sienna Blake's mystery man yesterday. Sources say he was instrumental in taking Marcus Aldridge into custody. We also heard rumors that he wasn't a new member of Sienna's security team but rather her latest boyfriend. Stay tuned for the latest in the unfolding saga of the Blake family and what is in store for them next."

"Looks like you're famous," Damian said from the next desk over.

"At least the Blakes have been successful in keeping your name out of the press," Tristan added.

"Yeah. Lucky me."

"Hey, you've had more than your share of luck lately," Tristan insisted. "In fact, the way things have turned out for both you and Sienna has been downright miraculous."

"You're right," Craig said. Hadn't he thought the same thing himself? More than once, he had looked at the situations Sienna had survived, knowing she could so easily have been taken from this life. The Lord had protected her, and Craig had been lucky enough to watch the miracles unfold. But now what?

He had been doing so well not letting himself dwell on her fame or public image, but with the constant news stories and increased presence of the paparazzi, it was hard to ignore it all. They hadn't even been able to go out to dinner last night like they had planned because the press had been so invasive outside the hotel. Instead, they'd settled for room service with her grandparents. Again.

He hadn't been lying when he'd declared his love for her, but how could he possibly keep a relationship with her going? From what his teammates had told him, he had to expect he would be deployed often, and he knew her movies usually took at least three months to shoot, sometimes on location and other times in LA. Either way, they would likely have thousands of miles between them because of their careers.

The office phone rang, and Damian picked it up. "Hey, Craig? Telephone."

Craig's eyebrows drew together. Not once since coming to work with the Saint Squad had anyone ever called him on the office phone. Craig crossed the room and took the phone Damian held out to him. "This is Craig."

"Hey, Craig. It's Charlie Whitmore."

"Hi, Charlie. What can I do for you?"

"I'm sorry to bother you at work, but I wanted to thank you for everything you've done for Sienna. Words can't express how grateful her family is that she's safe."

"I was happy to help." Craig leaned back against the desk and discovered Damian and Tristan had deserted the office, and he was now alone. A burning question surfaced, and he let himself follow impulse. "Can I ask you something?"

"Of course."

"I know you went through something similar with Kendra. How long did it take for the publicity to die down?"

Charlie chuckled. "It's a pain, isn't it?"

"Yeah."

"It isn't easy being involved with a Blake," Charlie said.

"I guess it was only a matter of time before that part spilled out too."

"Actually, William told me a couple weeks ago that you two were dating. Not that he needed to. I had a feeling you were heading that way when I saw you together before my wedding."

"How have you managed it, keeping your career and being involved with someone who was born famous?" Craig asked.

"It isn't always easy, but believe it or not, when the family chooses to stay out of the limelight, they're pretty good at it. The paparazzi are surprisingly easy to get rid of when you aren't doing anything exciting."

"You're an FBI agent. I'm a Navy SEAL," Craig reminded him. "Our lives aren't exactly scripted to be dull."

"Yeah, but we both work in secure government buildings." He chuckled again. "If you really want to drive the press nuts, marry the girl and move into on-base housing where the press can't follow. That would be fun to watch."

"Now you're starting to sound like her grandfather."

"I remember being in your shoes. It can be terrifying, although I'm not sure which is worse, dealing with the paparazzi while trying to make a relationship work or facing William's interrogations."

"What did you do?"

"I gave it a few months. I figured if Kendra and I could make it work with our crazy schedules and we still wanted to be together, then our love must be meant to last."

"Sounds like good advice."

"Only kind I give," Charlie said. "Kendra has a show coming up next month in Virginia Beach. I thought I might take off a few days and come with her. We'll have to get together. It sounds like we have a lot in common."

"I'd like that."

"And, Craig?"

"Yeah?"

"Don't let William scare you off. He's just anxious for great-grandchildren."

"Great-grandchildren?" Craig choked the words out.

"Like I said, don't let him scare you off."

After Craig hung up the phone, he stared at it for several seconds, his mind still processing the conversation. How had he gone from wondering if he and Sienna could date successfully to thinking about marriage and children with her?

He blew out a breath. William might be pushy when it came to moving along his agenda, but Charlie was downright sneaky. Craig liked him already.

37

SIENNA WOKE UP THINKING ABOUT Craig. It seemed she always woke up thinking of him. When was this going to stop? She loved him, but she kept expecting something to change between them. Part of her expected they would grow tired of one another, but after all these weeks of her affections for him growing, she now wondered if it all might go the other direction.

She could hardly believe they had known each other for five months any more than she could believe that today would be her last day of filming. The accidents and then the delays caused by hiring a new director had nearly doubled their production time, but Sienna hadn't minded the extra months.

It was time to move on to a new project, but so far she had been hesitant to commit to anything. She knew she was letting location play a huge factor in her decision, but she figured after everything she had been through at the beginning of this movie she deserved a little time off.

She knew her desire to spend more time with Craig was the dominating factor in her refusal of two promising scripts being filmed in California. Her agent wasn't particularly thrilled with her at the moment, but, she reminded herself, he worked for her.

She gathered her purse and cell phone, expecting George to arrive any minute to escort her to the set. Her cell phone rang, and she saw her agent's name illuminate the screen.

"Hi, Bill." She looked at her watch and did the math to see it was only four in the morning in LA. "What are you doing up so early?"

"I received an offer last night that I want you to consider."

The little bubble of excitement warred with the knowledge that the day would come when she would have to leave Virginia Beach in order to pursue her career.

"I thought I told you I need to take a few months off."

"This is a once-in-a-lifetime opportunity, and it's long-term, steady work," he said. "Sienna, I'm telling you, this could be the perfect fit for you. You'll also like the fact that filming doesn't start for six weeks."

Feeling the temptation dangling in front of her, she let out a sigh. "I'm listening."

* * *

Craig stood at the edge of the action, so many emotions flooding through him. This chapter of Sienna's life was now over, her movie complete despite the unique path to reach this point.

His palms were damp as he considered whether she was ready to begin a new chapter, one that included him in her future. He knew she planned to take a few months off to spend time with him, but he was more concerned with what would happen after her planned hiatus.

He glanced down at his watch; it was nearly eight o'clock, and the light was fading quickly. He worried that the filming wouldn't end today as planned until actors and crew members let out a celebratory cheer, then Craig watched Adam and Liam hug Sienna in turn.

He supposed it said something for his confidence in his relationship with Sienna that he no longer felt those jealous tugs when he saw her with her coworkers. He hoped that confidence would hold steady and prayed he wasn't about to undo what they had already built.

She saw him across the lawn and waved at him to join her. Already crew members were breaking down equipment, and talk of a party dominated many conversations. George stood a short distance from Sienna and nodded a greeting.

Craig reached her, his nerves settling a little when he saw the warmth in her expression.

"Hey, there." She reached up and gave him a quick kiss. "Your timing is perfect."

"I heard you guys talking about a party. When is that supposed to start?"

Several cast members laughed a short distance away.

"I think it's already started," Sienna said.

"Any chance I can steal you away for a few minutes before you join them?"

"Of course, but I was hoping you would come with me." She lowered her voice. "I may need an excuse to leave if they break out too much champagne."

"Understood." Craig took her hand and led her back toward his car, knowing George would follow from a discreet distance. Craig saw the surprise on her face when instead of opening the door, he popped the trunk and retrieved a picnic basket. "I hope you don't mind, but I brought you a little something to celebrate."

"That's sweet, but you do realize there will be a ton of food at the party, right?"

"Not like this." He tried to fight back the nerves warring in his stomach. "I brought your favorite dessert."

Her eyes brightened. "Apple pie?"

"Yep." He took her hand again and led her down the lawn toward the back of the house. He had worried the party would spill onto the beach, but so far everyone seemed content to stay at the house where the food tables were set up.

Determined to ensure as much privacy as possible, Craig led her away from the house, hoping the fading light would help mask their presence. He already knew the paparazzi were unable to make it onto the property, but he had checked their positions when he arrived to make sure their telephoto lenses couldn't get an angle on them.

"I can't believe this movie is over," Sienna said, smiling when she saw him set the picnic basket down and retrieve a blanket for them to sit on.

Craig waited for her to sit before he lowered himself beside her. "Are you ready for a vacation? Three months is a long time."

"Actually, my vacation may not last quite that long." Sienna fiddled with the edge of the blanket before lifting her eyes to meet his. "My agent called."

Craig's stomach dropped, a hollowness taking over and threatening to consume him. "I gather he had some project you couldn't turn down."

She clasped her hands together tightly. "Actually, that's exactly what happened."

Pain centered in his chest, and Craig prepared for the worst. He was on the verge of making an eternal commitment, and she was about to leave him. He took a steadying breath. "I understand."

"Actually, I'm not sure you do." Sienna shifted her legs so she was sitting cross-legged and leaned her elbows on her knees. "The offer isn't for a movie. It's a television series." Sienna kept her eyes on his, but she took a deep breath before she continued. "That means I'd be in the same place for nine to ten months out of the year."

"Oh." Craig didn't think things could get worse. He was wrong. How could they possibly be together if she was gone most of the year? And what if his deployments occurred during her time off? They could literally go years without seeing each other.

"Are you okay?"

"Not really." Craig pushed himself to a stand and took a few steps before turning to face her. "I thought we were going to have a few months together to figure out how far this thing between us can go. Now you're telling me we've hit the end of the road."

"No." She stood and closed the distance between them. "No, that's not what I'm saying."

"What are you saying? You can't possibly think we can make this work if you're gone most of the year, and it's not like I have a choice in where I work. I go where I'm assigned."

"Which is why I accepted the job."

"Just like that?"

"I hoped you would want me to accept it." She took his hand and held firm. "Craig, the job is here."

"What? Here?"

"Yes. Right here in Virginia Beach. I hope you don't mind if I stay."

"Are you kidding?" He pulled her closer and leaned down to kiss her. "I love you. I want you to stay forever."

"Are you sure?"

"Why don't you tell me." He released her to go collect the pie he had brought her. He lifted the to-go box and held it out to her. "See for yourself."

Her eyebrows drew together in confusion. "What does eating a piece of pie have to do with my staying in Virginia?"

"Open it and see."

She took it from him and opened the top. The piece of apple pie lay inside, but instead of ice cream on the side, an open ring box occupied the space next to the dessert, a diamond ring sparking from within.

Her eyes widened and then shot up to meet his. "Are you . . . ?" She tried to find her words. "Does this mean . . . ?"

"I'm asking you to marry me." He lifted the ring from the box and lowered to one knee, his heart pounding. "Sienna Blake, will you marry me?"

Her hands lifted to her mouth briefly, tears glistening in her eyes. Then she nodded and grabbed his hands. "Yes." The moment he stood, she threw her arms around his neck. "Yes, I'll marry you."

The ring still in his hand, he lowered his lips to hers, the kiss holding more promise and emotion than he'd ever thought possible. When he pulled away, breathless, he smiled and reached for her hand. "You know your grandfather has been after me for a long time to get this ring on your finger."

"Yes, I know." She watched him slide the ring into place before she said, "And just think, you already know how my dad will react when you ask for his blessing."

Craig pulled back enough to see the humor dancing in her eyes. "Not again."

"Oh, yeah." Sienna laughed. "But this time I'm going to be there to see the performance."

"What if he thinks I'm role-playing again?"

"Don't worry. He'll believe it's real as soon as we come out of the temple together."

Craig let that image take root. "What are the chances we can talk Kendra and Charlie into having a one-year anniversary party? Maybe a nice, intimate family affair where we can celebrate their marriage at the DC Temple?"

Sienna's smile bloomed. "I like the way you think."

"That's a good thing." He lifted her hand and kissed it just below her sparkling ring. "Because you're about to be stuck with me forever."

"You know what we call that in the movies, don't you?'

"What?"

"Happily ever after." Sienna reached up and kissed him once more.

Craig's heart lifted, and he let her words repeat in his mind. *Happily ever after.* Yeah, he could live with that.

ABOUT THE AUTHOR

Originally from Arizona, Traci Hunter Abramson has spent most of her adult life in Virginia. She is a graduate of Brigham Young University and a former employee of the Central Intelligence Agency. Since leaving the CIA, Traci has written several novels, including the Undercurrents trilogy, the Royal series, the Saint Squad series, *Obsession, Deep Cover, Failsafe,* and *Chances Are,* as well as a novella in *Twisted Fate.*

When she's not writing, Traci enjoys spending time with her family and coaching the local high school swim teams.